Living the Dream

LAUREN BERRY

virago

VIRAGO

First published in Great Britain in 2017 by Virago Press
This paperback edition published in 2018 by Virago Press

1 3 5 7 9 10 8 6 4 2

A CIP catalogue record for this book
is available from the British Library.

ISBN 978-0-349-00900-1

Printed and bound in Great Britain by
Clays Ltd, Elcograf S.p.A.

Papers used by Virago are from well-managed forests
and other responsible sources.

Virago Press
An imprint of
Little, Brown Book Group
Carmelite House
50 Victoria Embankment
London EC4Y 0DZ

An Hachette UK Company
www.hachette.co.uk

www.virago.co.uk

For Josh Jones, obviously

Part 1

1

Ten Thousand Spoons

The third floor of the Soho office block smelled of instant coffee and disappointment. Outside, London was in high spirits, alert and hectic. Inside the air was tepid, made of plastic and powered by static.

Emma Derringer was the first to arrive, because nobody at APRC was ever half an hour early for work. Motion-detecting lights blipped on as she passed through the office, which throbbed with the low sound of wasted energy. Smoky rainbow screen savers swirled and the air con hummed with electric persistence. The office was kept just short of warm in winter, and just short of cool in summer, so that everyone was slightly uncomfortable all year round. It made Emma's curly hair go fluffy and meant that everybody got everybody else's illnesses, regardless of how many Beroccas they drank.

The APRC Values had been engraved into the plaster-board that ran the length of the office.

INNOVATION
VALUE
QUALITY
PURPOSE

Emma was incessantly punctual; it wasn't deliberate, she was born that way – literally, on the morning of her due date. Time seemed to move differently for her friends, who plucked hours from Emma's life indiscriminately. Hours that she spent standing outside stations or alone in bars.

She played through the events of the night before. She'd been waiting for a mate in Soho Square, sitting on a bench and rolling a cigarette when a bike courier sat next to her. Glancing sideways at him Emma noticed that he was scruffy and handsome. He asked her for a light.

Twenty minutes later they were deep in conversation. Emma had calculated all the time she'd spent waiting for her friends and the fact that if she could take it back, she'd still be twenty-four. Instead she was twenty-seven, and sitting on a park bench with a cute courier, waiting.

He had smiled at her use of 'cute'. Emma allowed a cheeky grin to surface at the brief flashback that tingled through her system, happy that she had abandoned waiting and spent the night drinking and kissing and mucking about with him instead.

Innate punctuality aside, Emma was the first to arrive at APRC so that for the first half an hour of the day she could pretend the office was a sanctuary of quiet creation. Could start her computer on her own terms; could, for a brief moment, be a proper writer, and not an executive assistant.

She walked past the deserted PR department where the

desks were covered in sweet wrappers, cuddly toys, branded pens and photos; framed pictures of loved ones, pets in hats, nights out with the girls or couples embracing on the beach.

PR was comprised of eleven women whom it was near impossible to tell apart. It was a high-pitched minefield of femininity. They each had names that ended in 'y' and their desk drawers were filled with shoes, hand cream, Tampax and Nurofen.

Emma had specialised in feminism and women's media as part of her literature degree and worried that her contempt for them was inherently sexist. But she shuddered at their seemingly endless conversations about lunch. Whenever she walked past them she wished, briefly, that she cared enough to wear make-up or heels to work.

If the APRC carpet colour were on a paint chart it would be called Electric Snooze. Next to her desk there was a red swoosh in the carpet that marked the end of PR and the start of creative. She pictured the meeting where that decision had been made. Some horsey grey-brained office manager piping up with 'I've got it! How about a lovely red swoosh for the creative department? That will have SUCH impact.'

Whenever Emma thinks of the term creative department, her brain puts 'creative' in inverted commas.

She pressed the button on the back of her computer and waited for the techno sigh that signalled the start of the day. She typed in her password (Fresh_Hell) and shoved her jacket under the desk. (*DEAR ALL, Please keep your coats and bags out of sight and NOT on your chairs as they are unsightly. Thx.*)

In the kitchen, they had a coffee machine that ate aluminium capsules and spat out tepid, coffee-flavoured water. Emma had staunchly disapproved when they'd bought the machine and told the receptionists that it was the environmental equivalent of throwing ten thousand spoons at the moon. They had looked at her blankly, and walked away. She stood and waited for the machine to heat up, staring at the logo.

Built for life.

She pictured the advert: people holding cups and smiling – proud mums, executive dads, other gender archetypes and maybe an arty sort to mix it up, a rock climber, a skateboarder and someone not white for demographic and then blam, *built for life*.

That's how it would go.

Emma had been working in advertising for nearly a year, but had started thinking in straplines after a few months. She worried that her brain was permanently broken.

She made a professional-strength coffee, vowing to quit coffee next week. Her other perennial goals were to stop smoking, binge drinking and biting her nails. She'd made no progress with them either.

Aim high, she thought, and miss.

Back at her desk Emma sat and stared at her screen – a Mac standard image of a long white beach with crystal-blue waters and palm trees swaying in the breeze.

Fuck you, desktop.

She opened her emails, preferring the junk mail to any real messages about work. '50% off!' 'Book Now!' 'Last Chance!' 'Coming Soon!'

The first message she opened was from *Slick* magazine. She had submitted a sardonic opinion piece called 'Girls Gone Mild', a response piece to an article she had read about the 'empowering rise of onesie culture'. Emma wanted to address the idea that dressing as a cartoon tiger was only empowering until you had to strip naked to go for a wee. *Slick* were 'not interested at this time'.

She gave her disappointment a few seconds to subside, shut her mail and opened her blog.

She typed a new post and called it 'Bicycle Guy'. She stared at the empty screen for a moment, trying to pinpoint what about him had been so appealing ... Strength, maybe? His arms had been taut under his courier outfit. His light Scottish accent hadn't done any harm, but it may have been the enthusiasm with which he described his job and his concern for her safety – he begged her to wear a helmet if she took up cycling – that had made her lean forward and kiss him. Two bottles of red wine later, she had realised he was boring and walked away, but he had watched her go with a satisfying mix of glee and disappointment. She saved the post as a draft to her magazine blog, Stupid Shit Machine.

By the time the receptionists turned up and started bringing the office to life, Emma was ready to face the day as her alter ego: someone who worked in advertising and meant it.

2

Everything Tastes Better When It's Free

Somewhere over the Atlantic, Clementine Twist was on a Virgin 747 bound for London. She sat squidging a slice of lemon with a straw. Four mini-bottles of gin stood soldier-like, guarding her plastic cup from her neighbour – a shabby, bulbous businessman who was asleep against the window, mouth agape, tie and fly loosened. She looked over at him and rolled her eyes. Normally a hangover this bad would have stopped her drinking, but regardless of her headache she could never resist a free drink. Everything tastes better when it's free, she thought.

Clementine had pictured herself doing this journey in Executive Mode, wearing a trouser suit and carrying a briefcase. She would get upgraded just from the sheer fabu-lousness of her hair, and she briefly considered renting a limo to take her to the airport so that she might march up to the desk with a stretched-car swagger.

The plan had been reliant on having some money and an early night, getting a haircut and buying a briefcase and so, predictably, it had come second place to spending her last night in New York getting completely wasted with her now former friends and peers.

Four hours earlier she had been shaken awake with shouts of 'Your flight, Clem. GET THE HELL UP!' In a drunken flap, she had pushed as many things as she could fit into a rucksack and had run, without cleaning her teeth, out of the door to JFK. The last thing her roommate and best friend in the city had done was shove sixty dollars into her hand and insist she get a cab. Clem hadn't even had time to thank her properly, for everything. Standing on the corner of St Mark's Place and Second, in the pouring rain, she had tried to say it all with a look and hoped it had at least been cinematic. At the check-in desk she had tried to avoid breathing on the lady. Simultaneously she was trying not to be sick and searching for her passport and tickets, which were in her handbag by sheer fluke.

Clem allowed herself a smile. She must have looked, smelled and sounded ridiculous trying to check in. Scrabbling through her bag, wearing a Yankees T-shirt that was plainly her pyjama top. They had not given her an upgrade, they had given her the seat at the back, next to the toilet and another shambolic passenger, along with a dirty look and a series of condescending smiles. In the queue through security an overweight New York woman had whispered that she'd better have a splash of perfume to mask the stale booze, or the stewards wouldn't let her fly. She would have been insulted had it not been completely true.

Two hours into the flight, she was a bit tipsy and held a pencil in the hand that wasn't taking care of the lemon. She was making two lists. One of the things she would miss about New York, the other of things she was looking forward to in London. Under New York she had written 'Roommates / Pizza / Jordan' and on the other she had written 'Emma'. She looked past the sleeping beauty and out of the window at the clouds. Executive mode wasn't going particularly well for her so far.

Clementine had just graduated, top of her class, from her year-long post-grad course at Columbia film school, where she had been awarded a full scholarship. She'd made friends and produced work that she was genuinely proud of. She'd been to London once during her year in NYC and it had felt like a visit to a historic town, to the past. The past, which was now looming over her looking very much like the god-forsaken present.

The night before, Clementine had felt like a star; she and her friends had raised toasts to her future success. In her bleary flashback she was holding court in a booth in some snazzy diner that none of her small and geeky entourage could really afford.

'To high friends in good places,' she'd yelled across the floor. At the time she'd imagined a restaurant-wide cheer, but in retrospect she realised, she had probably just seemed obnoxious.

Her final submission to the course was a screenplay, her big hitter, called *Moonshiners*. It was a brooding period drama about English booze smugglers in the eighteenth century. It was '*Prince of Thieves* meets *Goodfellas*' and was on desks from London to LA. Her professor had sent an introductory email to Drake Jones, one of the leading agents in the UK, and she'd sent scripts to big names. But as she sat at the back of a plane making its way towards the UK, she felt sad and small;

all she really had to show for her time in New York was a few email addresses and several maxed-out credit cards.

She wondered when, if ever, she would start to feel like the big shot she was purportedly becoming. She scowled at herself and signalled for another gin. 'I'll have a big shot,' she muttered at the lemon. The lemon was Jordan and she was stabbing him repeatedly in the face.

'Here's a top tip ... ' she leaned over and whispered to her unconscious cohort, whom she had named Dirk. 'Don't shag actors, they don't have an honest bone in their body.' She cackled at the pun. 'And neither will you,' she finished, sloshing some gin over his oblivious leg. Then she stopped and felt a long cold hug of sadness stretch over her shoulders. For a moment she wouldn't have minded if the plane had started to plummet to her dismal end in the Atlantic. She crossed out 'Jordan'.

She wondered where she would go when they landed at Heathrow. She sighed, unable to picture her immediate future, and passed out. Her head dropped slowly onto Dirk's shoulder, and the rest of the gin, tonic and lemon sludge slid out of the cup and down through the gap in the seats.

3

Value Banner

As the volume in the office started to build, Emma sat silently at her desk and watched her co-workers. They conducted themselves with an air of urgency that Emma struggled to maintain.

Her enthusiasm was a mask, her efficiency a defence mechanism, her presence a scam. She was good at her job because she'd figured out after three months of negative feedback that life was simpler when she got things right the first time. She stopped short of excellent, because excellence seemed superfluous.

There were Post-it notes stuck to various piles of paper on her desk – 'Pls print proply' was attached to a document, which Gemma the intern had bound with most of the pages upside down.

Gemma was a twenty-two-year-old business studies graduate who couldn't give the faintest shadow of a shit about the job. It was an attitude that Emma admired.

The constant battle that their boss, Adrian, had with their

quite similar names was a joke that never wore thin; it occupied the same comedy cupboard as saying 'afternoon' when someone was a bit late.

Everyone laughs.

No one laughs.

Work laughs.

Under her coffee cup there was a printed presentation, with a note written in big black letters: 'SEE ME'.

He's gone out of his way to find a marker pen.

The document had started life as twenty-five landscape pages, scrawled in pencil during a group brainstorm. At APRC it was called an *insight* document, the product of an *ideation*.

In the beginning Emma had silently rejected the corporate vernacular. Now she said things like 'experiential' without flinching. She was gradually but conspicuously becoming one of *them*.

'SEE ME'. It was the 'We need to talk' of the office world. Emma sighed for the first time that day and then instinctively checked for an audience. She'd recently had a verbal warning about sighing; apparently people found her audible exhale demoralising.

Why even leave a note? she wondered, getting up and mooching through to the kitchen for a banana. The first thing that happens when he walks in the room is he sees me. I sit directly in front of his glass office. I literally see him all day.

She dropped the Post-it in the kitchen bin.

APRC was made up of five departments. Twenty-eight people spending forty hours a week under a collective 'value banner'. The term had been proudly coined by Adrian in

2005, and had made an appearance in every meeting since. The values existed in leather-bound books that the corporate department handed solemnly to each new employee, urging them to uphold the values in all that they did, at work or not.

When Emma had been initiated into the APRC way of life, she had taken her boxed set of values documents home and shown them to her flatmate, Paul, who took them from her and wordlessly threw them out of the kitchen window, onto the roof below where they remained, gently festering in the damp London outdoors.

Emma's department occupied the area with the highest denim count, where the shoe of choice was low-rise Converse. The 'creatives' sat at their 27-inch Mac screens and wore bulky designer headphones; they spent hundreds of pounds on plain black T-shirts, sneered at pop music and knew a lot about paper. They talked dispassionately about football and went on holidays to San Sebastián. They said 'gig' when they meant 'job' and had framed pictures of fixed-gear bikes.

The creative department surrounded Adrian's glass-box office. He called it 'his hub' and revelled in the idea that he was integral to the creative process. Emma's official title was executive assistant, but because her desk was closest to Adrian's office, and because the consensus at APRC was that the hierarchy was in constant flux, she had inadvertently become Adrian's PA. It meant that she arrived every day to an increasingly varied selection of tasks – a quality of the job she claimed, disingenuously, to enjoy.

The rest of the creative department was made up of Gemma; Ross, a freelance web guy; Drew, the director;

Jack, a designer with no discernible personality; and two Eds, glorified sales people who argued officiously about everything. They were best friends, but seemed to revel in each other's shortcomings. Emma didn't know if they hated each other or if theirs was just an executive's approach to friendship.

4

Team Meeting

At 11.05 Adrian Gilmartin entered the conference room and the group hushed. He was a formidable man – big in three directions. He was a proud forty-nine years old ('years young') and stood 6'4" in a dark blue suit and light purple shirt with white cuffs. His salt and pepper hair was on the right side of thin. He always looked a bit too warm.

He had studied economics at Oxford and admired, above all, capitalism's grip on humanity and its 'unique ability to tackle problems purposefully, meaningfully and for the greater good'.

He cleared his throat and glanced at the agenda that Emma had produced minutes earlier. She had a flash of panic that she'd done something wrong.

'Welcome, everyone. Firstly, there is a new face in the room, which is always exciting – it's great to get some fresh blood in the mix. So let's start by saying a big welcome to ...'

He glanced at his paper, flipping the pages theatrically,

searching for the information that only Emma knew was clearly written on the first page, when an American voice called from the back of the room, 'Hilary.'

All eyes turned towards the voice.

Hilary was small; she had bright eyes, and her hair hung in perfect, static curves around her shoulders. Her shirt was starched. She was chubby but she wore her weight with confidence. Her smile was sincere and instantly likeable.

She had her hand in the air and half stood at the back.

'Hi, sorry, did you mean me? I'm new – I'm Hilary. Hey, everyone.'

She trailed off and sat back down with a look that made Emma chuckle. Ross leaned in to Emma and whispered, 'She'd be an 8 without the waist.'

'I like the waist; she looks like she loves the taste of life.'

Adrian cleared his throat gruffly.

'Thank you for that, Hilary. A very warm APRC welcome to you. Hilary has joined our illustrinus PR department as our new head of social media.'

There was a collective cringe at the mispronunciation.

'OK, without further ado, this week's APRC moment is from Ross in creative. Ross, thank you very much for volunteering.'

The ritual humiliation that was the APRC monthly moment was obligatory and operated on an alphabetical basis.

'What do you have for us?'

Ross blushed as he shuffled up to the front of the room. His shoes squeaked, his jeans were loose and his T-shirt had two moth holes at the shoulder. Emma watched as he made his way through the room and wondered how men got away with being so wholly unattractive.

17

He cleared his throat and peered out over the group, his usually confident stance undermined by his obvious discomfort in the task.

In an English accent that suggested an extremely higher education, Ross spent the next ten minutes doing a monotone reading of a poem about blind guys groping an elephant. During which there were several thinly veiled giggles from the back of the room.

Six verses later there was a light spattering of applause as Ross folded away his printed pages and half stuffed them in his pocket, where they dangled as if gasping for air. Emma yawned exactly as Adrian caught her eye. Bugger. Emma knew that Adrian operated on a three-strike system and she had already had a twenty-minute meeting earlier that morning about attention to detail, following a typo on the SEE ME document. He wouldn't normally notice a typo, but she'd signed it 'Adrain', rather than Adrian, on his behalf and that was 'an unacceptable oversight, Emma'.

'Thanks, Ross, that was really something. Do you want to talk us through it? What makes that an APRC moment for you?'

Ross smiled benignly. 'Well, Adrian, I wanted to read this poem today because I think it's a really beautiful metaphor for what we do here at APRC.'

The collective eye-roll was felt, rather than seen.

'Because at the end of the day, if we don't communicate . . .'

We'll be molesting elephants?

'We'll never know what we can achieve, together. This poem is about the Big Picture, and I think that's very APRC.'

He said it as though he'd delivered a punchline and was expecting rapturous applause.

Get back in your box, Ross.

He got a slap on the back from Adrian that might have been congratulatory or might have been a nudge back to his seat.

'Is there anything else we need to talk about today? Any birthdays we've missed?'

It was an APRC tradition to mention any birthdays that week in the team meeting. It was Emma's job to collate those birthdays and include them on the agenda, but she had decided, early on, to never actually do this.

'It's my birthday on Wednesday, Adrian,' said a voice from amongst the gaggle of PR department women.

Of course it is, thought Emma bitterly. She couldn't have kept quiet and had her gluten-free cake later.

'Great stuff ... ' said Adrian with forced enthusiasm. Deciding who to blame for the oversight, he glared at Emma who grimaced an apology at him.

Ross leaned in to play 'Guess the PR girl'. He whispered in Emma's ear, 'Julie?'

Emma shook her head slightly. 'Ellie or Jenny.'

'I'll take Poppy or Posey.'

'Next time do make sure you mention it to Emma ... Suzie?' Adrian said.

Emma and Ross both stifled laughs.

With the bets placed the disgruntled voice at the back corrected, 'Lizzy.'

Ross shrugged. No winners.

'Righto,' said Adrian. 'Off we go,' and leading with his Oxbridge-trained tenor, he began: 'Haaaaaaaaappppy

19

birrrrthday to you ...' At 'day' the rest of the company joined in and pushed it through to the bitter end.

They were making their way back to their desks when Emma felt a tap on her shoulder. She turned to face Hilary, who beamed at her.

'Hi, I'm Hilary, I don't think we've met. Adrian said I should ask you for the tour.'

'Right. Well, shall I show you the kitchen?'

'Actually, I think he meant the neighbourhood, if you have time?'

'What, like, outdoors?'

Hilary laughed a wide, confident laugh at Emma. 'Yeah, honey, outside – you know, London and whatever? You into it?'

'Sure, why not.'

Emma got her coat and Adrian gave her a thumbs up from his office.

Emma added 'Tour Guide' to her job description.

Hilary seemed to operate at 100 miles per hour. She was practically skipping down the street as Emma rolled a cigarette.

'You smoke? That is SO retro of you.'

'Thanks. I find it brings out my inner '90s.'

Hilary stood with her hands on her hips, staring up at the buildings of Soho Square.

'God, I love London.'

'Where are you from?' *Minus ten for originality, Emma.*

'I'm from California, but I've been here a while.'

Emma lit the cigarette and blew the smoke away from Hilary. 'So why d'you need a tour?'

Hilary laughed. 'Adrian is so confused to have a black American in the office, he thinks I'm fresh off the boat, so he told me to "get to know the area". Even though I've worked in Soho for three years.'

She linked arms with Emma and still laughing, guided them across the road towards a coffee shop.

5

Ealing

Clementine stood outside the door of her childhood home, pausing to take in the unfamiliar light blue paint, cracked at the edges, the additional locks, a black bin marked 'No Hot Ashes'. There was a cluster of spiderwebs in the awning over the door and a flyer hanging leisurely from the letterbox. She had the key in her hand, but she didn't feel she quite had the right to let herself in.

The patch of land in front of the house was well kempt: a squared-off hedge, grey slabs, some kind of bush growing neatly along the wall. A place where nature met OCD. A snail made its way across the top of the wall towards a raspberry plant protruding from the neighbour's garden. Clem could picture her mum's husband muttering darkly about the unruly fruits. Malcolm was the kind of guy who thought a man should pay for his raspberries, not get them in a front garden.

She lowered the rucksack from her back and rang the bell.

Malcolm appeared at the door and greeted Clem with a polite nod. She followed his brown corduroys and soggy grey shirt through the hallway, wondering if he'd bought a single item of clothing in the year she'd spent away. He always dressed like he shopped from a catalogue of burlap sacks.

The house was a testament to her mother's contempt for style as a concept. Brown carpets, gilt-framed mirrors and framed pictures of her brother, Callum, and his family. Clementine's sole appearance was in a school photo, aged five, frowning suspiciously into the camera. She could hear Callum talking to her mum in the kitchen. Callum was the family success story. He had done well in school and then in his degree, and he had a fancy job title at a leading bank, a mortgage and an attractive wife with two healthy sons. He was dutiful to his mother and had a good rapport with Malcolm. He had done everything the way it was supposed to be done, left for university and had never come back. Clem knew that she loved him, but they had nothing in common and since the birth of his second child the cavernous space between them had become a canyon. She'd been forced to ask him for a loan to get back from New York and he'd put a grand in her account, with an email that said 'saves you asking Mum for it'. She would attempt to pay it back although he would probably never ask her to. His email had made it clear that he expected her to babysit on demand and had given her a stiff warning about being cordial to Malcolm when she came home. He was *such* a grown-up.

Clem dumped her bag in the hallway and made a mental wager with herself: in thirty minutes or less Malcolm would mention her getting a job, her mum would tell her about some wonderful Callum achievement and Callum would say something belittling about films. She glanced at the clock.

Starting . . .

She entered the kitchen where Callum glanced up smugly from the *Financial Times* and her mum stood, dumpy and proud, with her hands clasped together happily.

Now.

6

A Large Parsnip

The door to Emma's apartment building was solid metal; it had no number, no doorbell and no letterbox. She stood in the street rummaging through her bag for the key, aware that she looked ridiculous, because nobody would assume that behind the door was a home.

Six months earlier, she and Paul had stood in the same spot, with those same misgivings, waiting for the landlord's 'guy' to show them around. He had shoved the door with his shoulder and they had nearly walked away. It seemed like the perfect place to take someone and kill them. Behind the ominous metal door was an unlit wooden staircase, splintering at the edges with age, dust and neglect.

'Don't worry,' The Guy had reassured them as he led the way, 'we'll get a bulb in here before you move in.'

'Don't worry' was something they'd heard a lot during their hunt for houses and it was usually an early indicator of something unacceptable.

The building was registered as a storage facility, a claim

supported by towers of brown cardboard boxes, each full of cellophane-wrapped handbags, lining every available space on the staircase. It was on a side street off Commercial Road, 'the largest thoroughfare in London' according to the description on Gumtree. The rent included council tax, all the bills and giving up the right to vote. Also, they shouldn't register with a local GP and wouldn't need a TV licence. The rent would be collected in cash, at the end of the month.

They climbed the three flights of stairs, past several hundred bags, and up to a solid white door. As The Guy fumbled with the keys they looked at each other sceptically. When the door opened to reveal wooden floors, high ceilings, a mock fireplace, an open-plan kitchen and lounge and two massive bedrooms, Paul put his arm around Emma's shoulder and squeezed her happily.

'We'll take it.'

And they did.

Paul and Emma had met a few months before moving in together, at the party of a mutual friend where Paul was DJing. His speciality was playing minimal/funky/deep house/techno/dubstep to rooms full of drug-addled teenagers/Shoreditch hipsters/Italian tourists/sexy gay guys. He had consciously crafted a look that was sexually ambiguous to achieve equal success in gay and straight club worlds. He kept his love life private despite being of some interest to the press. His love life was pretty easy to be discreet about since he never seemed to see the same girl twice. The *NME* had named him amongst the top 100 coolest people in the music industry. He was 75th, which was a source of constant amusement to their friends. Emma had started the conversation with flirting, quickly realised he was a child in a man's body and they'd spent the rest of the night pointing and laughing at the crowd. When Emma mentioned she was house-hunting, Paul had suggested they look together.

Six months later Emma climbed the stairs and opened the door, pleased to find Paul on the futon sofa watching *Come Dine With Me*. On the counter was an oven pizza waiting, she assumed, for her to come in and stick the oven on. She did this, before taking a seat on her side of the sofa. He cracked the top off a beer and pushed it towards her. On the TV a pasty-faced woman was trying to carve an equally pasty-faced piece of meat.

'She's got no chance,' Paul said, tipping his head at the telly. 'It's supposed to be coq au vin.'

'Why is it pink?'

'She's put rosé in it – the voice-over's ripping strips off her.'

'How was last night?'

'Pretty good. I got in at 4 a.m., and I dunno who I was with, but I found a mystery vegetable in my bag this morning.'

'Really?' Emma frowned, getting up to investigate. 'What is it?'

'I have no idea. What happened to you last night?'

'Some sexy Scottish guy ... '

Paul wolf-whistled.

Emma plucked a large, grubby parsnip from the bottom of the fridge.

'Why is it muddy?'

'They're born that way,' he said without looking up. 'You

should've come to the club. There were loads of sexy boys you could've blogged.'

Emma grinned mischievously.

'I was blogging elsewhere. What are you up to tonight? Clem's back from New York if you fancy joining for a pint.'

'Maybe. I'm playing at eleven, so just powering up.'

She put the pizza in the oven. 'Hey, should I roast the parsnip? I could make it into sort-of chips.'

'Calm down, Derringer, you're not on the telly.'

7

Pinchos

Clementine was perched on the barstool of Pinchos, a small, dimly lit tapas bar near Old Street. She was staring at the second email she had sent to Drake since she'd arrived in London exactly one week earlier.

'Hi Drake, just checking in. I'm in London for the foreseeable, it'd be great to meet up and talk *Moonshiners*. Let me know if you're around?'

She hoped the desperation she felt hadn't somehow seeped into her words.

She had dressed to look like the star of an Edward Hopper painting: heavily black eyes and dark red lips, her long auburn hair styled into dramatic waves and a black dress that was fitted and elegant. One shoe was delicately balanced on the base of the barstool, the other pointed outwards. The only giveaway that she wasn't a famous screenwriter, but an impoverished, twenty-something London girl, was a ladder in her tights that started at the toe of her shoe and wound up and around her leg, disappearing at the knee. Clem was uncharacteristically early to the bar, eager to get away from her mum's house. She was wistfully stirring a martini that she couldn't afford and hoping Emma wouldn't get caught at work. If Emma couldn't buy the drinks, Clem would have to run for it.

Emma walked in and paused in the doorway. The bartender, seeing a familiar face, nodded.

Clem rushed over and threw her arms around Emma, squeezing her tight and lifting her up a little. 'Looking gorgeous as always, Emmy D.'

'You too, Twist. Jeez, you've lost so much weight – I thought you said you only ate pizza.'

Clem had lost more weight than looked healthy to Emma, but this was traditionally how their meetings started and they were damned if a few pounds up or down would change that.

'I wouldn't worry.' Clem noted the expression on Emma's face as they hoiked themselves onto the tall leather barstools. 'My mum's on a mission to fill me with pudding; I'll have my happy pounds back soon ...'

Two months earlier, Clem had sent Emma a strangely hysterical email: she had broken up with The Actor – a mysterious figure that Emma knew very little about – and was going on a road trip with her roommate. Emma wasn't to worry if she didn't pick up her phone. Emma had worried until Clem posted dozens of road trip pics and seemed to be having a brilliant time.

Emma waved at the bartender. 'Hello, mate – two martinis please.' She turned to Clem. 'Dry and dirty? As if I have to ask.'

They watched while the bartender stirred the drinks.

'It's been too long,' Clem said happily.

'It really has,' Emma agreed.

Two olive-garnished, ice-cold martinis slid across the bar. This was their drink – the official sponsor of Girl Talk with Em and Clem, a tradition that predated New York by years.

Emma let out a long sigh of pleasure. 'You look so glamorous,' she said, motioning to Clem's tight black skirt. 'Is that how fabulous New York screenwriters dress? I should've got out of my work clothes.'

'Jesus, are they your work clothes? Where do you work? Gap?'

'Says the high-class hooker.'

They were two drinks in when Clem mentioned Yasmin.

'She's coming down in a bit, by the way.' She said it with a hint of apology. 'She's got news.'

Emma resisted the urge to roll her eyes. 'That's cool, we're besties these days.'

Clementine and Yasmin had grown up together and their parents were old friends. When Yasmin's parents divorced she had hidden at Clem's house. Their mutual contempt for dads as a concept bound them together in their early teens. Unable to escape the clutches of her friendship, Clem had introduced Yasmin to Emma at sixth-form college and, since then, Emma and Yasmin had embarked on a now decade-long battle for Clem's heart and time. When Clem had left for New York, Yasmin and Emma's friendship had developed, to their surprise, into something above circumstantial.

'She still doesn't know about the Cotton Club,' said Emma reluctantly, blushing slightly.

'Yikes.'

'Yeah. And they're pretty serious now – she's met his parents and they go on mini-breaks. They bought a cat, Clem; they called it André.' Emma looked pained.

Clem leaned back on her chair and plucked an olive from her glass. She put it in her mouth and spoke around it.

'You can't tell her now.'

'I know, right? It's been too long, but ... When *can* I tell her? Do I even need to at this stage?' She lowered her voice and said with impending doom, 'What about when she marries him?'

Clem laughed and then frowned. '*When* she marries him?'

'Yeah, don't tell her I told you but she booked the venue months ago *just in case.*'

'Oh my god, this is so ridiculous. You have to let it slip, make it innocent – don't "confess", just say something like, "Well I wish I'd never made out with him, ha ha ha." Something like that. Say it like it's no big deal and it won't be?'

She posed it as a question because they both knew that Yasmin's inclination to make a big deal out of something was wildly unpredictable. She might, for example, go ballistic at a waiter for bringing lukewarm water to the table, and in the same restaurant she would practically ignore having a glass of wine poured in her hood. Nobody could guess how she would react to the fact that moments before she had met her now serious boyfriend, he'd been kissing Emma in a corner of the club. They'd broken apart just as she'd arrived and Emma had introduced them saying, 'Yasmin, meet some guy, some guy, meet Yasmin,' before wandering back towards the dance floor. When she had next seen them, a few weeks later, the relationship had blossomed into something tangible. The couple had moved in together a few months previously. The prequel had never seemed necessary to mention, but it weighed heavily on Emma's conscience.

'I dunno ... I guess it doesn't matter. I just don't want to be his dirty secret, you know? It feels icky.' Emma looked at Clem imploringly but could see her mind had wandered.

'Why hasn't *he* told her?' Clem said distractedly. 'Maybe he doesn't want to get between friends? Which is admirable, I guess ... but someone should probably tell her ... ' She trailed off and her eyes were wet.

Emma signalled for more drinks. It was time.

'Come on then,' she said to Clem, who looked up at her sheepishly. 'Tell me everything about this cock-sucking motherfucker. Start at the beginning. I've got all night.'

Jordan Guillermo was an actor. He'd been in couple of low-budget films that had done well and he was studying writing and directing at Columbia. He'd been called a rising star in the industry, and he was recognisable.

'One of the twenty-something Manhattan luvvies set,' Clem told Emma.

Clem had met him in a lecture theatre after she'd pitched a script idea to the class.

He had asked her out and when she said no he had pursued her, utilising all of his Hollywood charm and disarm tactics.

She was resistant at first because she was wary of dating actors. 'Clingy drama queens, the lot of them,' she said. But eventually she gave him the benefit of the doubt because he was also a writer, an artist, a deeply ambitious person, and so absurdly handsome.

Jordan had taken her to exclusive parties and introduced her to industry people. She was proud to have been cropped out of *Hello!* twice. He had pulled her all the way into his life with such ease that she barely had time to drop her guard.

'I think I slung it out the window of a limo on our second date.'

They dated for five amazing months, and then it suddenly got serious.

'One day he just switched and got really intense; he said he loved me for the first time and he just kind of upped the ante. I got carried along. I started to enjoy it – he was so *present* all the time, you know?'

Emma nodded.

'It stopped being fun, but I assumed that proper relationships matured that way and this adult, slightly tortured thing was the next phase.'

'He would call constantly ... You know me, Em – normally I would find that irritating, but because New York was so alien to me, it actually felt good that there was someone who gave a shit about where I was going and who I was with.' She stopped and sighed, rubbing her eyes. She took a napkin from the holder on the bar and wiped under her mascara.

'He would bring up these deep philosophical questions, like, what we wanted from the future and why we had come to be together. He would get metaphysical and talk about parallel dimensions, and I thought he was just trying to really get me. I thought he was saying those things *gratefully*, like he was so pleased the universe had brought us together, and I would say how pleased I was too.'

Emma looked mortified.

'I totally fell for it – the needy puppy act got completely under my skin. But it wasn't love, it was guilt. Because that whole time he was seeing this other girl, his friend, who was *my* friend by then. And now when I think about all those conversations, where I basically told him everything about myself, I think he was looking for something that would let him off the hook and give him an excuse to treat me like a total bastard.'

Tears were threatening to spill onto her cheeks, but she remained composed. Emma, full of fury, sat speechless.

'Even right at the end, I didn't suspect anything. They fell in love right under my nose. *She* was the one in the spotlight and I had absolutely no idea. I just thought they were really close, because they had been friends for years. And I liked being part of their friendship, part of a group. I really liked her. Can you image how stupid I must have looked? She let me raid her wardrobe. She was fucking my boyfriend and I was wearing her jeans.'

She stopped for a sip of her martini, anguishing at the memory. Emma flinched.

'Honestly, I think he must have loved the drama of it. All the lying and intrigue. And I really never suspected. Credit to him, the man can act.

'You know I even asked him, I remember it clearly. We were in bed at my apartment and I said, "How do I know this isn't just a role you're playing?" And he said, "If this is a performance I hope the show never ends."'

Emma made a gag face and Clem laughed, switching to a Yonkers accent: 'Wadda guy.'

She sighed and went on, 'I feel like such a dick, because I *knew* it would end like that, with drama and heartache. He's an actor, how else would it end? I thought it was a romcom and I was the leading lady, but the whole time it was just another break-up movie happening right under my nose ... They took me to a Broadway musical for my birthday – together, like I was their kid or something! Who does that?'

At the memory she stopped talking and pursed her lips, and two large round teardrops landed on the bar.

The bartender put two shots of tequila on the bar. They clinked and knocked them back. Emma was aghast. 'Why didn't anyone tell you? Didn't anyone else know?'

Clem shrugged.

'I guess people knew, but they were *his* friends. He made them choose and all they knew about me was that I was just some scholarship bitch from abroad. He's this gorgeous New York starlet who's already being cast in stuff. I don't blame them really; he'll be on the A-list before the year's out and I will be no one. Even if I'm rich and famous, I'll be a famous writer. No one gives a fuck about the writer, Emma.'

'What do you mean?'

Clem laughed bitterly, and smiled at her friend. 'Who wrote *E.T.*?'

'Umm ...'

'I'll tell you exactly what you're thinking – Spielberg directed it and Drew Barrymore was one of the kids. Maybe you know who the main kid was, but the writer? No one gives a fuck.'

Emma took a too-big gulp of her martini. Clementine went on.

'So I was totally nailing New York; I had a great place, cool friends, my boyfriend was in magazines. I was top of my class, my tutors loved me, and everything was awesome.

For the first time in my life I was actually doing more than just surviving, you know? And then in one day, he just tore the heart out of it . . . '

She paused for breath and composed herself, sighing long and deep. She looked at Emma through her hair and smiled softly, shaking her head.

'Do you want to hear it? The roof story?'

Emma laughed nervously. 'Sounds dangerous.'

'Right? Of all the places to dump someone . . . So it's Saturday night, and we're going to a party on the Upper West. He insisted on coming all the way downtown to pick me up in a town car, and he looked so cool. He was wearing a dark blue T-shirt and he smelled all clean and sexy. And he seemed kind of uptight but I just assumed he had pre-party nerves. All the guys from our course were going to be there, and get this – it's at *her* house, the other woman. He's taking me right into the snake's nest and I don't even know it.

'I'm in this gorgeous dress, it's dark blue, and it's a coincidence but I feel really good that we match. I've borrowed shoes from my roommate that are too high but fuck it, right? I don't have to get the subway and it's a house party, I can always take them off.

'So when we arrive we walk up to her apartment. It's on the seventh floor and there's no elevator, so I'm pleased when we get there because the shoes are already killing me. I'm about to knock on the door and he says, "Let's keep going, I want to show you something." He doesn't even say, "We need to talk," so I could have maybe braced myself. No, he goes, "I want to show you something."

'So we go up another four or five floors and then he opens the fire escape door and it's really like something out of a movie, and for a second, for this tiny second I think he's going to propose. I know it's stupid and I totally don't want him to, but for this little moment I entertain the idea, and I grin. My feet hurt and it's cold but we're together and we're in love and we're up there, on top of Manhattan. I actually have this thought – "I am so happy". Can you believe that? I actually remember having that thought.

'And then he sucker-punches me right in the heart. Bang.

'He waits until I've taken it all in, like a deep breath, and then he says it, quietly, with his back to me: "Clem, I'm seeing Elise." There's no build-up, and for a second I think he's being literal and she's there, on the roof, so I look around for her. But then I hear it, in the way he said her name, this name I've heard and said a hundred times. It sounds different, *Elissse*, as if the 's' now stands for sex.'

Emma says it: 'Eleessss.'

'Yeah, exactly. I'm actually surprised he didn't take a photo when he said it. I must have had full-on shock face.'

'I can't believe he ... I mean ... on the roof?' Emma didn't know what else to say. She chewed an olive. Shocked.

'I know, that was his *actual* plan. And then he delivers this fucking monologue. He talks about how it was because of me that his eyes were opened to her, and how he's so glad we met and blah blah blah. And it's all about him. It's all about how amazing he is and how much he's learned and how much he's been through and how hard it's all been for him. And I stand there thinking he must be joking, because why am I wearing this dress? Why did he make me get in the car? Why didn't he just do this when we were at my place, like, half an hour ago? Why make me get ready and go to a party, just to have this conversation? I absolutely cannot understand it.

38

'And then he kind of steps away from me, and delivers his closing lines out to the New York skyline, like he's playing Macbeth or something. And I'm just standing there, with my mouth hanging open, like a complete idiot. And then he comes over and touches my arms, looks into my eyes and he whispers at me, "Never change who *you* are," and then he just walks away! He goes through the fire escape door and he's gone, I hear him go downstairs, and I think, his pace was actually pretty jaunty, you know? He skipped down those stairs. And it must have been minutes before I could move. And all I could think was, I'm on her roof. She's nicked my boyfriend and I'm standing on her fucking roof!'

She necked the last of her drink and looked at Emma. There was a long pause.

'True story.'

Emma couldn't help it; she laughed. 'Oh my god.'

Clem looked at her earnestly.

'Never change who you are? What does that even mean?'

Clem shook her head. 'I honestly don't know.'

'That might be the worst break-up story I've ever heard.'

'I think it was the classic "it's not you, it's me".'

Emma nodded. 'It's not you it's me me me; never change who *you* are.'

'Yeah he's like, I'm the actor, I'll do all the changing in this town.'

'He sounds like a dick.'

Clem nodded solemnly. 'He's king of the dicks.'

When the laughter had subsided and the sadness of the story kicked in they went quiet. They ordered two more drinks and when they arrived they clinked glasses.

'So, what did he expect you to do?' said Emma, taking a sip.

'Maybe he wanted me to jump. Imagine the attention he would have got.'

'I'm so sorry I wasn't there. I'm so sorry there wasn't someone there who could've punched him in the face.'

'Yeah, me too.'

'So what did you do? Did you say anything to her?'

'I had to leave the roof on my own, and walk down like, a hundred flights of stairs in these beautiful shoes that I didn't want to take off in case I bumped into someone I knew on their way to the party. I had to walk past the door where they were *having* the party. When I got to her floor I stopped and thought about going in, just getting drunk and being normal, and I stood there for what felt like ages. I was debating it when everything inside went quiet, and I thought I heard my name, and I thought it was followed by this huge laugh and I couldn't stand to go in, but I had this killer dress on and these tall shoes, and they were supposed to be my friends too.'

The image broke Emma's heart.

'It's a shame you're not an actor too – you could have gone in and made a massive scene.'

'After that party I got relegated to the geek squad. For the rest of the term I sat with a Hungarian guy called Boris who only wrote sex scenes . . . He's actually doing quite well now though . . . ' she added.

'Aww, Clem, I'm so sorry you were there on your own.'

'I wasn't totally alone; I had a flatmate, a barrel of gin and a camera with a "look at me being cheerful" filter.'

Emma laughed. 'You did look pretty happy online.'

Clem nodded, rueful. 'You know how it is. I over compensated. I completely bankrupted myself trying to prove I was fine. But I was competing in this one-player game because he couldn't give a fuck.

'So Jordan and Elise were now this golden couple. I wanted to smash her face in, but I couldn't, because I'm nearly thirty and I was surrounded by *children*.

'I kept thinking if I was twenty-two it would have been fine to go mental at them, but instead I was just this dignified ghost lady. I was just killing time, waiting for it to end so I could come home, to my city, where I'm the boss and he's the stranger.'

'And now you're back.'

'And now I'm back, and I live with my mum ...' She laughed bitterly. 'But at least my best friend is here,' she added and leaned over for a hug. 'I missed you so much.'

Emma hugged her back. 'I missed you too. I'm so sorry.'

They sat silently, taking a moment to realise how much they had missed each other.

'So what are you going to do? Work-wise or whatever?'

'God, I don't know. I've got the impoverished artist bit down, that's for sure. So drinking heavily and feeling guilty, mostly.'

Emma signalled for more drinks.

'There's just one thing I need to know ...'

'Shoot.'

'Who wrote *E.T.*?'

'Dude, I don't know, google it.'

Another martini later and they were both firmly hammered, when their dulcet-toned conversation was shattered.

'Hey, ladies!'

Yasmin Attali entered the bar with a flourish, brandishing bags and wearing clacky heels. The bartender immediately stood up straighter and ran his hand through his hair.

'Clemmy! Welcome back, my darling.'

Emma winced at the shrill sound and shot an embarrassed look around the room.

Clementine stepped down off her barstool for a hug and Emma rolled her eyes at the bartender.

'Hi, Emma,' said Yasmin, theatrically kissing her on both cheeks and pulling a barstool up into the middle of the two.

'So,' she said, winking at the bartender, 'can I get a glass of red?' She beamed at her friends. 'How are we?'

Clementine shot Emma a warning glance across their drinks, a long-established expression that said *game face, bro.* When they didn't answer, Yasmin rolled her eyes.

'Emma, *how*'s Paul?'

Yasmin's insistence that Emma should hook up with Paul was one of the many reasons she never would.

'He's good, he's playing somewhere central tonight – he might swing by on his way in.'

'Cool, I'd love to see him.' She squirmed her shoulders seductively.

'Oh, Emma. By the way, I have the BEST news for you,' she squealed, pinching Emma hard on her arm so that she flinched and rubbed it.

'So Tammy, from *Experiamental*, has just signed as dep. ed at *Get Up.*'

Clem mouthed, *O. M. G.* behind Yas's back.

'I don't know what any of those words mean,' said Emma sullenly and Clem let out a short sharp laugh.

'Don't be obtuse, Emma. You know my friend Tammy, she's the new deputy editor at *Get Up* online magazine. I told her about your blog! You can send her articles or whatever … Because, writing and all that?' Yasmin rolled her eyes at Clem.

Emma groaned.

'*Get Up* though, really? What will I write about? Celebrity flip-flops?'

'You could write 157 ways to sell out,' Clem suggested.

'Or you could write ten ways to be massively ungrateful, Emma.' Yasmin glared incredulously from one to the other.

Clem shrugged. 'It's a bit like getting me a writing job on a soap, Yas.'

'Yes? And? So, what – we're too good for the mainstream now? You're too cool for a glossy, are you? These things are popular culture! Jesus, Emma, I thought you'd be pleased.'

Emma stared out of the window of the bar. She wasn't tall or thin enough for women's magazines. 'I am. Sorry, Yas – that's awesome, thank you.'

Clem saw despair kicking in and changed the subject.

'So, what's new, Yas?' Clementine asked, draining her martini as if it were the last she'd ever have and pretending not to have noticed the massive diamond on the hand that Yasmin held conspicuously out of sight.

'Your hair looks nice,' she said, to neither of them. Her mischievous grin told them she was enjoying the attention and was going for the slow build.

''Scuse me,' she flirted at the bartender. 'Can I get a glass of water as well?'

Catching Emma's expression she added pedantically, 'Please.'

'Have you had it cut?' She directed the compliment towards Clem.

'Not this year.'

'So . . . ' Yasmin straightened up in her chair.

'Come on then,' said Clem. Yas took a deep breath. It was like theatre curtains opening.

'Well. Last night, Adam took me to The Boulevardier in Canary Wharf, and he was all nervous . . . '

Clem put her head in her hands. 'Uuurgh.'

'So ANYway,' Yasmin continued – she was not going to let them spoil her moment. She stopped abruptly. 'Emma, why are you wearing all black?'

'Fat week.'

'I like you in colours.'

It was a classic Yasmin *non-pliment* and Clementine sniggered.

'I've got pink pants on if it helps.'

Yasmin took a deep drink of wine and put the glass back on the bar, sneering at it. House red was not her normal drink of choice.

'He ordered a bottle of champagne, and I just KNEW what was coming. And THIS was in my glass.' She brandished her manicured hand to reveal the most predictable diamond ring the world had ever seen.

'Whoa, that is a massive rock.' Clem took her friend's hand and Yasmin squealed with delight, 'I KNOW!', alarming a lady at a table behind them.

'And you said yes?' said Clem with thinly veiled disdain.

'OF COURSE! My mum's gone BONKERS! And it's so perfect because I've got the venue already! I knew I was right to get it done!'

Right on cue Yasmin's phone rang, and smiling widely she held it up to show them that instead of Adam's name, it now said 'Fiancé'. She stood and took the call, moving over to the door where even more people could hear her.

Emma looked at Clem with 'I told you so' in her eyes.

'She'd put a fucking heart over the "i" if she could,' whispered Clem, bitterly.

Emma shrugged. 'She's marrying a guy who once called an Ikea shelving unit "too wacky".'

They watched Yasmin hang up the phone and clutch it to her chest like a kid with a new doll. 'At least she's off the market,' said Emma.

Yasmin returned to the bar and sat down. 'He just called to make sure you're being nice to me.'

Clem leaned forward and said seriously, 'Yas, before you changed his name to "Fiancé", he was in your phone as "Boring Adam". You literally knew two more interesting Adams – wouldn't you rather marry one of them?'

Yasmin was blissfully oblivious to their concern.

'Don't be silly, Clem. Adam B is shorter than me, and Fit Adam is gay!'

Shouting gay across the room ruffled a few feathers and Emma frowned at Yasmin's complete lack of decorum.

'Congratulations.' Emma got up and they hugged.

'Thanks, Em.' She said it sympathetically, as if Emma's single status was a massive tragedy.

Clem stayed seated, looking exasperated. 'Are you sure you want to marry him though? Are you sure you're not settling?'

A flash of anger crossed Yasmin's face and she turned to Clem.

'Well I have to get married this year because Adam wants to have kids before he's thirty-four and he thinks I should have the first one before I'm thirty, and we want at least two so . . .'

She drifted off into thought, with a calm look of resignation you might see on someone who's just been told they're terminally ill. Clem shifted uncomfortably in her seat. She felt stung. She was suddenly and acutely aware that she was single and broke. She thought briefly about her own lack of a 'life plan'.

She sighed and smiled at Yasmin, whose plan was bang on track.

Yasmin shouted at the bartender for a bottle of bubbles. They popped the cork and clinked glasses: 'To Yas and Adam and the future.' Clem and Emma's eyes met as Yasmin added, 'And to the hen night!'

8

Nougat Sticks

'Ready then, magic makers?' Adrian projected his voice across the creative department. The Eds hopped up eagerly and swaggered, cocks first, towards the boardroom.

Emma, pale green and dishevelled, necked the end of her coffee, wished she hadn't, and got up to follow. Adrian walked along behind her, putting his huge arm over her shoulders.

'Rockin' and rollin', Em?' he said cheerfully. She kept her mouth shut and nodded, hoping he couldn't smell the vodka she was definitely doused in.

As she passed the PR department Hilary called out, 'You need a cheeseburger, Emma. Let's do lunch.' And the rest of the PR girls rolled their eyes and chewed their gum like a herd of cows.

Emma sat at the back, somehow, despite the circular set-up. Notebook in lap, pen tapping the chair's arm. On the whiteboard Gemma was hastily writing 'Nougat Sticks'. Nobody laughed.

'So . . .' Adrian beamed.

His expression said that whatever they were about to do, they were going to make a lot of money doing it.

'New client.'

Pause.

'A great new client with a great new product.'

Gemma dropped her notepad and mumbled sorry. Emma stared at the clock on the wall.

Seconds

Took

Ages

To

Tock.

'Who's the client, Ade . . . drian?' asked an Ed.

The 'Ade' rattled around the room. Much as he'd like it to, 'Ade' just wouldn't stick.

'It's a big one, Eddy baby, and if we get this right, we're going to become their primo people. We'll roll out our brand strategy across ALL the products. And that's a lot of products.'

He licked his lips, an expression of gleeful greed. Emma stifled a groan, Gemma stifled a yawn, and one of the Eds stifled an erection.

Adrian tapped the whiteboard loudly. 'Because this isn't about the product percy.' Per se, thought everyone.

'They're looking for a way to engage their people, and they feel, thanks in large part to Drew, and myself . . .' He said this reaching over his own shoulder and patting himself on the back. Everyone noted the large sweaty rings under his arms. Nobody laughed (nobody ever laughs).

'That it's the man on the ground that matters – and how do you influence the man on the ground?'

A strong desire to get this over with led Emma to recite in sardonic monotone,

'You start at the top.'

'That's right. Thank you, Emma. You start at the top. This campaign isn't about getting people to buy a new sweetie. This is about getting everyone from the leadership to the shopkeeper to really believe in it. And to do that we need to . . . ?'

'Start at the top,' said four or five voices with pantomime enthusiasm.

'Now obviously most people don't want to eat sweeties all day.'

Emma shuddered. *He has got to stop saying sweeties – he sounds like an utter paedo.*

She bit her nails, wondering if she could stomach a bloody mary with lunch. Gemma walked around the room distributing Nougat Sticks.

Emma examined the box. 'Is this aimed at kids?' she asked, barely bothering to conceal her contempt.

Adrian answered in earnest: 'I think we should be thinking about the broadest spectrum of appeal. Apparently they have fewer calories than a Big Mac,' he laughed.

You're a fucking Big Mac, Adrian.

He looked out at them, making eye contact with each person.

'There are eight people in this room . . . '

Emma counted ten people but assumed the Eds counted as one and Gemma didn't count as any. Gemma made a note on her pad, which Emma could see said '8'.

'Drew and I met with the client to talk about our approach,' Adrian went on.

Drew was Adrian's second in command. He'd started his career as an ideas guy with a coke habit, back when designers still used scalpels and cutting mats and mounted ideas onto card. In his spare time he was writing a kids' book about a one-eared rabbit called Hutch, whose life went round in circles. Emma knew this because she'd once asked him, 'What do you do in your spare time?'

Now, he was sitting quietly in his chair and waiting for Adrian to do his thing. Emma wondered if he took Xanax.

Adrian went on: 'So, we've decided to take the core team away, a couple of days together where we can crack this thing, talk about the next big opportunities for us as a company and really fuse as a team. We need to love and trust each other.'

Girl guide games and grinning for forty-eight hours. Emma's heart sank and she pictured Adrian in a life jacket leading the way down white water rapids (suitable for ages twelve and up).

'This is a great opportunity to get out of the office and really get to know each other. I really hope it's something that we can all really grow from.'

The room filled with insincere smiles.

'What about the PRs?' asked Emma. 'Is it a company-wide thing or just us lot?'

Adrian seemed grateful for even the most vague display of interest.

'This one's for the creatives,' he said happily. 'You guys are where the magic is and I want you to really take the opportunity to give this your best shot.' He looked triumphantly round the room. You could almost see the calculations going on: *Will I get paid?* (Emma) / *Will I get days off?* (Gemma) / *Will I get to boff Emma?* (Ross).

'In the meantime, get your sweetie thinking caps on, and let's get sticky! Hey, I think I've got something there!' He looked at Emma for reassurance. *Absolutely*, she nodded at him.

Emma cupped her chin and let her arms hold the weight of her hangover. She stared at the words: Nougat Stick.

Stupid.

Emma played some word association, or 'idea mapping' *if you're a dick*, so that she would have something to show them if called upon.

Nougat > nugget > chicken > bbq > cheeseburger > bleurrrgh. Stick > sticky > stickers > joystick > stick up > sticks and stones . . .

After twenty minutes the room had descended into corporate anarchy; they had put their pens down and were replying to emails or reading the news on their phones. Emma's eyes jerked open when she heard the others do the 'look busy' shuffle.

Adrian sat front and centre and looked at them expectantly. The Eds kicked off proceedings, standing at the front of the room and shouting at each other.

'Action.'

'Adventure.'

'Kids.'

'Cartooooons.'

They stopped in unison, turning from bouncing jackasses into serious moneymen.

In her peripheral vision Emma could see Adrian grinning, his hands squeezed between his knees. *His inner child runs awfully close to the surface.*

Emma's attention faded out of the room, and she pictured

Clem at that moment, working on her script, taking calls from agents and drinking black coffee in fancy meeting rooms while people cooed about her talent. She stared at the trees lining the street outside the office and was jealous of them, standing there, growing. She wondered if trees communicated, would it be in super slow motion? Not unlike this meeting . . .

Adrian was standing up and seemed very happy with it all. 'Emma, you're on.'

She felt the hairs on her neck bristle and her ears start to burn. She prefaced each sentence with a nervous 'Umm' that was designed to imply 'I'm just the assistant so ummm you don't have to listen but . . .'

'Well, I figured from the packaging that it's a more adult product.'

Ross winked at her and smiled.

Ewww.

'Through word play I got to Joy Stick, which could be the basis of a social campaign . . .'

One of the Eds pulled a 'la de da' face and rolled his eyes but kept quiet. Emma visualised punching him in the eye, and went on: 'That supports an overarching strategy . . .'

I say the same three lines in every meeting.

She could barely listen to herself and went on without caring what came out, trusting she'd been there long enough to get it right.

' . . . help to engage the leadership . . .' She moved to the front of the room, knowing that delivery was Adrian's G spot, and wrote on the whiteboard: The Joy of Sweets.

Adrian leaned back in his chair and clapped his hands together once. Emma thought he was going to slow clap her, but he simply stopped. She went on, knocked off course for a beat.

'They could position themselves as treats for grown-ups. And if they were using this product as a starting point, they could use Joy Stick to line up the campaign . . .'

She stopped talking; her voice had sunk into a depressive monotone and was shrivelling into the hollow peanut shell it called home. Fully flushed by this stage and sensing a lurch of nausea she trailed off and shrugged, 'That's as far as I got.'

She sat down and everyone turned to Adrian for his reaction.

'Brilliant, Emma, well done you,' Adrian said.

Patronise me more, babe.

'Thanks, everyone. This is certainly food for thought. A great starting point, well done.' He led the rest of them in a smattering of applause.

As Emma headed back to her desk, her phone rang. When she saw it was her dad she picked it up.

'Dad Derringer indeed. How the devil are you?'

'Hi Emma. All good, thank you. Are you at work?'

She sat at her desk and woke up her computer. 'I am, Dad – can't really chat. What's up?'

'It's a bit embarrassing actually.'

'Oh god, what? What is it?' She screwed up her nose and braced herself.

'Well, someone has sent me some footage to score . . .'

'Don't they know you're retired?'

'Oh yes, but it's only a little job, I'm happy to do it really. Anyway they've sent me a memory stick but I don't know what to do with it. I was hoping I could post it to you and you could help. Do you need to see it?'

Emma laughed, and then stopped – she didn't want to hurt his feelings. She wondered if she could talk him through it rather than go round.

'It's a memory stick, like the card that goes in your camera. You need to connect it to your computer ... '

'Yes, I thought as much ... '

'It's a USB.'

'A U-S-B. Righto. Which stands for ... ?'

'God knows, Pops. But you stick it in the computer and then you should be able to see it on the main screen.'

'Yes, I've put it in. But now I'm at a bit of a loss ... '

He drifted off, clearly not wanting to ask, but not knowing what else to do.

'I'll come over. After work. About seven.'

'Thanks, Emma. I'm sorry. I'll make dinner'

'No, Dad, I won't be able to stay. I'll pop in for a coffee – it won't take more than a couple of minutes.'

'Sorry, Em.'

He sounded completely wretched, and she wished he were stronger.

'No, don't be, it'll be nice to see you. I'll look forward to it.'

Sounding slightly perkier, he thanked her again and hung up.

She texted Paul that she wouldn't be back after work and checked online to make sure the trains were running. Her dad only lived forty-five minutes from her office, but it always felt like travelling through a wormhole to get there. The closer she got to zone 3, the younger and more inadequate she felt. Her education had crippled her parents' finances, dredging their tiny savings and exhausting their credit as well as her own. Her mum had got bored and moved to Spain when Emma was at uni, which seemed like the best outcome for everyone, but meant that Emma kept a closer eye on her dad.

She sighed but stopped abruptly when she caught Adrian's eye mid-breath.

Must stop sighing.

She opened her Nougat Sticks campaign folder and tried to remember what the hell anyone had said in the meeting.

9

Clem the Temp

Clem woke up in the attic room of her mum's house in Ealing. She had been in London less than a week and already New York felt like little more than a film she had seen. Her waking thought was of money; the night before she had surreptitiously felt behind the sofa cushions for quids. This was a new low. The bank had been calling, Malcolm had warned her – they wanted to talk. She had nodded breezily to cover the cold flush that ran up her spine at the thought of talking to the bank. She wished that she had a job like Emma's, where all she had to do was turn up, look interested and get paid. She had absolutely no idea what time it was, wondering how long she could keep attributing her lack of vigour to jet lag.

She rolled over and checked her emails, willing there to be something she could embrace as a career development. The closest thing to news was a message from a temp agency that Emma had recommended, inviting her to a meeting.

Tempted to pretend she hadn't seen the message, she closed her eyes against it.

She was more used to working in bars or restaurants to make ends meet between projects, but couldn't face minimum wage and late nights. Emma had offered to put a word in with the agency that had arranged her current role. Clem pictured herself in a creative meeting and thought it seemed easy enough.

She went downstairs hoping her stepdad was out and the house was empty. She felt a pang of resentment when she heard the page of a newspaper being turned with Malcolm's trademark aggression, as if those pages were his sworn enemies.

Malcolm sat at the dining room table with a cup of tea, reading intently. He looked up at Clem as she entered the room and then at the shoes she dropped by the door. She padded through in her socks.

'Morning, Clementine,' he said, with a glance at the clock. 'It's a nice day out – have you got any plans?'

'I've got a meeting with a creative recruitment agency about a job, on Oxford Street.'

'Is that what you're wearing?'

She ignored him and his banal rhetoric and walked through to the kitchen to put the kettle on.

Who calls a baby Malcolm? she thought as she stared at the kettle.

'I'm going into town in a bit if you'd like a lift?'

Clem was torn between her stubborn refusal to accept favours from him, and not wanting to take a bus.

'Yeah, cool, thanks.'

He nodded, seeming pleased that she had acquiesced, and

went back to beating up the paper. Clem watched him and wondered what her mum saw in him; he was a middle manager in a textbook publishing house and he always smelled like an old suitcase.

Malcolm pointed the rusty Ford Escort towards central London, and then let fate take the wheel. He spoke over his glasses, leaning forward as if to spur the vehicle on. Clem sat in the passenger seat on the white-knuckle ride of near misses.

She looked down at the clunky work shoes she had found in her mum's wardrobe; the heel was dense and they were obviously less than a tenner's worth of pleather. They had the disquieting effect of making her feel like a thick-tongued teenager.

She hissed 'Shit' as the wing mirror skimmed a cyclist.

'Don't swear, Clem.'

She resisted the urge to huff and sulk in her seat, knowing that would only reinforce his notion of her as a surly teenager. Instead she pictured grabbing him by the hair and ramming his face against the steering wheel.

When they pulled up behind Marble Arch, Malcolm handed her a twenty-pound note and smiled with mock hope.

'For luck.'

She took the money and muttered thanks. Embarrassed, she slammed the door as if that gesture could slam him out of her life.

She arrived at the recruitment office sweaty and perplexed and was asked to take a seat in a low red chair. She filled out a set of forms that asked her to reiterate everything on her

CV and included a spelling test. With her eyes unfocused, she tried to think what to say if asked such banalities as 'Where do you see yourself in five years?' or 'Which three words best describe you?'

She felt a bead of sweat pursuing its own career path down her spine. Clem had constructed a CV out of lies and possibilities. The email from Gabby Pickard Recruitment Specialist had managed to be accusing and obnoxious before it even had an introduction.

Clementine
I tried to get through to you but you don't have voicemail?? Call me on the number below and I can arrange for you to come to the office and talk about your experience.
Gabby

Clem glanced at the girl sitting to her right. She was a nervous strawberry blonde teenager and Clem dismissed her as one of the general public.

Clem yawned and looked around to see if she could spot a coffee machine. The office smelled of MDF and perfume. People tapped keyboards and stared intently at their screens. There was a low murmur of invoice-chasing and an exaggerated sense of urgency. From where she was sitting Clem watched the receptionist, clacking away in a pencil skirt and kitten heels. A slogan ran the length of the opposite wall in giant pink Helvetica letters:

TOMORROW IS TODAY WAITING TO HAPPEN.

Clem repeated the phrase a couple of times, trying to make sense of it. Her hangover was taking hold, and this place was exhausting. She closed her eyes and when she opened them Gabby was standing in reception staring at her. Their dislike was instant, and mutual. Clem built her character profile: she was twenty-four, had a ponytail that had probably been in the mouths of many Central Line commuters as she flicked it back and forth. She drank G & Ts (which she called G & Ts). Her metrosexual boyfriend worked in ... experiential marketing. She had a degree in media, hailed from the Midlands and lived in Stoke Newington. She was wearing skinny jeans and box-fresh trainers and she couldn't be arsed to do anything friendly with her face. She was utterly content in her two-tiered existence, which consisted of work and the weekend and fourteen days' holiday to Thailand every January. She was completely satisfied with her contribution to society. Clem's smile aimed for enthusiastic but had an unmistakable air of 'let's get this over with'. Together they walked the length of the office; Clem stood tall, trying to project confident employability.

In a shiny white plastic meeting room, Gabby sat on a low black lounger, tucking one trainer up under her bum and tapping her clipboard while scrutinising the CV in front of her. Clem tried to remember what she'd written and cursed herself for not revisiting the document before she left this morning.

Clearing her throat, Gabby put the CV on the table and folded her arms. Clem discreetly glanced at the clipboard to see which version of herself she needed to present. 'So you've just returned from America?'

'Yeah, I've been back about a week.'

'And what were you doing there?'

'I was at film school, Columbia, in New York.'

She was used to having people be impressed by her stint as a scholarship student. Evidently, however, Gabby was not one of them.

Gabby cleared her throat again. 'And did you work, at all? In America?'

Her intonation rose at the end of each sentence and Clem could not figure out why she said 'America' like it was something Clem had invented.

'Not legally – I only had a student visa.'

'So, if you were at *film school*, why are you applying for office work? Don't you, like, want to work in film?'

'Yeah, that's the idea.'

'We don't have any jobs in film.'

Clem fought to keep the tone of her voice level.

'Sorry, I misunderstood. I studied screenwriting, so when you say *work in film* I mean, I already work in film – I'm basically waiting to see what happens with my scripts; I have a couple in the pipeline. But right now I'm not fussy about the industry, I can do admin anywhere.'

'Oh, can you?'

Can't anyone? Clem thought.

'So what *actual* experience do you have? Because before you went to America there's a big gap in your CV. What did you do for that year?'

Got housing benefit, went to Greece, had my stomach pumped, she thought.

'I freelanced in quite a few capacities – I did some screenwriting classes and I worked for my stepdad a bit ... I basically had my fingers in a lot of pies. I was doing quite a bit of bar work but I didn't put it down because it didn't seem relevant.'

'Yeah, well, I hate to break it to you, Clementine, but you can't have gaps like that in your CV. Employers are looking for a solid employment background, not just someone who flits about.'

'OK, well, I can update it. I did some data entry and other administrative bits at my stepdad's publishing house – I can expand on that. I mean, I haven't forgotten the alphabet and I've been answering the phone since I was five, you know?' She grinned, aiming for enthusiasm.

'Why don't you just go back to your dad's place, then?'

'It's my stepdad, and I was there for ages – I'd like to try something different. My skills are very transferable.'

Gabby openly scoffed.

'Riiiight ... Well, under a year isn't considered *ages*, actually.'

It is when you're sitting with Malcolm doing data entry, Clem thought.

'So what are your salary expectations?'

'I'd be happy with anything on or around 25k, I guess. What's the industry standard?'

Gabby pointedly put down her clipboard, uncrossed her legs and retracted her face into her chin, like an incredulous turtle. It was not a good look. Clem braced herself.

'Look, Clementine, I'm not sensing any *real* enthusiasm from you. Why should I put you on my books if actually what you want to do is make films or whatever? I'm look-ing for candidates with energy and passion for what they do ... You need to go away and make your CV suitable for someone who *actually* wants a job. You need to pull your finger out of your *pies* and be realistic about your expectations or I'm afraid you'll be looking for work for a very long time.'

Clem was taken aback.

'I'm looking for temp work, to keep me going while my scripts pick up pace. I'm clever and competent – isn't that what employers are looking for? I mean, sitting on a reception desk for a week doesn't exactly demand a PhD, does it?'

Clem's head was spinning at how quickly this had turned nasty. She couldn't figure out how to get back on track.

'Actually, Clementine ...' Gabby responded with her eyebrows furrowed.

Clem wanted to beat this woman to death with her two-toned Converse, she wanted to take her eyebrows off with a shovel, she wanted to pick her up by her perfect fringe and sling her out of the window.

'There are a lot of highly qualified people looking for these roles. The job market is more competitive than ever and with this level of *experience* I don't see you earning more than, say, 18k and I definitely don't think you're going to get very far when you have year-long gaps on your CV.' She leaned back smugly.

Clem took a deep breath, then she locked eyes with Gabby with her best knowing smile.

'Right. So, tell me, Gabby, why did you ask me to come here and meet you? You've got my CV; you could see there were gaps and that I'm a screenwriter. If I'm so completely unemployable, what am I doing here? In your EMPLOYMENT agency. Did you just fancy calling someone a loser today? Because frankly, you could have saved us both an hour and either given me this "feedback" in an email, or even better, not contacted me at all, don't you think?'

She picked up her bag and stood up, wishing she was wearing fabulous shoes after all. *Damn it, Mum.*

She walked as tall as she could across the office, resenting with every step the ugly clump of the rubber heel. Gabby emerged from the office door behind and watched her leave; across the room eyebrows were raised and curious.

'I'm only being honest with you, Clementine,' she said from the doorway.

Without looking back, Clem shouted, 'Shove it up your arse, Gabby.'

She heard a couple of sniggers and the fading sound of Gabby's outrage as she marched past the receptionist, whose thin lips were agape, and down the stairs onto Oxford Street with a satisfying slam of the door.

I've been too long in New York, she thought, remembering fondly the way New Yorkers yell casually at idiots. Fuck creative recruitment, she thought, I'd rather work in a bar.

10

Glycaemic Index

Hilary stood and stared at Emma's screen, which was full of a PowerPoint presentation called 'Rediscovering customer loyalty – market research base points'.

She raised her eyebrows at the screen and turned Emma's chair slightly away from it.

'Jeez, I thought this was the creative department. Can you tear yourself away for lunch?'

Emma nodded gratefully.

Outside Hilary linked arms with Emma. 'I need a bacon double cheeseburger, stat.'

'You'll shatter the PR department's glycaemic index.'

'Nah, it's Friday, it's our treat day – chardonnay for everyone!'

They sat in a booth and ordered two burgers, and fries to share. Hilary was good company. Emma liked the way she spoke to the waiter, and listened while she gave Emma a run-down of her *deal*.

Hilary was thirty-four, married to a banker, liked PR and loved social media, so enjoyed her job. She wanted her first kid (of three, please) in the next year.

Emma told Hilary she was a writer with an accidental career in marketing. 'I started at APRC as a temp, to cover some girl's maternity leave, but she never came back.'

Hilary smacked her lips. 'So what are the perks?'

'Free fruit, a lifetime's supply of inverted commas, a Christmas bonus. It could be worse.'

'Could it?'

'Yeah, I could be in the PR department.'

Hilary laughed. 'It is a bit like being on a bachelorette.'

'And Adrian's the bride to be.'

Hilary added ketchup and mustard to the burger in front of her. She moved with the confidence of a real grown-up.

'Adrian sent the PR department an email saying you were a creative genius and to go to you if anyone was short of ideas.'

'Are you serious?' Emma was genuinely shocked. 'No wonder they all hate me.'

'They don't hate you; they feel sorry for you, being Adrian's right-hand girl. Do you like him?'

'Not a lot.'

Hilary laughed. 'He's kind of an asshole, right? In my interview he said he's never met a black Hilary.'

'Good grief.'

'He's also mentioned diversity twice since I started, but I can forgive him, I guess. He's just . . . '

Suddenly protective, Emma blushed. 'His heart's in the right place.'

Hilary chuckled and took a big bite of the burger. Emma, not knowing why, came to his defence.

'The thing about him is the APRC values are, like, his life guidelines and their profits are his quality of life indicators, you know? He's a nice guy but his faith in capitalism is completely unshakeable, that's why he seems like such a dick.'

'And what are you? Anti-capitalist?'

'Well, for example, he's always saying shit like "you can't stop the march of progress" but I think you can stop it and maybe you should. He thinks growth and progress are the same thing and I absolutely disagree. But I don't care enough to argue with him, and I know him well enough to know that if I did it would just hurt his feelings.'

'So are you, like, a hippy, or something?'

Emma ate a chip and thought about it. 'Don't you think it's sinister how they've reappropriated the term "hippy"? How it now means someone lazy and unwashed. Don't you think that's clever? The yuppies won.'

Hilary rested her chin on her hands. 'You're weird.'

Emma was surprised. 'I don't think so – am I?'

Hilary nodded apologetically.

'I'm only a hippy because I don't have any money.'

'Well, Emma, money doesn't buy happiness.'

'But it does buy Audis, and golf clubs.'

'And lunch.'

Hilary signalled for the bill and put her purse on the table.

'So what else do I need to know about Adrian to get by here?'

'Well, at some point he'll probably ask you, "If you were a brand, which brand would you be?" so you should probably have an answer prepared for that.'

'What was yours?'

'I've never answered him, but my surname's Derringer, so

he just said I was a handgun, because I could go off at any time.'

'What does that mean?'

'I have no idea.'

Hilary took two notes from her purse and put them under the bill. Emma added her card to the pile but Hilary pushed it back over the table. 'This one's on me. But let's do it again soon.'

11

Memory Sticks

An off licence and a chicken shop flanked the top of the north London street where Emma had grown up. The pervading smell was a rich combination of petrol, vinegar and fried chicken. Even in summer the street was dingy; shadows lurked behind other shadows. The residents of this road tended towards paranoia and the average age was sixty. The houses were all yellowed curtains and plastic doors. 'No Junk Mail' and 'Beware of the Dog' stickers.

Emma's house was a red-brick terraced with two bedrooms. Outside was her dad's knackered Fiat.

Daniel and Liz Derringer had bought the house in 1985, under the illusion that the area was 'up and coming'. But thirty years later it was still rough.

On the wall of the house opposite theirs, some bright young thing had scrawled 'Nisha Loves Neils Cock' in red spray paint. Someone had made an amend using a black spray can, and now passers-by would think Nisha had a thing for socks.

Although she had a key, she rang the bell. Her dad's hearing was shot and if she let herself in she ran the risk of scaring the crap out of him. From the doorstep she heard him click off Radio 4. She could see through the bevelled glass that he was making his way down the hallway. When he opened the door a gust of warm familiar air joined his welcoming smile. She was surprised to see how old he looked. His hair had thinned since her last visit and was now all the way grey. He smiled warmly and ushered her inside.

'Emma, lovely, thanks for coming. Don't I feel like a total dinosaur.' The house smelled of baked beans and dust; it looked like he hadn't hoovered for weeks. They'd used to keep a very clean house, but that had been down to a weekly cleaner who had long ago left the area. Evidently nobody had picked up where she had left off.

Emma headed directly for the computer in the music room. At one time it had also functioned as a lounge, but had gradually been taken over with instruments and recording equipment.

Until a few years ago, Daniel Derringer had been a BBC session musician and sometime composer. The house was covered in pictures of him with TV stars from the '80s and '90s and he had almost done well for himself. But when his hearing started to go so did his *joie de vivre*, and he had gradually, then completely given up on the BBC, and spent his savings on pianos, trumpets and various instruments that were as much for procrastination as for composing. He had tried to work independently, composing long and old-fashioned pieces that he didn't have the contacts to sell. He claimed incapacity benefit alongside his pension, because of his hearing.

Emma fired up the computer and drummed her fingers on the table. 'What's the job, Pops?'

Daniel moved some sheet music out of the way and sat on the sofa, then picked up an acoustic guitar and started tuning it. 'It's for the title sequence of a short film.'

'Whose film?'

'She's a student. Very talented, apparently.'

Emma put the stick into the side of the computer and opened the file. 'Are they paying you?'

'I didn't like to ask for money, really.'

Emma resisted the urge to tell him off. 'Let me show you where I'm saving these files. Do you know how to open the film?'

'I think so. Let me grab a pen anyway.'

They watched the opening sequence of the film together.

'Looks cool,' Emma said.

'It does look cool. I'll have to get the Gibson out. Thanks for doing this, Em.'

'No worries, Pops.'

12

Shabby Saturday

At home Emma sat on the sofa next to Paul. The table was covered in a generous layer of crisp packets, Rizlas, bottle tops and aspirin – all the hallmarks of a traditionally productive day in Paul's life. She wondered why he didn't feel guilty about wasting the day on junk food, TV and weed.

'Good day, dear?' he asked.

She leaned back on the sofa and emptied her bag, boxes of Nougat Sticks falling out onto the table amongst the detritus. 'I had a hangover and we got free sweets at work. Oh, and Yasmin's getting married.'

'Sounds eventful. I did a whites wash.'

'Good for you, Paul. I'm proud of you.'

Paul picked up a box and examined it.

'Nugget stick.' He looked at her blankly. 'Nugget stick?'

'It's pronounced "Noo Gar",' she said, although it occurred to her that actually nobody had said it out loud all day. How was that possible?

'It's spelled nugget.'

'No, nugget is n-u-g-g-e-t, like a chicken nugget. That's a Noo Gar stick – the 't' is silent. Like French.'

'I don't think it is,' he said, opening the top of the box and taking a bite. 'Yuk – it's like an old man's teeth.'

'Well, that's branding challenge number one, in a nut-shell,' she said, getting up to see what was in the fridge.

'In a nugget shell.'

Emma made a cup of tea and sat back down, too tired to bother making dinner.

'So who is sexy Yasmin marrying? The lucky bastard ... Or is it the poor bastard?' he mused.

'Boring Adam.'

'Yum, he sounds like a catch. You jealous?'

'No.'

'You a bridesmaid?'

'Don't reckon.'

'Gutted.'

Emma picked up her stuff and headed for her room. In the doorway of the lounge she stopped and looked at Paul, his face lit by the TV.

'Do you want to get married?' she asked curiously.

'Not right now thanks, busy.'

'Generally, though?'

'I dunno, Em, maybe. I do look shit hot in a tux ... '

Emma rolled her eyes.

'Are you around for dinner tomorrow? If I cook.'

'You're not going to propose, are you?'

'Not to you, knob-chops – you don't look that good in a tux.'

'Phew. Then yeah, I'm here till ten.'

*

Later that night, Emma was in bed trying to sleep while her mind bounced between the events of the week like it was channel-hopping. She had spent all day exhausted but now that the house was empty and quiet she was lying in the dark in a caffeine frenzy of alertness.

She tried to control her breathing and empty her mind.

1 in

2 out

3 *How do you say nougat?*

1 in

2 out

3 *Why can't I be like Clem?*

1 . . .

2 . . .

3 . . .

4 *I am going to die.*

How did I end up in advertising?

Sweeties.

Who says sweeties?

If I died I wonder if my dad would cry.

She opened her eyes and listened to the soothing sound of the largest thoroughfare in London.

For the first week in the new flat they'd found the constant flow of traffic annoying. Now Emma's head rang with the emptiness of its absence when she slept elsewhere.

The sound reminded her of bedtime as a child, when she would be hustled off to bed and lie listening to the muffled sounds of her mum on the phone or the baritone and beeps of Radio 4.

Her parents had once been the kind of adults who had a landline and a car; they booked family holidays and owned an ironing board. They were a kind of grown-up that no longer existed for Emma. The jovial parent role had gone when her mum had left, and it was replaced with responsibility, bosses, landlords and guilt. As Emma moved through her twenties she was starting to understand that nobody's life was easy, it just looked that way to kids.

At 4 a.m. she heard Paul coming up the stairs and her brain, still whirring, was pleased to have something to distract her. She thought about getting up and talking to him but when the door opened she could hear that he was with a girl. They whispered and giggled as they went into the lounge. Emma lay still and tried to relax. She heard him open the fridge and the clink of bottles, then the vague rumblings of their speech. She wished he'd come home alone so she could go and join him in the lounge. Then she heard the unmistakable silence of kissing. The sound of pleasures shared seeped into her room and she clamped a pillow over her head, trying to avoid the invasion of their privacy. She hummed to herself, a monotone sound that covered at least some of the repetitive spring creaks that crawled under her door from his bedroom and through the walls.

Emma woke up to a bright Saturday morning, annoyed that her body clock was programmed to wake up early, even at the weekend when she could have legitimately slept until noon. She moved around the flat quietly, remembering Paul had a guest and not wanting to inflict her corporate hours on them. When she appeared from the shower Paul was outside the door. 'I am desperate for a piss,' he said, pushing past her and into the steam of the room. When he emerged Emma was waiting for him under the guise of making tea.

'Who's the lucky lady?' she said in a whisper.

His bedroom door was open and she could see a long leg protruding from under the duvet.

He shrugged, overplaying the casual by a degree.

'I met her at the club last week. She's wicked hot.'

'Do you know her name?' Emma asked, referring to the several instances when he hadn't.

'Lucy, I think, or Lacey? Is Lacey a name?'

'It might be New Zealand for Lucy.'

'Lucy then. Pretty sure. She's wicked hot.'

'You said that. I'm guessing she's pretty hot then.'

'Pretty, hot, whatever you want to call it.'

He pinched her chin and winked. 'Not as pretty as *you*, though,' he said, sneaking back into his room and pushing the door shut quietly.

On Saturdays, Emma liked to pretend she lived alone in some sleepy town in France, with a typewriter and a dog. She hoovered and tidied her room, made coffee and sat at her desk staring at a desktop full of unfinished articles, half-drafts, short stories and miscellaneous ideas for books.

At university she had been co-editor of a feminist newspaper called *The Rag*. The other editor was now halfway to becoming a publishing big shot and always promised Emma that if she ever submitted a novel, it would go to the top of her reading list. That promise had so satisfied Emma's ambition that the actual writing of the novel felt almost superfluous.

She opened her blog; her writing name was The Smallest Cog. She had 450 followers, mostly made up of her friends from uni, or people she had met when she used to introduce herself as Emma The Writer with much more gusto than she could usually manage now. Corporate was gradually eroding her sense of indignation, or her ambition, she wasn't sure which.

In the early afternoon she called Clem.

'What are you up to tonight? Shall we see a movie or something?'

'Emma, I can't, I haven't got two dimes to rub together ...'

'I'll buy.'

'Sorry, kiddo, I can't do any more Emma credit until I at least have a job. So, listen, do you remember meeting an American dude called Michael Duke Smith when we were at Pinchos?'

Emma downed her coffee and refilled it from the cafetière on her desk.

'Doesn't ring a bell, is it someone from New York?'

'He is from New York, but I don't remember meeting him there. His message went ...' Clem broke into a comedic NYC accent, 'Hey girl, this is Michael Duke Smith, director; we met at that bar. So listen, call me, let me know you're free or whatever, we'll get dinner, I'm buying, we'll chit-chat, that bullshit – talk to me.'

Emma laughed.

'It's an English number, but I have no recollection of meeting a director. Do you?'

'I basically can't remember anything past the fourth martini,' Emma responded, honestly. She heard Clem take a sip of a drink.

'Yeah, it's a bit blurry.'

'So are you going to call him back?'

'Yeah, I guess. He might be somebody.'

'Does he sound sexy?'

'Not particularly, but he has the confidence of a handsome fella. I'll call him – everything in the name of comedy, right? Not much to lose, is there?'

'Apparently not. Good luck, Twist.'

'Yeah, you too, Emmy D.'

Emma went back to staring vacantly at her screen until later that afternoon when Clem called her back.

'So I'm meeting him on Friday, outside the Hippodrome at 7 p.m.' She said it with a mix of pride and dubiousness.

Emma smirked. 'We Londoners like to call that the worst time and place known to Western civilisation.'

'Yeah, fuck, you're right, and I'll have to be early because it's basically a blind date ... '

'Everything in the name of comedy, right Clem?'

'Right,' she muttered, hanging up.

By the end of the day Emma had entered a piece of flash fiction called 'Temping for the Lizard King' to a writing prize, paying £7 for the privilege. *Less than 2 pints*, she reasoned, pre-emptively spending the prize money (£500) on pints.

She sent a pitch to *Hurrah* magazine called 'What your sandals say about you', then she sent it to *Slick* in case it was too sardonic to be taken seriously at a women's magazine. Then, following advice she'd read in *Hurrah*, she did ten sit-ups.

Looking through her phone for something to do, she found that nearly all her recent calls were work related. Thinking on it she realised that most of her nights out were impromptu trips to the pub with colleagues. She had spent more time socialising with the receptionists than she had on dates so far this year. This was not a happy stat.

She had sent a few texts, feeling like she was missing out on some city-wide fun, but everyone who replied was parading their relationship along the South Bank or working on freelance projects, meaning they had no concept of Saturdays. She was just starting to feel lonely and unpopular when her phone finally jangled on the table, making her jump.

Yasmin, queen of perky, shouted in her inimitable high pitch down the phone, 'Emma what are you up to come to the theatre with me Adam stood me up.'

'I dunno, Yas, I'm super broke at the moment.'

'Boring! You always say that.'

'It's usually true.'

Yasmin hung up in a sulk. Emma wondered what 'broke' meant to Yasmin, who'd had a job since they left college. It had become a running joke that nobody really knew where she worked. She played on the joke and always masterfully changed the subject when anyone quizzed her on it. More recently however it seemed to have stepped up a notch and Yasmin was often abroad on business. She spent all her spare time with Adam and the cat, drove a company car and despite consistently claiming she couldn't afford nice things, nobody ever saw her in the same outfit twice.

Emma would have been jealous if she had wanted any of those things, but finding Adam to be intolerably dull, having no driving licence or desire to live in west London, get married or look after a cat meant she didn't use Yasmin's life as a bar against which to measure her own. Emma knew that

Clem found Yasmin's mystery success deeply galling and frequently lamented her own choices for the lack of tangible payoffs. Emma and Clementine usually agreed that in many respects Yasmin had had a head start, career-wise, but they really did think they might have caught up by now.

Yasmin hailed originally from West St Leonards, a small town next to Hastings, and moved to London aged thirteen. It was less than a year after moving that she stopped trying to explain where her hometown was. When abroad she would say she was from London then sling a furtive squint about to make sure nobody was going to undermine her. If asked while in London she would say she was from Swiss Cottage, then giggle prettily if someone mentioned that her accent was distinctively coastal.

Emma considered the offer of the theatre. She wanted to get out of the house, but Yasmin never ever shouted a bill, and Emma knew an evening in her company would be more expensive than it was fun.

Instead she plunked herself down on the sofa, resigned to the evening. She opened a bag of crisps and flicked on the TV to watch hapless members of the public have their dreams shattered by B-list celebrities.

13

The Ionian

Clem sat in front of the rickety piece of crap her mum called the computer and stared at her bank balance. She was fucked.

But in the adjacent window she was re-reading the best email she'd got in weeks. It was from Drake Jones.

Hi Clem,
I've just read your script. You've got potential, kid!
Have you got any other treatments I can have a read of? Let's meet up.
Drake

So far he'd only read *Moonshiners*. Clem tried not to worry about the popularity of *Moonshiners* being a fluke. She wasn't old enough to be a one-hit wonder. Also she hadn't had one hit . . .

Her other projects were under-developed by comparison, and needed some serious time and attention before she could send them to Drake Jones.

Nonetheless, she was fucked – it said so right there in the other window. It was the mathematical representation of fucked. Potential or not, she was right royally financially fucking fucked.

Malcolm had offered her a temp job at his company, and she had politely declined. She needed some income, fast.

She left the house without saying goodbye, plucking a few quid for the underground from the change jar where they kept their keys.

Waiting for the Central Line, she watched a man with a toddler wipe his child's face and shake a toy. Clem had stood on the same platform as a kid. She had vague, pastel-toned memories of the era; there had been shiny cars, new shoes, holidays and dinners for Clementine and Callum.

When the train arrived she found an empty carriage and stood at the end. Clem's father had made his fortune in the stock market crash of the '80s, while everyone else was declaring bankruptcy. He had surfed the wave and come out of it glistening with wealth. Then he'd decided that his family were depreciating his stock and left. *What a gigantic cliché.* He'd supported their mum financially for a while but then, by Callum's tenth birthday, he'd decided they'd had their dues and evaporated altogether. Their lives from then on seemed like a collection of cheap shirts and small change.

In New York she'd struggled at first, but when Jordan took her under his wing he found her poverty bohemian and always made her feel like it was something she could be proud of, because it was all in her past . . .

As the memory crossed her mind the train whizzed past a poster for a film and she thought she saw his name. At Tottenham Court Road, on her way out of the station she passed the same poster and stopped abruptly, causing a man in an overcoat to swerve suddenly and tut at her.

'Piss off, dickhead,' she muttered at him as he hurried on, shaking his fist for effect.

The film was called *Mind Games* – 'the best thriller this year', apparently – starring Bradley Cooper and Gene Hackman. Jordan's name was underneath with the other supporting cast members. So he finally made the B list, she thought. Bugger.

Soho was teeming with sweaty, aimless tourists as Clem pushed open the heavy black door of the Ionian. The entrance smelled of last night's party and of cigarettes smoked two decades ago; it snuck out of the walls, cushions, curtains and carpet, reminding them each morning that what they did was dirty and cancerous. Clem noted mournfully that walking in there felt more like coming home than her house had.

There was nobody sitting at the front desk so she padded through to the main bar, a windowless homage to speak-easy chic. Heavy burgundy curtains were draped from floor to ceiling, the lights were dim and the room had a dingy air that made you feel like the glamour had left the building – which technically it had, in the '80s.

As Clem rounded the entrance to the bar, she saw a familiar figure stocking shelves. At the sound the girl turned and her double take made Clem's grin widen. 'Ferocious T, no less – how's it going?' she said.

Tina was an old cohort from the bar scene and had started bartending at the same time as Clem had joined the Ionian as a fledgling waitress. Their bond was made of hard booze and late nights.

'Well if it isn't Clementine Tits. What are *you* doing here?'

Clem gave her a rueful smile and T looked at her sympathetically. 'For a job?'

Clem nodded. 'Is Alan about?'

'Yeah, he's here. How's London treating you?'

'Could be worse, just a bit bankrupty. Do you know if he's hiring?'

'He will be now you're here, Clem, I reckon.'

They hugged and Tina turned back to her work.

Alan was sitting in his tiny office, concentrating furiously on making a rota and tutting loudly as he typed with a single digit. Alan was an Albanian who was deeply proud of his heritage – he would often ask people to guess where he was from. He would get disgruntled if they guessed anywhere outside of the Balkans and downright angry if they guessed a country within the Balkans that wasn't Albania. It was a risky game with no winners. The bar was co-owned by some deeply sketchy characters, but Alan himself was a nice guy; he was kind to his staff and in love with his wife. He treated people well, unless his drugs, business or finances were involved, and then he was a nutter.

The Ionian's staff called it the Onion. Alan got mad when he heard it referred to as such, until they explained that it was counter to the Gherkin; their London, Clem had told him, was constructed of pickles.

Clem knocked gently on the door and pushed it open with a sheepish grin.

'Hiya, is Alan here?'

At the sound of a voice he recognised he spun round eagerly.

'Clementine, darling, you back!'

His accent was thick and he stood, 6 foot high with a powerful body that he carried like a gangster.

'Hopefully.'

He laughed a belly laugh and pulled her in for a hug. It was like being cocooned in a wardrobe.

'But you're big star now, no? You come to book the bar for your premiere party, yes?'

'Well, you know, not so much.'

'Ah, Clementine.' He pulled her back into his hug. 'Soon though, darling. You want to work?'

'Have you got anything?'

'Clementine, for you, always. I put little Polak on reception but she's no good – she got too much attitude, you know?'

Clem flinched at Alan's free-flowing racism. He had once claimed that he wasn't racist because he hated everyone equally, including his fellow Albanians. The only kind of person he respected was a rich one, and they could be whichever colour they liked.

'Not attitude they like, but *bad* attitude, you know? Not like you – they want you, they come here to see you. You want the job?'

Her internal voice said no, her real voice said, 'That'd be amazing – thanks, Alan. When can I start?'

'You have to do one trial shift, Clem, unpaid – make sure you gots what it takes.'

He threw his head back and laughed a big, hearty laugh, which Clem hoped meant he was joking.

Clem said goodbye to Ferocious T, who could barely contain her glee that Clem was back. She left the Ionian feeling both elated and depressed, and headed to Primark to buy a pair of the black trousers she'd put in the charity bag when she'd set off to New York, full of certainty that she would never need them again.

As she made her way through the relentless hubbub of central London she tried to work out how long, in bar shifts, it would take until she could afford to move out of her mum's house.

14

Martini

On Monday, after a team meeting full of the usual feast of humiliation, boredom and banalities, Emma returned to her seat with her trademark lack of enthusiasm. Clem called it her clipboard face. She clicked on her email and had a new message from *Slick* magazine. The subject was 'You'.

It wasn't from 'admin' or 'info', it was from Matt. Someone called Matt at *Slick* had sent her an email.

Eeeeeeee.

She opened it, trying to contain her excitement, when Ross slid across on his chair and looked over her shoulder. She minimised the window and turned towards him.

'Fancy a cocktail tonight? The wife's given me the night off,' he lied.

Emma rolled her eyes. 'Maybe,' she said, non-committal. 'Let's see how the day pans out.'

He smiled eagerly and rolled himself back to his desk.

Emma turned back to her email . . .

Hi Emma,

Thanks for your article about sandals, we thought it
was bloody funny. I wonder if you fancy meeting for a
drink and a chat? Let me know your availability.

Matt

Eeeeeeeee.

She left it an hour before replying to set up the meeting, in
a pub near Old Street. The excitement powered her through
the rest of the day. The team even noticed she was upbeat.

As the sun dipped behind the low-rise offices of Clerkenwell,
Ross and Emma sat in the corner of Porter, a small, smart
cocktail bar. Emma didn't know when they'd started going
there, or why.

The waitress carried their drinks over, holding Emma's
martini where the V of the glass met the stem.

'You only twizzle one side of your hair, you know that?'
Ross said, nodding towards the curl twisted around her
finger. 'You should do the other side, so they match.'

In the mirror behind him she could see he was right. She
crossed her arms on the table.

To Emma, Ross was never anything more than a gentle
ego massage. Her mind had zoned in on the glass as he
talked about his old days, when he went travelling and music
was the most important thing in his life. He was thirty-eight
now. When he talked about those times he called his wife
by her name, instead of saying 'my wife', because they hadn't
been a couple back then, they'd just been friends. Emma had
seen pictures of her when she was on a beach in Australia;
she had short hair and toned arms, and she looked good.

Ross had been wearing the same metal band T-shirt he was wearing now and Emma thought he should be grateful for her. She had settled 'down'.

The cocktail stick in her glass was fully loaded, six olives squashed together like Central Line commuters. She stirred the vodka and watched the filmy brine patina twist into a smoky spin. Ross was talking but she wasn't listening now.

She took the martini glass in her hand, holding it lightly. She wished suddenly and acutely that she had long nails. Her bitten fingers looked stunted and inappropriate, like a baby clutching a diamond necklace. She raised the glass and sipped the serious, frosty, salty, savoury, delicious . . .

Ross finished his sentence and then spurted out urgently, 'Can I kiss you, Emma?'

'What? No.' The spell of her drink was broken by his stupid half-beard and aged desperation. He was like a cheap steak, he was like a warm beer, he was just . . . god, no. 'Your wife would mess me up for a start,' she added, to soften the rejection.

She looked at him and wondered what it would take. She found him physically unimpressive and no amount of vodka would change that. She only humoured him because she couldn't get through a day at APRC with no one to talk to.

And she could admit that there was something about him: he never patronised her. He seemed to find her age delicious and intoxicating and she wondered if that's what she got from him. He made her feel attractive and appreciate her life, her body, her age; he made her proud of it. Also, she thought, he buys me martinis.

Ross had enough pride simply to nod in agreement. 'She probably would.'

*

Two drinks later and Emma was leaning, drunkenly on her elbow.

She wanted to keep the email from *Slick* to herself, but excitement and booze got the better of her.

'So we're meeting next week, and if I can get a regular column with them, I can jack in this executive assistant bullshit and be an actual writer. Maybe, fingers crossed, I can be happy.'

She sloshed a bit of her drink on the table. 'I was supposed to have got there by now, you know?' she said. Ross had heard this a dozen times before but he listened patiently, enjoying the attention.

'I honestly think if I do this job much longer I'll just be a PA for the rest of my life. I'll get married, knocked up and die without ever having *done* anything. You know?'

He nodded sagely; the grown-up of the two, she was pretty much describing his life.

'It's just so hard to actually do anything I'm proud of. The weekends are for hangovers and the evenings just evaporate. Maybe I should just quit and see what happens. I won't have any excuses. I'll go to Paris and sit around and write all day; I'll wear a black beret and I'll be poor, but at least I'll be happy.'

'Why don't you then? Just quit?'

'I will, I have to; I'm watching myself trudge towards death one team meeting at a time . . .'

'You won't do it. Adrian won't let you – you're his protégée.'

'I'm a glorified receptionist and they're ten a penny – he can get some unambitious bimbo to write his insight documents. They'll just have to be fluent in bollocks.'

She drained her glass and Ross signalled for another round that he couldn't afford. He could listen to her all night. He could look at her all night.

'I'll do it, I swear.'

He laughed at her gently. 'I bet you don't.'

She was practically slurring as the waitress tentatively placed two more drinks on the table, along with some pistachios she hoped would sober the girl up a bit.

'I will bet you . . . anything you want . . . '

He looked at her with open lust.

'Yeah, I will blow you on the away day if I haven't handed in my notice by the end of the month. How about that?'

She held out her hand to shake on it. He shook it eagerly, laughing in a way that caused a wave of regret to wash over her. Her inner voice whispered to her, *You're an idiot*.

15

The Curzon

Emma was sitting in the lounge of the Curzon Cinema waiting for Clem. It was a relatively quiet place, for the heart of Soho, with mellow acoustics and arty types. Around her sat various denizens of the film industry, directors and writers discussing projects in hushed tones, and young hopefuls with no money tapping away on laptops, looking up expectantly whenever someone new came down the stairs. The punters – people who could afford £15 for a film and a fiver for a green tea – perched on stools, smelling expensive and shooting condescending looks at anyone wearing trainers while privately wondering if that scruffy tyke was famous.

Clementine arrived dressed for work at the Ionian, in tight black trousers, a low-cut, long-sleeve T-shirt, a wafty scarf and eyeliner that bordered on gothic. She saluted the bartender and threw herself onto the sofa next to Emma. 'Sorry I'm late.'

Half a bottle of house red later, Clementine was looking sympathetically at Emma following a brief synopsis of the blowjob bet.

'Risky strategy, sweet pea. Although fuck it, quit the job. I'm jealous – at least you can get corporate when you get desperate. I'm back at the Onion making peanuts.'

Where Emma had spent her summers in uni temping, Clem had always opted for the service industry, such was her commitment to free drinks. Before her stint in New York, Clem had worked at the Ionian for six months. In that time she managed to save exactly one week's worth of New York rent.

'So, are you going to quit? Or are you going to actually blow some dude because of a bet. You can always come and work with me; waitressing is about as much fun as it looks.'

At seven they ordered another bottle of wine. When it arrived, Clem's tone dropped a note.

'I went to Yasmin's at the weekend. Did she tell you about it?'

Emma shook her head and sipped the wine.

'So she called me up to see if I was free for dinner, and she made this big deal about what I should wear, so I said, "I'll wear something suitable for dinner at a friend's house" – you know? I mean, I don't tend to turn up to places in my gym kit, do I?'

'Not since the '90s.'

'I get there a few minutes late, no big deal, and as soon as she opens the door she is completely hyper, you know how she gets. But this was next level – I mean she was squealing and running about and shouting at the cook. By the way, they paid someone to do the cooking, this tall Brazilian girl called Juanita. You couldn't make it up. Yas kept ordering her about for no reason. It would have been funny if it wasn't so uncomfortably colonialist.

'So I got a bit weirded out; I thought maybe it was some special event I'd forgotten, maybe it was Adam's birthday or something? And Adam, you know how he is, he just sat pencil straight on the sofa. I thought he was staring into space for ages because their TV is so flat it's invisible except from the front. God he is such a nothing, and she's doing this whole crackers housewife bit – it's like *Abigail's Party* or something. So I thought fuck it, I'm gonna get drunk.'

'Seems reasonable,' Emma conceded.

'Right? But I'm pouring my second glass and she rushes over and wrestles the bottle out of my hand and screams at me NO MORE BOOZE CLEMENTINE. So then I'm sort of freaking out because I think it's an intervention or something. When the doorbell went I honestly thought it would be you, and you were all going to read me a letter about how my alcoholism affects your lives or whatever.'

Emma laughed.

'That is honestly what I was thinking when this dude walks in. And he's all dressed up and he's blushing, and Yasmin says, "Clementine, *this* is Timmy."'

'And that's the moment I realise it's a set-up. I can't believe I didn't see it coming. And she delivered it as if I had known all along, which I guess I should have. But there's Timmy, like, super thrilled that I wanted to meet him ...'

Clem paused, partly for effect, partly for a mouthful of wine. She shook her head at the memory.

'I still don't get why she didn't just ask me. If she wanted to play blind dates, why spring it on me like some kind of joke, right? I was already in her house, at least say something before he walked in.'

'Since when does she do matchmaking?'

'Since the engagement. She keeps saying shit like, "I want you to be happy, Clemmy, you can't go to the wedding single!" She knows I'm dating, so obviously she figured I'm fair game.'

Emma laughed again.

'So? How was it?'

Clem grinned. 'You know exactly how it was; I had to sit there and play little miss princess while Yas and Adam just stared at us. Every time we started to talk Yas would interrupt and randomly change the subject, or embellish what I had said. She was easily the most nervous person there. Totally nuts.'

'So how was he? Timmy? Any future?'

'Seriously? You have to ask?'

'Just being polite.'

'I mean, honestly Em, what grown man calls themselves *Timmy*?'

'Someone who works in finance?'

'Well, yeah, I suppose. He had this flaccid handshake and his body was forty, but his face belonged to a cherub. He was all apple cheeks and kiss curls. When Yasmin introduced us she said, "Timmy, this is Clementine Twist," and he laughed at my name.'

She shook her head and exhaled. 'It's hard not to take it personally when someone sets you up with a total flannel of a man.'

'He sounds like a winner.'

'He was a *massive* winner. He kept talking about his car – he told me the mileage, Emma. How many miles his car has gone. Seriously, it might have been the conversational low point of my life. At one point I said, "Actually Timmy, I ride a bike." And Yasmin basically screamed. I think she meant it to come out as a laugh but she was so unhinged by that time she was basically wailing. Adam just sat there watching, like the inanimate knobject he is … Anyway, she said we'd be seeing each other at the wedding, so I couldn't be anything but polite. It was well awkward.'

'At least it wasn't just wedding chat,' said Emma optimistically.

'There was plenty of wedding chat, obviously. You're looking at the maid of honour, by the way.'

'Wooooo,' said Emma supportively. 'Yaay,' she added, less so.

'Fuck off.'

'Wait, what about me? Am I not a bridesmaid? What did I do?'

'I think you've gotten away with it, kid – she said the bridesmaids are Adam's sister and some girl I've never heard of. Maybe she knows you've tongued the hubby.'

Emma felt a pang of ouch that Clementine saw in her expression.

'Seriously buddy, count yourself lucky. Don't feel left out.'

Emma felt left out.

16

Squash Hotpants

When Adrian arrived he was sweating. He walked triumphantly along the corridor swinging his PE kit. He stripped
in his office, forcing the creative team to pretend his office
walls weren't made of glass. Emma looked up at the wrong
moment and caught a brief glimpse of his gargantuan belly.
She cringed.

Blonk. An IM from Ross, which made her shudder.

Looking forward to showing you my nougat stick.

Jesus.

He was grinning at his screen. In profile he was even less
attractive. Adrian appeared in his doorway buttoning his
shirt, emperor of all he surveyed. Emma's muscles clenched.

'Adrian, do you have a sec?'

'For you, always.'

Ross looked up, both eyebrows raised.

She got slowly out of her chair with her heart racing. She

wished she hadn't worn clothes that could be rightly relegated to pyjama class.

They took their seats at the small round table in Adrian's
office and she braced herself for battle. Adrian eyed her from
over his glasses and took the lead.

'So tell me, Emma, do you like working here?'

Emma's impulse was to answer honestly; they literally had
to pay her to be there. Instead she said, 'Yeah, course. I love
it, Adrian.'

She made a mental note to say his name every time he
said hers. She wondered if she actually wanted to go through
with this meeting, but the image of Ross's toothy grin
spurred her on. She had no intention of putting his limp sadness anywhere near her face, or any other part of her body
for that matter.

Why didn't you bet him a tenner like a normal person?

Adrian pushed himself back on his chair and revealed his
doughy white thighs. His top half was all pink chequered shirt
and expensive glasses, but he'd kept his gym shorts on under
the table, like a newsreader that wouldn't be standing up.

He put his hands behind his head and his belly peeped out
between the buttons of his shirt. He looked like a cake.

'What do you like about it?'

Weekends.

'Brand strategy is an exhilarating world, Adrian; I learn
something new every day . . .'

He tapped his pen on the table. Emma was reminded of
the time he'd conducted a conference call while sucking a
red lollipop.

'So, Adrian, I wanted to talk to you about my role here
because—'

'Yes, I'm glad you brought it up because I've been meaning to have this conversation with you.'

Is he going to sack me? She felt a pang of panic. Her bank balance flashed through her mind. *Oh shit. I need this job.*

'So tell me, Emma, what do you want to *do* with your life? Hmm? What do you want to *be*?'

'Well, I studied literature and I've got a blog. People seem to like it.'

'Blogs, is it? If you applied yourself, you could probably make a very nice living as a copywriter.'

A very nice living. It rang in her brain. *Sounds nice.*

'What do you write a blog *for*, Emma?'

'Well, Adrian, it's cathartic, I guess, and it makes people laugh. It's the only thing I do that isn't a fundamental waste of ti ... ' She realised too late in the sentence that she was outing herself as a hater. 'I write for the fun of it. For the art of it, really.'

He practically spat on the floor at the mention of art. 'For art, Emma? Really? People who serve themselves have no place in humanity. Of your four core values, only one can be aspirational, Emma.'

You're an Ass piration, Adrian.

'What are your core values?'

Habit said, 'Innovation quality ... '

'Not *our* core values, your own, what are yours?'

Bullshit, sadness, anger, booze ...

She forced herself to look receptive but she could feel her sadness rising.

'Let me put it another way ... If you were a brand, which brand would you be?'

She didn't react.

French Connection, because FCUK you.

'Well you can think about it and get back to me.'

'What brand would you be?' asked Emma.

Pedigree Chump.

'That's a great question,' he beamed at her.

If you say so yourself.

'Well, Emma, I position myself as an Armani but everyone knows I'm just a big Haribo.' He laughed and banged a meaty paw on the table. Emma pictured Giorgio Armani standing behind him, shaking his head. She wondered if this was actually worse than freelancer fellatio.

'So you want to be a writer and that's your goal in life?'

'I try to live in the present – my dad always taught me to be happy now. I've always kind of held on to that. I'm not "goals orientated", and I like it here, but sometimes I feel frustrated by my role.'

And I hate you and I quit.

Suddenly her heart was in her mouth, her palms were sweating and she realised she wasn't actually going to do her resignation speech.

'Well, Emma . . . '

Get fucked, Adrian.

' . . . A lot of people blame their childhood for ideas they have as adults. But you've been here for nearly a year, and you've proven that you could be a really valuable asset to us.'

She stared at the damp meat scarf he called a neck.

'And just between you and me, we might be moving into the energy sector.' He leaned forward, as if the sentence deserved a round of applause.

Emma wanted to leave the room and hide in the bathroom until the sadness subsided.

'When you started at APRC you weren't really a team player, but since our performance review you have really upped your game and so I want to make you the copywriter for the Nougat Stick project. I want you to really grow as part of the APRC family. Your Joy of Sweets work so far has been insightful. I think it shows you're capable of great things, and I'm excited for you, Emma. You've got a style that cuts through the bullshit, you see the world without spin.'

I DO! That IS how I see the world! Damn it, Adrian.

'If you continue to apply yourself, you can be an integral part of our forthcoming Dubai proposal and whatever projects might come out of it? How does that sound?'

Fresh hell.

He was beaming.

'That sounds really good.'

'You might be an ideas person, Emma.'

I am! I am an ideas person, Adrian! But you're a dick and I hate my life!

'I might . . . So will someone pick up my other work?'

'Not for the time being; this will be a trial run. You should try and give as many things as you can to Gemma, though.'

Emma glanced out at Gemma sitting cross-legged on her swivel chair, shoes off, in mismatching socks. She was swinging gently from side to side, staring gormlessly at Buzzfeed. The pile of unsent mail in her out tray had been there for days.

Brilliant.

'We'll still need you to hold the fort in creative, but you will be the junior copywriter. It also means a raise.'

Emma perked up, now genuinely surprised at the outcome of the meeting. Bemusement, more than anything else, forced her to nod. 'That sounds good. Thanks. I . . . umm, thanks.'

He went on for a while longer, while she tried to calculate how much extra cash it was likely to mean. She had a flash of Clem's face in her mind, shaking her head at her. She stood up to leave but Adrian stopped her.

'There's one more thing actually. Now that you're an *integral* part of creative. We need to bring someone from the PR team on board for these new projects so I thought, in your first job as the new junior creative, that you might like to have some input.'

She didn't need to think about it. 'I know she's new … but I've had a couple of meetings with Hilary … She has great insight, and she's very ambitious. She really understands communication.'

She deliberately used buzzwords she knew Adrian would respond to.

She closed the glass door, leaving Adrian sitting at the table in his shorts, and made her way to her desk. She'd been there less than a minute when a new email dropped into her inbox. It was from Adrian to everyone, subject: Emma.

Emma has just accepted a new role as the junior
copywriter for the creative team. She will be
managing the tone of voice documents for the Nougat
Sticks project as well as having some great input into
new client projects. Please make sure she's involved in
any branding work you do in the future and be sure to
congratulate her!

Any pleasure that she felt evaporated as she watched the reactions unfold. Gemma rolled her eyes, Ross smiled at her with undisguised lasciviousness and Drew sent her a look that said both 'congratulations' and 'sorry'. The Eds sent emails without missing a beat: 'Well done!' and 'Well done you!'. Twenty minutes later she received an email with each of the APRC values documents attached and the subject heading 'Great opportunity'. Her heart withered and shut down for the day. The email said, 'Hi, Emma, great to have you on board for this. Please find attached the insight documents! Would be great to have you read and edit them for consistency. About time we had a fresh pair of eyes on these. Please let me know your projected timescale to get them back to me for review!'

Emma didn't groan out loud, but her body gave her a nice big headache by way of response. She didn't reply, in the vain hope that it would simply go away.

At 3 p.m. Gemma walked triumphantly into Adrian's office carrying a plastic bag full of Calippos. From where she was sitting Emma watched Adrian drop his head into his hands and shake his head. Gemma left his office visibly disgruntled, clutching the bag angrily. On her way past she scowled at Emma.

She walked around each department with the carrier bag asking people 'what flavour they wan'ed,' from a choice of red, yellow and orange.

By the time she had done the rounds she had learned two things: the first was that yellow was the least popular flavour of Calippo, and the second was that twenty-five Calippos wasn't enough Calippos for everyone.

Blonk.

An email from Hilary made Emma laugh out loud.

Are you aware that your intern is dealing Calippos? Is 'ice-cream van' in her job description?

Emma replied on the internal IM.

I think they sent her out for a cake. God knows how they phrased it.
She should have got Cornettos.
She should have got a cake.
Ha. Well, I've got a red Calippo under my desk if you want a lick.
That's what she said.

17

I'll Have What She's Having

Clem arrived at the Hippodrome at 6.45 p.m. and wondered if it was actually the busiest place in the world. She stood and watched the swathes of people, directionless amongst the chain stores, fast-food holes and souvenir stands. She leaned against a lamppost and admired the architecture; the buildings seemed austere, looking down their ornate noses at the nonsense below.

She was wearing a small black cardigan over a lacy green vest, skinny jeans and biker boots. She looked cool and she felt pretty good about herself.

At 7.05 she called Emma.

'I don't know what I'm doing here. Should I just leave? Are you nearby?'

She was turning on the spot when someone approached her from behind and kissed her neck. She clutched her phone to her chest and turned, fury rising, to face him. The evening they'd met came back with a flash. This was her guy.

Damn.

Clem mumbled into her phone that she would call later and took stock of her date for the evening. He was in his forties and wearing tight leather trousers and a sagging white T-shirt. Several small grey hairs were peeping out from under the cotton. He had brown eyes with flecks of green, which would have been pretty if they'd been younger or kinder.

'Hi?' she said loudly, sceptically, posing it as a question. In response he reached out and took her hand. His now familiar New York twang opened with, 'Hey, I recognised those eyes from miles away – you've got such beautiful eyes.'

'Yeah, right. Thanks. So umm . . . Where are we going?'

He seemed flattered by the 'we' in the sentence and guided her by the small of her back towards Long Acre and the throng of Covent Garden. She wished she had worn something less pretty. He looked the wrong way down the road and stepped out in front of a cab that blared its horn and just missed taking the tip off his snakeskin shoe. Whoa, she noted. That is an extreme loafer.

When he asked if she wanted to try Bella Pasta she laughed and wondered if he was serious. Eventually they walked down Monmouth Street and passed a small, sweet-looking French restaurant. Clem paused at the menu. It was 7.15 and she was already bored. She was due to work at 9. Two hours to kill with this chump; she texted Emma to see if she was in the neighbourhood. Inside, Michael slid his arm around Clem's waist and demanded a table.

The maître d' looked at Clementine as if to say, 'Why have you brought this *American* in here?' Clem wondered if she looked like his hooker. They were led to the back of the restaurant and seated in a corner. Michael picked up the wine list and scrutinised it, holding it at arm's length in a gesture that reminded Clem of Malcolm. She suppressed a shudder.

'So, what kind of films do you direct?' she asked quietly, to which he didn't respond. Instead he held his index finger close to her face and said, 'I'm choosing wine right now, OK? We'll get to talking when I'm done.'

Clem checked her phone while he stared at the menu. She had a text from Emma:

'Is he The One?'

She replied, 'He's wearing leather trousers, he might be fifty and he just shushed me. So yes, definitely.'

Emma replied with a turd emoji.

When the waitress approached Clem fell instantly in love. She was round, rosy and beautiful and smiled at them shyly. She asked quietly if Michael was ready to order drinks. He turned the menu away from Clem and shouted, 'Is the chablis any good?'

Her delicate French lilt assured him that it was a very fine choice and he pointed to the menu: 'We'll take this one.'

The waitress looked confused. 'This is the house wine?' she said softly.

'Yeah, whatever – we'll try it; if we don't like it we'll get something better.'

Clem smiled at the waitress who had taken the menu and was walking away. He brazened it out. 'There's plenty of her to go around,' he said at her back. Clem felt a strong desire to jab him in the eye.

He leaned forward and stroked her knee, moving his hand upwards. She moved her leg out of reach; he leaned back in his chair and spread his legs wide. She wondered if he was really a director, and if she valued her career enough to stick around.

She thought of a way to make a swift exit. 'Do you smoke?' she asked. 'I could really use a cigarette.'

'Sure, baby, but after dinner, OK? We'll wait for dessert to smoke.'

Clem ordered the sea bass and Michael, leaning back in his chair and staring at her said abruptly, 'I'll have what she's having.' His tone made it sound like an accusation: 'what *she's* having'. It was a strange sentence and Clem had a flash-back to an early date with Jordan, who'd playfully ordered for her. She remembered with a wistful pang how sexy she had found it.

'Why don't you try something else? We can share,' she said, regretting it instantly.

He spent the next five minutes deliberating over his deci-sion while the waitress stood patiently. 'So I'll have the monkfish, and she'll have the sea bass, OK?'

Eventually the exasperated waitress said, 'I will bring them, you will have them on the table, OK?'

She walked away and had reached the middle of the room when he shouted after her, 'Tell the chef, bring it medium.'

The waiter, Clem and the whole restaurant stopped and looked at him.

'Do you understand me? I want it cooked MEDIUM,' he said in a French accent that was somehow all the way racist.

The waitress came back to the table. 'It's a fish,' she said gently.

Clem smiled at her, signalling she could go and turned to Michael.

'It's not like steak, it comes as it comes.'

He cleared his throat, took her hand, leaned in too close and said quietly, 'Hey, listen, don't you tell me how to be in here, OK? Don't talk to me like I don't know. What you just said made me look dumb. Don't do that again, OK?' He said the last sentence slowly, a warning.

She swallowed and leaned as far back as she could. The realisation that he might be an actual psychopath, as opposed to just a total dick, caused a rush of sweat to her palms.

Holy crap, I'm going to die for a monkfish, she thought.

He started talking and settled into his stride. The wine arrived and was poured, and by the time he'd stopped to take a breath and a sip, Clem was filling her glass for the second time. She had adopted the expression of avid listener, to mask her horror at almost everything he said. She surreptitiously checked the time: 8.05. She worried that the longer she stayed, the more aggressive he was going to become. She cursed her decision to be there at all and pictured her body, broken and bloody in a skip somewhere. She hated him for making her miss Jordan. She had never met anyone, ever, who had actively made her want to go to work. She looked at the maître d' with an expression she hoped conveyed the thought 'Please don't let that dude kill me after dinner'. He seemed to understand and she felt a bit better. She was in London, after all; the city had her back; no way would her town let some thug murder her in an alley, right?

Game face, bro.

'So what do you do?'

She looked at him and thought, What does it matter? but said, 'I'm a screenwriter, I just—' He interrupted with a loud laugh. 'Why do I *always* end up with writers?'

She looked at him through her increasingly thinly veiled contempt; he was duller than a Liverpool sunset.

Clem was relieved when the food arrived, willing the whole experience to end. Her sea bass was delicious, and she forgot for a moment that she was on a date with a murderer and let herself enjoy it. By the time they'd finished eating it was 8.40. She was rapidly losing the will to humour this man, whom she had crowned the biggest fuckwit she had ever met. While he was wiping his plate with his finger and licking it with his moist, crumb-laden lips, she had examined him more closely and decided, at the very least, this would be the worst person she would ever go out with. She was actively looking forward to seeing Emma and recounting this.

As the waitress cleared the plates Michael reached over, touched Clem's hand and said, 'You're much hotter than her, you know that?' He signalled with a nod that he was referring to the waitress, who looked at Clem, surprised and hurt. Clem was horrified by the unbelievable meanness of it. She looked at him as if he was a total idiot and she hated him, which was easy, because he was, and she did. When the waitress asked if they would like dessert, Clem answered quickly for them, 'No.'

While they sat and waited for the nightmare to end, she asked for the cigarette he had promised at the beginning.

He leaned back in his tight, tight trousers, and spat the words, 'Why don't you go ask that guy at the bar?'

Realising that he didn't actually smoke, she saw her opportunity. Discreetly she picked up her bag and went over to the bar where the maître d' obliged her with a wink. She left the restaurant. It was exactly 9 p.m. She looked down the road, deciding which way to run, when she remembered her cardigan on the back of the chair. She did some mental maths and decided it wasn't worth getting killed for an £8 Primark cardigan.

Allowing herself a strained laugh, she handed the cigarette to a homeless guy, turned and walked towards Soho, towards the Ionian, Ferocious T and free drinks.

18

Slick

Emma shut her computer down and edged gently out of the office. Adrian gave her a thumbs up and jabbed it into his cheek, under the illusion she was headed for the dentist. She bounced through the double doors towards east London and the bright shiny world of *Slick* magazine.

She wore her skinniest jeans, heels and a wildly overpriced T-shirt. Even so, as she entered the Shoreditch pub, she felt overweight and out of touch.

Her meeting was with Matt Attic. She knew what he looked like because his shiny eyes and scruffy haircut were the face of *Slick*, the coolest, rudest and most abrasive magazine on the market.

Slick had quality writing; it was full of outrageous stories of drunken antics and witty, pseudo-political banter. It had an impressive range and was considered by the hipsters to be intelligent and engaging. It was also 75 per cent adverts and had more boobs per capita than spring break.

Matt Attic looked her up and down as she approached.

She pushed her shoulders back, sucked her stomach in and hid her bitten nails, wishing she were taller or thinner. They shook hands and he sat down, pushing a bottle of water slightly in her direction.

'So, *Slick* magazine – thoughts?' His tone was abrupt.

'I love what you guys do. I've been a fan for years and—'

His phone rang and he held up a finger to stop her, answering gruffly, 'Attic.'

Whoever was on the line said something that made Matt throw his head back and laugh. His voice was cashmere and his accent alluded to wealthy parents and a charmed life. When his phone call was over he cleared his throat and said, 'So, what makes you think you're right for *Slick*?'

'I guess I have that irreverence that people associate with *Slick*, and I think I have a tone of voice that is complementary. Not the same exactly, but, umm ...' she trailed off, losing the pitch and knowing it.

Put your marketing face on, dickhead.

'I've got a style that resonates, I think because I cut through the bullshit and spin, but also because in a brutal way, I'm a positive person ...'

He made eye contact for just one in every three seconds. The rest of the time he spent staring over her shoulder. She looked behind her in case there was a celebrity, or some other reason his attention was directed over there.

Nope, just rude. He's Adrian, but in better shape.

'I think *Slick* is energetic, and that I could be a part of maintaining that pace. Potentially ...' she drifted out, not sure he was actually absorbing any of her chat.

'Have you got any real ideas, though?' he said to the space behind her.

'Ideas for *Slick*?'

He rolled his eyes and ran his hand through his hair. 'Yeah, ideas for *Slick*. Like, we want pieces, you know? Of writing? For *Slick*.' He said it slowly, as if explaining to a child.

Emma felt a glimmer of anger rising, but couldn't decide what to do with it.

'Well, I, I have a lot of ideas but I haven't prepared ... I mean, umm, what makes *you* think I'm right for *Slick*?'

'I don't know that you are.'

Emma tried to channel her inner Clem: what would Clementine do? She would tell him to get fucked, for a start.

They sat in a stalemate silence for a moment until Matt said, 'OK, well since you didn't bring any of your *own* ideas to the table, I had a meeting with Carina, who's our new features editor, about some stuff you might be capable of. She's a big fan of your blog. *Slick*'s a men's magazine, but we're looking to widen our scope and appeal to both sides of the market.' He glanced at Emma's boobs. 'We really like what you do with the sex stuff. Obviously we don't want like, feminism or whatever, but some of your slutty stuff is quite funny and so Carina and the guys came up with ideas for columns you might be right for.'

Emma nodded; this was more like it.

'We like your whole sexy singleton thing, and you can use your secretary stuff, but being a slut should be a positive thing. We celebrate girls who like it dirty. That's our brand, do you get it?'

Emma took a small sip of water and interrupted.

'But, do you think that's going to appeal to women? That brand? I mean, I am all for celebrating sexuality, and I'm not shy about being promiscuous, but that all sounds a bit reductive, don't you think?'

He nodded eagerly.

'Yeah, bang on. Sex, promiscuity, reductive. That sort of shit ... So we bounced some titles around – tell me what you think.'

He picked up his phone and scrolled through to his notes. He seemed enthused for the first time since she'd sat down.

'Let me know what blows your hair back, yeah?'

She held her pen, ready.

'Minge Monologues?'

He saw her expression and went on.

'The Daily Slut ... Sluts Talk ... Snail Tales ...'

Emma's mouth hung open. *What does* 'Snail Tales' *even mean?*

He stopped to register the look on her face again, cleared his throat and calmed down. He put his phone on the table. 'Or, we could call it something based on your appearance? What do you think of Short and Curly?'

He clearly thought it was pretty good and added it to his list.

'Honestly, Matt, I don't know what to say.'

'Say yes or no, it's not that complicated.'

His phone vibrated loudly on the table. Matt picked it up. 'Hang on a sec, Rob.' Turning to Emma and pushing his chair back he covered the mic on his phone and said, 'I've got to take this call so I'm going to bounce. Why don't you give it a think? BTW we pay a penny a word and we want stuff on spec, yeah? I'll be in touch.' He dropped a business card on the table and then turned and walked off. As he exited he shouted at his phone, 'Roberto, you king of cunts, tell me everything.'

Emma sat and stared at the bottle of water

'BTW' takes longer to say than 'by the way', by the way.

She felt like she'd been in a fight that had gone really badly. She replayed the conversation, adding things she should have said, including the moment where she told him to go and fuck himself. She left the pub and walked home deflated.

When she got in Paul was packing up for his night at work. He looked up distractedly, moving around the flat and slinging things in a bag.

'How was it?' he asked as she sat on the sofa and watched him get ready.

'It was a total mind grope.'

'Did they give you a job? Please take it, I love *Slick*, it's cool.'

'You only think that because they said your album was seminal ... you know they were probably referring to jizz, right?'

'Well yeah, but it's funny, and it's full of tits.'

'You're full of tits.'

'Tits!' Paul exclaimed happily, throwing his hands in the air. 'So what did *Slick* offer you?'

'Nothing, I think. A chance to pitch, maybe.'

'But that's amazing, Emma.'

'Is it? I already have a job I hate, but at least that one pays the rent. *Slick* pay a penny a word.'

She could see Paul trying to work out how much that equated to.

'It's sod all,' she said, helping him along.

'Standard.'

Emma was glum. 'One of his article ideas was called "My Minge and Me".'

Paul threw his head back and laughed. 'I'd read that.'

'It's not even grammatically correct – it should be my minge and I, or me and my minge. Either way, I'm not sure what it means.'

'I think it means you take that,' he pointed at her crotch, 'on a little tour of the town.'

'Holy fuck.'

'Yeah that would work – you could shag a monk. That'd be a good column, pitch that.'

Emma grabbed the remote and turned on the TV.

'Is there somewhere I could work that isn't overrun with dicks?'

'The countryside? You could be a farmhand.'

'I could give *Slick* a go, I suppose. But I think it means I have to get a ketamine habit and write about anal sex.'

Paul laughed and nodded at her.

'I might just fake it. How hard can it be? I'll talk in circles and walk into walls; they'll never guess I'm just high on being totally unfashionable. I get a proper buzz from wearing Uniqlo jeans.'

'I think that actually might be hipster; are they ironic?'

'Not deliberately.'

'Post-irony, it's the new hipster – I think I actually read that in *Slick*.'

'What shall I do, Paul? Just tell me what to do and I'll do it.'

'OK, tell *Slick* to shove it up their bum holes, tell your boss thanks for all the fish, get housing benefit and come raving with me every night. You can carry my records.'

'Your records are on a memory stick.'

'Easy work.'

'I'm pretty sure we can't get housing benefit here – we can't get a doctor or any post.'

'Sell your body?'

'I'd rather sell my brain, it's in better shape.'

'Blackmail the stalker from work?'

'He can barely afford a weekly martini.'

'God, you're so negative, Emma. I thought you were going to do whatever I told you?'

'I have since rescinded that idea as misguided.'

He sat down on the sofa, letting his head flop onto her shoulder. He smelled nice.

'Honestly Em, I don't know what you should do, I only know you definitely shouldn't stay at APRC until you're old and fat and sad. It was only supposed to be temporary.'

Emma hid the tears that surfaced uninvited.

'Come out with me tonight anyway, we're going on a journey through sound. It's going to be epic, and other music magazine tropes.'

'That actually sounds like fun.'

'That's why we do it, Emmy D.'

While Paul was planning his set, Emma typed a blog about her meeting with *Slick*. She called it 'Matt, My Minge and Me'. And saved it to drafts, not sure it was a bridge she should burn just yet. She cracked a beer and clinked a toast with Paul. 'Fuck 'em! To Friday.'

19

Sexually Transmitted Regrets

Emma could feel daylight on her eyelids.

She could feel the warmth of another person.

Then she felt her whole hangover.

She lay with her eyes closed for a few more moments, piecing the evening together. *Dinner with Yas, dancing with Paul, kissing who? A cab to where?*

The feel of the sheets, the smell of the room and the quality of the light were unfamiliar. She sat up and glanced over at a mop of curly brown hair.

Ah, shit.

It was the quintessential boy's room. A flatscreen TV was mounted opposite the bed; the dusty parquet floor was strewn with socks, boxer shorts and T-shirts. There were two familiar-looking posters stuck loosely to the wall, a festival line-up from 2009, and a Page Three girl with the Joker from *Batman*'s make-up. Emma cringed. There were framed pictures leaning against the wall, waiting patiently to be hung: a Tarantino movie poster and a line drawing of a girl holding a gun. A layer of dust along the frames suggested they'd been waiting a while. Emma noticed the pairs of ragged trainers that were heaped in the corner and felt a sharp pinch of a memory.

It smelled like a boy's room, like a boy with a disposable income, pretending to be a man.

Her mind had stored only snippets of the night before – a low-res, musical (dubstep) montage. A glass of water, bubbled with the passing of time, was on the floor next to the bed. She leaned over carefully and picked it up, plucking out the strand of hair that floated on the top. It looked like one of hers. She drank gratefully from the glass and then gagged – it had been there a while.

She had met someone; Yasmin was cross with her. A memory struggled to surface. She felt a surge of guilt.

She could see her bag out of reach across the room, and her shoes, skirt and bra at various intervals between there and the bed. She peeped under the covers; she was wearing pants. She checked to see if there was any evidence of having had sex, any remnants of pleasures or aches. Nothing detectable. *Hi, denial, long time no see. I've missed you, how've you been?*

She pushed the covers back and stepped up and into her skirt. She wondered what would be the least clichéd next step. She could sneak out, leave a note, wake him up or go and make tea. Pulling her top over her head she looked around for her tights.

She held her breath and tiptoed tentatively around to his side of the bed.

She looked at the sleeping form of Lee Freeman and stifled a groan. *That bastard*. She hadn't seen him for more than a year.

Lee was a pro skateboarder. He was physically exquisite, but intellectually ridiculous. It had been an acrimonious break-up. He had cheated on her and had had the audacity to have the final word. She had eventually given up on hating him, but it had taken several furious months.

Since they had broken up they had never bumped into each other. Until now.

Lee Freeman, of all the exes.

He was sexy though, she conceded, looking at him, a man-boy breathing softly, mouth agape. She noted the spent condoms on the floor and tutted. *God damn it, Lee.* She had a flashback of nudity and decided to deny the sex she knew they'd had.

She wondered if he was really asleep, because pretending to be asleep and waiting for her to leave was bang on brand for him. Even when they were together he had frequently woken up the next day and demanded that she immediately and unceremoniously get out.

A rush of unpleasant memories from their relationship had resurfaced and she wanted to get away before he ...

Damn.

His eyes unstuck and he yawned widely. When he saw her standing there he held out a long, sinewy arm from under the duvet.

'Come baaaack.'

'No thanks,' she said, pleased to have an opportunity to reject him.

'Don't go, stay here ... give us a hand job.'

'Where are we?'

'Bethnal Green. There's a bus stop outside.'

He rolled over and pulled the covers back over his head.

'What happened last night?'

'I dunno. Who cares? Stop shouting or you'll wake up my flatmate.'

She didn't bother responding. Self-loathing had already kicked in. Had he lived alone she might have stopped and had a tea, maybe even looked around for something to steal; not for profit, just to get on his nerves – something like the TV remote or the base for the kettle. It was a Clementine-trademarked move, and Clem had a cupboard full of phone chargers, tin openers, game console handsets, oven gloves and random cables. One guy she had dated for a couple of months thought she was an actual kleptomaniac, not realising that his missing stuff was a manifestation of her disappointment in him.

'Bye then,' she said, checking her bag for keys, wallet, phone. Relieved to find them all present, she took his grunt as the best she was going to get and left, slamming the bedroom door, which was the closest she was going to get to retribution.

Pretty feeble, actually.

Emma emerged from the flat to find herself outside an orange-brick cul-de-sac. It was a nice day and she wanted as much distance between her and the night before as possible, so she ignored the bus stop and decided to walk.

Her legs and lower back were aching. A symptom of sex, she wondered, or just dancing hard? She was enjoying the feeling of the breeze washing him off her. *There are worse exes it could have been*, she conceded. She wondered if it counted as a one-night stand since she had a history with him, and gave herself a little pat on the back for the fact that it had been a revisitation as opposed to a full-on random.

A lady passed with a trolley and looked Emma up and down. Emma wondered how walk of shamey she looked.

Sometimes the walk of shame is a marvellous thing, the unmistakable gait of someone who's had a night full of pleasure and luxury and orgasms. Strutting home in a ballgown, holding your heels happily, eyeliner intact, a smug glow and a (not so) secret grin. At other times it feels like you need a long, hot shower and a darkened corner to share with your regrets. Today was the latter.

She stopped at a shop and grabbed her customary hangover cure of a bag of Hula Hoops (red) and a Cherry Coke. When she opened her wallet she was surprised to find a hundred quid in it, most of which took the form of rolledup tenners.

Jesus.

She snapped the wallet shut quickly and rummaged around in her bag for some coins.

Why did she have so much money? She must have been on some kind of rampage. Oh god, how much had she spent if she had a hundred left over? She tried to remember who had paid for dinner but she had been with Yasmin so it was safe to assume the majority share had been her own.

Emma was tempted, vaguely, to call her up and find out what had happened but she still felt pretty tenderised by the Lee Freeman horror and didn't particularly want to layer on any additional embarrassment just yet.

Sipping her Coke she walked slowly towards home, thinking about the best approach to getting some clarity. Yasmin was one of those friends who really seemed to enjoy retelling all the embarrassing details from the night before. Clem, on the other hand, would phrase things with a tactful 'You were so funny, do you remember saying ...' but Yasmin would opt for the outrage tack; she had been known to pile on fictional events, if the real story wasn't juicy enough.

It was, Emma thought, a quality of spiritual generosity, to go easy on people the next morning. Nobody wants to hear their mistakes during a hangover, that's why they got drunk in the first place – to be outrageous without inhibition. What was the point if somebody appointed themselves the official record-taker and held you to account for everything in the morning? Her headache was doing a damn fine job of that anyway.

Emma realised she was deliberately blaming Yasmin for something that was undoubtedly her own fault.

She felt a wave of relief as she climbed the stairs past the handbags. She could hear music coming from her flat and knew that Paul was home. Hoping he might be a reliable source of information she opened the door and was surprised to see a tall blonde girl in the hallway. She was wearing one of Paul's T-shirts and a pair of tiny red pants and squealed with embarrassment when Emma walked in. 'Oops, sorry,' she giggled, dashing into his room and hiding behind the door.

The squeal made her head ring.

'No worries, nice pants.'

Paul chuckled from where he stood in the kitchen waiting for the kettle to boil.

'The wayward hero returns,' he grinned. 'What happened to you?' He grabbed another cup from the cupboard and popped a tea bag into it.

Emma flumped onto the sofa, dropping her bag on the floor. 'I was hoping you could tell me.'

The girl reappeared in a pair of jeans and came over to sit

with Emma. 'Hi, how are you feeling?' She was blushing slightly; she was, thought Emma, extremely pretty.

'Hi, I'm Emma. Nice to meet you.'

'Yeah, I know, we met last night. You were telling me all about how amazing Paul is.'

Emma groaned.

'Don't you remember, Em? This is Lucy. Thanks for the rave review, by the way.'

'Sorry. I can't remember anything past meeting up with Yas. I woke up at Lee Freeman's house.'

'Yeah you brought him to the Cotton Club, you kept saying you were going to avenge your relationship with him by having sex.'

'I see. Well, that plan backfired.'

'It wasn't watertight.'

Paul put the milk away and started wiping the surfaces in the kitchen. Emma resisted the urge to ask why he was breaking the habit of a lifetime and doing something useful.

'Who else was there?'

'Clem turned up while you were barfing in a corner. You arrived with Yasmin – where did she go?'

'Jeez, I have no idea. I'm worried I told her about Adam.'

Paul came over to the sofa carrying three cups of tea. Sitting opposite the girls, he looked healthy and happy. He looked the diametric opposite to how Emma felt.

'Do you remember inviting everyone you met to a party today?' he asked.

'No. Is there a party today?'

'Apparently you're going to stay up all night and go straight to a rave on Commercial Street. You've got a fan club you're meeting there at three.'

'No. Jesus, no way. That was optimistic. I'm gonna stay exactly here.' She made a circle around where she was sitting on the sofa. 'What are you guys up to?'

She wondered if Paul was going to tactfully get rid of this girl, like he had with so many before, or if he was going to draw it out a bit longer. As long as she'd known him Emma had never known Paul to get attached. This girl was particularly good looking, though, she noted, and friendly – a lot of the girls she had met were mean. Lucy had cropped blonde hair in animé-style spikes. She sat in skinny jeans with her legs folded up underneath her; Emma thought it was probably a yoga pose. She smiled broadly at Emma. She had a tight white T-shirt that hugged her perky boobs and adorable mini-paunch stomach. Her toenails were painted a dark, glittery blue and she had taken her make-up off. She looked fresh-faced and her eyes smiled even when she didn't.

'We're going to go for breakfast and a mooch about I think, if you fancy it?' Paul added in a way that meant 'definitely don't fancy it'.

He reached out and touched Lucy's knee and she smiled at him, a goofy smile that made Emma send him a set of 'Oh really?' eyebrows.

'No thanks. I'm going to lie on my face and lament my life choices.'

'Sounds like a plan.'

'At some point I might take an aspirin and find out what I said to Yasmin.'

'Good luck with that.' Paul got up – 'I'm gonna have a shower' – and left the girls sitting on the sofa.

'So, what do you do?' said Emma, and then sighed at

herself. 'You don't have to answer that; I think I left my good chat in a cab.'

Lucy smiled her broad, open smile again. 'I'm an environmental scientist . . . I'm working on a film about the Arctic.'

Emma knew there were dozens of potential questions that could follow that, but her brain was not up for supplying any of them to her mouth. 'Wow. Impressive.'

'Thanks. What do you do?'

Emma hated her for asking. She groaned and leaned over until her face was pressed into the sofa. Through the dusty, smoky fabric she muttered, 'I contribute my ideas to companies that don't deserve them and in my own special way make the world a slightly worse place for everyone.'

Lucy laughed. 'Have you ever thought about maybe, like, *not* doing that?'

'I've thought about it, yeah. Still trying to come up with a better idea though.'

'Paul said you're a writer?'

'That was generous of him.'

The music that had been playing stopped and was replaced by the repetitive click of used vinyl. The room got suddenly heavy with silence. 'I'll just change the record,' said Lucy, getting up.

You and me both, she thought. Change the bloody record, Derringer.

When Paul and Lucy had dressed and left in a whirl of shower-scented, friendly goodbyes, Emma made another cup of tea, took her bra off and lay on her bed with the curtains half drawn. Resolving to deal with Yasmin and the night's mistakes later on, she lay back and opened her laptop, checking in to her blog. She was surprised to find she had a bunch of new followers. She created a new post – a short but effective description of the feeling she had caught from Lee Freeman. She called it 'Sexually Transmitted Regrets', and pressed publish.

When she woke up several hours later her hangover had condensed. It felt like a ball of spiky glue pressing on her eyes, looking for an exit point. She had missed calls from Clem and Yasmin and tried to decide which to deal with first.

The phone rang and Clem's voice groaned down the line.

'Emmmmmmmmmaaaaa, please help me, I can't move.'

'I've just woken up from a lovely snooze, I highly recommend it as a course of action.'

She could hear Clem shifting in her seat and swapping her phone to the other ear. 'Top tip. Did you wake up at home?'

'No. Did you?'

'I did, yes, because I'm not a filthy slutbag like some.'

'Like who?'

'Like you. Obviously. How was revenge sex?'

'I don't think it counts as total slut-duggery when it's an ex, right? I don't even know if we did anything.'

'You kept shouting "Avengers Assemble!" and snogging him in front of everyone. It was pretty spectacular stuff. And you called Yasmin a gold-digger or something, I dunno – she was pissed off, though.'

'Did I tell her about Adam?'

'I don't think so. Did you? I hope not. I think it was all money based; he didn't come up when I spoke to her just now.'

'How did she sound? I'm scared to call.'

'I think she's fine, actually; she wasn't angry. Just call and play it like everything's fine. She might not even bring it up.'

They hung up and Emma called the pizza place. Her justification for getting a large was that she had to go up and down three floors to get it: exercise.

Then she braced herself and dialled Yasmin. When she answered, Emma could hear she was driving.

'Oh. Em. Geee. Emma Derringer, you dirty whore.'

She sounded cheerful at least. Emma could hear the click of her e-cigarette.

'Yas, are you driving, smoking *and* on your phone right now?'

'Yeah, I just went for lunch with my mum.'

'Shall I call you back? I don't want you to crash your car.'

'No it's fine, you're on Bluetooth darling.'

'So . . . I feel like I owe you an apology, but I literally can't remember anything past dinner.'

'Yeah it was really weird, you got totally obliterated on two glasses of wine. You were whooping and everything . . . '

Emma had a well-documented contempt for women who whooped.

'You were on a total mission to get munted. What do you remember?'

'Seriously nothing at all – please tell me everything you know.'

'Well . . . ' she started gleefully. Emma imagined her wiggling in her seat, getting comfortable.

'First we went to that new cocktail bar on Frith Street, and you had a manhattan I think, but you kept shouting at people so the bartender asked us to leave. Do you really not remember that? You owe me a tenner, by the way.'

'I really don't.' It sounded out of character and Emma wondered how much was embellishment.

'Well, anyway, we left there and you bumped into Lee Freeman, and I tried to make you get rid of him but you just kept shouting at me that I should hook up with his friend because Adam is boring – which was mean, by the way. And the friend wasn't even fit.'

Yikes.

'So we went to the Cotton Club and you went bonkers – you said I wasn't any fun because my life was too serious.'

'Jeez, Yas. I'm sorry, buddy.'

'No, it's all right, it was kind of funny and I bet I feel a lot better than you do today.'

'Damn straight you do.'

'I left when you and Lee Freeman were getting too slobbery for me. Adam's back tonight anyway so I thought I should get some beauty sleep. Sounds like you could use some too.'

'I woke up at Lee's house.'

'Ha haaaaa, I thought you might. He's really mean though, you know? He wasn't being nice to you. I kept trying to get you away from him but you told me to leave you alone.'

'I woke up with a mystery hundred quid on me.'

'You were on one.'

'Well. I feel totally diabolical today. I've been feeling really guilty all day. I could just remember you looked cross.'

Yasmin laughed and Emma could hear the indicator ticking in the background.

'Don't worry, we all have nights like that; you seemed like you needed to let off some steam. Did you have sex with Lee?'

'If I did it was 100 per cent forgettable.'

'Well I hope you were careful, Emma.'

'There were rubbers on the floor.'

'Oh Em, I wish I could have talked you out of it. You know he actually pulled someone else right in front of us.'

'What? Wow, that's pretty low.'

'It wasn't good. You threw up in the corner; the whole thing was just very, like, five years ago. Listen I've got to go, I'm parking. Have an early night. I'll speak to you soon.'

She hung up and Emma sat in silence in the dark, with nothing for company but regrets, a ringing in her ears and a twenty-pound note for the pizza guy.

She decided to spend the few weeks until her birthday being clean, sober and healthy. I'll hit twenty-eight running, she thought. The doorbell rang. I'll start tomorrow.

Part 2

20

Issue 28

Emma had mixed feelings about her birthday; mini-tweaks of excitement preceded a swell of self-loathing until she settled on benign indifference. The passing of a year at APRC felt like a year wasted, except for glimpses of a bank balance in the black. At the end of last month her balance had been £550 in credit, and she had delayed withdrawing her rent by a couple of days, to really enjoy it.

She could feel her twenties sliding away, like a raw egg down a plughole. A spectacular decade reduced to a swirl of memories that threatened to blend so completely they'd become a flat colour. But as she played a mental montage of some of the highlights, she smiled. No, if her twenties were reduced to a colour, it would definitely be neon.

Right now life felt like a beige monotony of paydays, rent days and lost Saturdays. She remembered as a teenager thinking that twenty-eight meant a proper adult, that it was the age by which people had everything they wanted and had firmly established who they were. She didn't feel like a grown-up and looking down at her trainers, decided she didn't look like one either.

This was her chain of thought during the team meeting's weekly rendition of 'Happy Birthday', with Ross serenading in her ear. She resolutely hadn't put it on the agenda but when Adrian had done the shout-out, Hilary had piped up from the back of the room.

Adrian had made a joke about the 27 Club, reeling off an apparently pre-supplied list of famous deaths at twenty-seven. The Eds gleefully joined in until it became morbid.

The meeting's APRC moment had fallen to one of the receptionists, who took the opportunity to show them slides of her trip to Majorca. The highlight of the presentation was a photographic nipple slip. Adrian blushed and guffawed and tried to think of something funny to say that wouldn't qualify as sexual harassment.

When the meeting was over Hilary caught up with Emma in the corridor. 'Happy birthday, baby face. You OK?'

'Yeah, starving though. You?'

'I'm fine. You look kind of pale – you hungover?'

'No, I've been sleeping really badly – got APRC anxiety I think. Nothing a cheeseburger won't fix.'

'Awesome. So, I've got a present for you.'

'My birthday's not until tomorrow but don't let that put you off giving me gifts.'

'I know – it's for tomorrow,' she beamed at Emma. 'I hope you don't mind.' She handed Emma an envelope. 'It's a spa day!' she giggled, unable to bear the suspense.

'Wow.'

'Have you ever had a massage?'

'I never have, no, but I've always wanted to,' she lied. 'Thanks, H.'

'No problem. Just make sure you give me a nudge when they bring you a cake today, OK? Oh no! I ruined the surprise,' she said with mock horror.

'Shall we lunch?'

'Definitely.'

They sat in a booth in The Burger Place, looking out at the Holborn traffic. Hilary ordered a bottle of sparkling water and a bottle of rosé, which they had established as their drink of choice for celebrating. They had found cause to celebrate on most of their lunch dates.

When the bottles arrived they lifted their glasses to clink. Hilary made the toast.

'To the best copywriter at APRC, to this year being your best and to the coolest twenty-eight-year-old I know.'

'I'm twenty-seven until tomorrow.'

When the burgers were done and taken away Hilary ordered two glasses of prosecco.

'We'll be hammered,' said Emma, nervously.

'It's your birthday, so relax,' Hilary replied. 'Plus I booked you out for a meeting.' She winked.

'Nice.'

There was a pause while they watched a cyclist swearing at a cab driver.

'What's wrong, Emma? Your usual level of despair seems particularly heightened today.'

'It's just like, every Friday I walk out of the office, and think, well that was shit, but at least it's over. And every Sunday I wake up and remember that I have to do it all again, exactly the same week again, and I wish I was old enough to retire. Like, I'm twenty-eight tomorrow and I wish I was turning sixty-five, just so I could stop doing this shit.'

'Well at least you've got something to look forward to. Are you OK, though?'

'Just birthday blues I reckon; I guess I never thought I'd actually make it to twenty-eight.'

Hilary laughed. 'Aww, bambina. Why do you put so much pressure on yourself?'

Emma felt a wave of wine-induced tears press against her eyes.

'I really hate my job, Hils. I hate it there.'

Hilary looked shocked and moved to Emma's side of the booth to hug her, which made the tears Emma was holding back cascade. She snuffled, embarrassed.

'Don't be sad, Em, you're really talented – you just got promoted! Adrian knows you're amazing, everyone does.'

Emma stuck her lip out and fiddled with a sugar sachet on the table.

'I hate advertising, it's so futile. I'm just coasting towards nothing.'

'We all are, Em, this is what life is like.'

'Is this it? Doesn't it at least get better with age?'

Hilary looked at her with an adult concern.

'The only difference between your twenties and your thirties is you'll get more cabs and tip bigger.'

'Can't wait,' Emma muttered into her glass. If that was the case, what was the point? Hilary had been doing this for a decade and was content. All that meant, to Emma, was that Hilary lacked depth. How was she not bored to the core of it all?

'Isn't copywriting what you wanted to do? I mean, isn't it near enough?'

NO.

'It's a bit like wanting to be an artist but doing painting and decorating instead.'

'Yeah but, you know, you're using your materials? You're painting word pictures, kind of? Why don't you try and monetise your blog or something?'

Emma sighed, bored of trying to explain the difference. 'I don't associate getting paid with anything I like. I've been working since I was fifteen. I guess I associate financial survival with boredom. I don't know if I can combine writing, which I love and do for myself, with work, which I do for money. I'm worried that if I start getting paid to write, it'll become like every other job I've had and I'll hate it. Writing is the only thing I do for the art of it and I want to protect that.'

A flash of contempt crossed Hilary's face and she twiddled a fork.

Emma continued: 'I get overwhelmed by the number of words in the world. Everyone's got a blog, everyone's got a pen. Everyone with an internet connection is a writer, there are all these billions of words flying about. I just think, why add to them? None of it makes any difference anyway.'

'Wow, that is impressively self-destructive.'

'Thanks.' Emma grinned.

'There are worse places to work. At least at APRC they're using your talent a bit.'

Emma nodded.

'In my experience,' Hilary started, moving back to her side of the booth, 'there are two types of people. The first don't know what they want, so they're defined by their job. They get good at it and progress and enjoy it. That's the type nobody likes. The other is doing it because they have to; they want the stuff that money buys – the houses and holidays and cars. You're neither, you're the elusive third kind; you know what you want to do, and you're not materialistic. So I don't really know what's stopping you, I don't know why you're still here – unless it's because secretly, you like it.'

Emma shrugged.

'You'll figure it out, Emma. Maybe you don't feel it, but you're only young. You still have passion and drive, just don't give up on yourself.'

'You're good at reading people, H.'

'I'm a type one kind of gal.' She smiled.

At 3 p.m. Emma sensed the office gearing up for birthday time so she headed out for a smoke, wanting to avoid the covert operation that was getting the card signed and candles lit, all while the recipient pretended not to notice and feigned surprise.

She was still reeling from the lunchtime booze and the cigarette made her gag so she stubbed it out on a nearby bin and was standing aimlessly watching the world go by when Yasmin called. She had her executive voice on and barked at Emma, 'My friend at *Get Up* wants you to send them something, they've got slots to fill this week. This is a real opportunity, Emma. You can at least send them a pitch, can't you?'

'Pitch what?'

'I don't know, you're the bloody writer ... Something girly, try not to be sarcastic about it. She likes your stuff.

Ping something over to her now while our chat is fresh, yeah? You're welcome.' Yasmin hung up without saying goodbye.

When Emma got back to her desk the cake was alight with five candles and everyone was gathered around. Adrian clutched a card.

'Happy birthday, Emma. We hope you have a great year.' The Eds cheered and Ross lead a weak round of applause.

Emma thanked them and smiled politely, trying to enjoy the sense of discomfort.

After they'd all wandered back to their desks Hilary blonked on the IM.

Hungry Caterpillar cake? What are you, 8?
I 8 its face.

21

Drake Jones

Clementine sat at a table in a members' bar in Covent Garden waiting for Drake Jones. She was trying to exude an air of calm but just under the surface there were nerves, tingling the palms of her hands and drying the roof of her mouth. His email, when it arrived, had been so blasé she'd felt more ridiculous than elated. It had made all her attempts to elicit a response from him seem desperate and juvenile.

Hi Clem, let's do lunch. My assistant will set it up.

She glanced up whenever anyone entered the bar.

The irony that she would go from the meeting to her own job at a bar wasn't lost on her. That morning the bank had called to collect. Her mum said they had rung the house weekly for a couple of months. Before she'd left for New York Clementine had arranged a business loan, which was the only type she qualified for. Under the terms of the loan, she was the business and the Columbia course was her initial financial speculation. At the time having 10k in her account had been deeply liberating but as it began to dwindle and the real cost of it became clear, she had stuck her head deeper into the illusion that everything would be OK. Now she was practically bankrupt, and the bank had been calling to explain just how completely screwed she was, and to make sure she wasn't enjoying herself at all.

She was reading Emma's blog on her phone, an entry called 'Money Buys Happiness – if Happiness Is Made of Denim'. Impressed with the piece, she felt a sense of despair that Emma was so seemingly unwilling to take a leap of faith and be a writer.

When Drake arrived Clementine stood up, smiling. He was tall and Hollywood handsome with slick blond hair. Even to her untrained eye she could tell he worked out, and his suit was expensive and his smile charmed her into a nervous shudder. He shook her hand firmly; his voice was deep and confident and oozed charm, and he was a bit of a cliché but utterly unembarrassed by the fact.

The waitress came bounding over, having actively ignored Clementine for the last twenty minutes, and simpered at Drake as he asked for a coffee.

'Make that two,' Clem added casually as the waitress started to walk away.

'So, Clementine, welcome back to London. How are you finding it?'

'Great, thanks, it's nice to be home. I do miss the pizza though.'

Drake glanced at her slender body, which made her immediately grateful for her shape.

'Yar, I love New York. I don't get there as often as I like, much more West Coast action for me.'

'I like LA as well.'

'Mmm,' Drake murmured, giving Clem the impression that he would rather do the talking. She shut her mouth and waited patiently.

'So, Clem, your professor happens to be an old mate of mine, and he sent me *Moonshiners*. Which I love, by the way, although I do think you need to work on the name ...'

Clem tried not to beam at him while high-fiving her professor in her mind.

'I've got lots of ideas for names; *Moonshiners* is a working title.'

'Good, that's great. Can't be too precious about these things while we're still in the process of building your PB.'

He put 'PB' in air quotes with his fingers and although she tried to disguise her bemusement he caught a glimpse of it.

'Personal brand.'

'Ah.' Clem nodded and had a flash of Emma's clipboard face smiling smugly at her as if to say, *Branding, babe, told ya*.

'So I'm up for sending it out to some of my contacts and see if we can't get you optioned,' said Drake

He leaned back as the waitress put their coffees on the table, giving Drake a generous dose of cleavage in the process. Clem raised an eyebrow at her.

'That would be magic.'

'You had a great class at Columbia, huh? It was a gold mine this year – we've got Jordan Guillermo on our books and we've just signed a kid called Boris.'

Clem flinched at the mention of Jordan.

'Boris is cool.'

Drake fixed her with a curious look and went on, 'I'm going to ping you over a contract; you just need to sign and send it back over to me and we can get things going. Yar?'

Fuck yar.

22

Exotic Treats

Emma's appointment for the spa treatment was at 12. She had never had a facial or a mani-pedi. Her nails were too bitten to paint, she didn't own a hairdryer and she had never understood blusher. It occurred to her that, on her ascent into adulthood, she might try to act more like a lady – but even the voice in her head said it sarcastically.

In the glossy waiting room Emma felt like an intruder and watched the women walking about in dressing gowns, chatting and sipping cucumber iced water.

Hilary's birthday gift was called Exotic Treats and involved:

Wellness consultation

Head massage and facial refresh

Therapeutic Peruvian mud soak

Foot and ankle massage

Deep-tissue hand and forearm massage

Fire and ice stone therapy

Refreshments included.

A small Chinese lady led Emma to a room and pointed at a leather chair in the corner, under which sat a small silver bowl of water. The room was brown, low lights and mahogany. It was warm and smelled of soap.

Emma took off her jeans and T-shirt and put on the dressing gown. She looked at herself in the full-length mirror along one wall.

No one looks sexy in a dressing gown.

She sat in the chair, with her feet either side of the small silver bowl of oily water. The woman returned and looked at Emma, surprised. Emma decided to name her Dolly.

'Put feet.' She pointed at the bowl. Emma put her feet in the bowl of tepid water as Dolly knelt in front of the chair and said, 'How are you?'

'Good, thanks.'

Emma wondered if that counted as the 'wellness consultation'.

She sat trying to contain her embarrassment. She wasn't big on being touched. Her little toes were ticklish and she had to strain against the kick reflex whenever Dolly touched them.

Emma's vision of the spa day had been based on chick flicks, so she was picturing that the mud soak would involve cucumber eyes and cling film, but when Dolly said 'extract of mud in here' and pointed at the bowl, Emma regretfully let the image evaporate. She wondered if Hilary had got the voucher at a heavily discounted price.

Once the water in the bowl was all the way cold, the woman lifted each of Emma's feet, and placing them on her knee, wiped them gently with a towel. Emma had the uncomfortable feeling of being the oppressor in some colonial nightmare.

Dolly stood up, put a dollop of oil on her hands, and stood behind Emma, pushing her fingers through her hair. As she yanked her way through the curls Emma's eyes watered.

Next she moved around to stand in front of Emma and then gently pressed each section of her face. Emma kept her eyes closed to stave off the discomfort of staring directly at Dolly, though Dolly did not appear remotely bothered.

She took each of Emma's arms, kneading them down to the fingers. Then she took each of the fingers and turned them clockwise, then anticlockwise. Emma thought about what everyone else in the world was doing at that moment. How strange was it that she and this small woman were in this intense little room together and she was having her fingers wobbled, for money. She realised the situation was both girly and funny and that it would be perfect for her *Get Up* pitch. She decided to pay more attention to the details and instantly began to enjoy it. *This wasn't embarrassing. It was espionage! She was undercover, a writer at large.*

Dolly wiped her hands with a towel and pointed to the gurney. Emma had a sip of water, took off her dressing gown and lay face down on it. It didn't have the hole in the pillow for her face so she lay looking out at the mirror. She felt a bit of a tit.

Dolly tried to take off Emma's bra. It wasn't a bra, though; it was a crop top that had no clasp. Emma was suitably embarrassed, not only that she was wearing the kind of underwear popular with eleven-year-olds, but also that it was probably eleven years old. If it were a person, her underwear would be starting secondary school. She tried to take it off with due modesty but Dolly got a solid eyeful of boob.

Dolly pounded her back and tickled her side panels; their

bellies had an audible grumble about lunch and they shared a giggle. She slathered Emma's back in various oils, inviting her to smell each one as she poured them into the cup of her palms. Emma wished there was some gentle music they would put on to cover the sounds of hunger pangs and the gentle slapping of skin on skin.

Using an oven glove Dolly placed the stone on the small of Emma's back; the skin sizzled and Emma yelped. Emma could sense Dolly's boredom and felt guilty for wasting her time. When she was done, Dolly completed the wellness consultation. 'How you feel now?'

Greasy, burnt, tugged, pummelled and embarrassed, thanks – you?

'Amazing. Cheers.'

Dolly left the room wiping furiously at her oily hands, shutting the door behind her and leaving Emma to get dressed. Emma took a seat for a moment and looked down at her shimmering body: she was coated in a thick layer of oil and she envisioned sliding, like a surfboard, along the marble corridor. You could fry her into an Emma tempura right now.

On her way out of the spa she took a bright green apple from a fruit bowl that was obviously for display purposes only.

Refreshments included.

She walked along Bond Street chuckling to herself.

Everything in the name of comedy.

She headed directly to a nearby coffee shop and took out her laptop. She was a writer. She was submitting a piece to a magazine. She wondered if this is what it felt like to be proud of your job. When she was happy with the article she sent it to Tammy, who replied immediately with an email full of hearts and exclamation marks.

Emma! Yasmin said you were a genius! Thanks a bunch for this! I'll send you a link when it's up on the site! Love it! ♥ ♥ ♥ ♥

Excited in spite of herself, she headed towards the underground. She was freelance, she was published, she was practically a journalist. Fuck *Slick*, she thought happily, picturing herself collecting a Pulitzer and making a speech.

Emma Derringer, writer at large.

23

A Soggy Twenty

'Hi, Dad – nice cardigan, very OAP chic.'

Daniel Derringer stood in the doorway and laughed at her. 'Yes, thanks; well, it gets a bit chilly.'

They walked through to the kitchen where Emma instinctively went first to the fridge and then to check the contents of the cupboards. He had own-brand cornflakes, cat food and some sorry-looking vegetables. He kept his tins in the drawers under the sink.

They sat at the kitchen table and he plodded over to the kettle as Emma looked around, noting the mess and feeling guilty that she hadn't been there more, and helped him tidy up.

'It's a bit of a state in here, Pops,' she said. He couldn't hear her. He couldn't hear anyone unless they spoke loudly and slowly.

'How are you?'

'I'm good, Dad. I got a massage for my birthday and I'm writing for a website.'

He nodded and started to make tea, putting two sugars in her cup although she had never taken sugar.

'That sounds nice – part of your job, is it? Writing?'

'Just a side project; I'm trying to branch out from marketing.'

'Good money though, isn't it? Marketing?'

'It's good for the bank balance, bad for the soul.' She was shouting slightly.

He nodded knowingly. 'Often the way.'

The cat, Tumnus, an ancient, bad-tempered tabby, walked in through a flap in the back door, looked at Emma with an air of contempt and then mooched out of the kitchen.

'I got you a birthday present,' said her dad, clearly just remembering; he left the room and she heard him in the living room, rummaging amongst the heaps of crap. She wanted to get up and start tidying, but the task was over-whelming and it would take hours to get things really straightened out.

He called through from the living room.

'I won't be able to give you a lift home, Em – will you be all right on the bus?'

'Fine thanks, Dad,' she yelled as he made his way back down the hall.

'Did you do anything nice for your birthday?'

'Just the massage, but Clem's coming over for dinner with Paul and me tomorrow, nothing fancy.'

'Which one is Clem again?'

'The one from Ealing who writes films – the tall one, the pretty one.'

'Oh yes, Clem,' he said, walking back into the room, clearly none the wiser. He handed her a small box that he had wrapped in brown paper; it was comically shabby and she laughed at him.

'Nice wrapping, Dad.'

He smiled vaguely. 'Not my strong suit, as you know. It's like ironing to me.' He swept his gaze over the room and added, 'Or keeping things neat.'

'Do you want me to come over next week and give you a hand?'

'No no, not to worry, I'll do it.'

She opened the package and inside was a small, carved wooden box.

'I couldn't believe it when I saw it.'

Curiously she opened the box and a small plastic dancer, worn completely white with age so that she looked naked, span slowly while a song tinkled at the wrong tempo.

'Wind it up, Em,' he said.

She spun the winder on the back and opened the box again, now recognising the tune.

'I wrote it! Do you remember? I wrote it when you were a little baby, you were in a cot by the piano, do you remember?'

'I know the song, Dad; I guess I was too young to remember the actual writing.'

He put his hands between his knees and grinned at her.

'You were there, though, and I had to finish it before we went to the opera, your mum and I. To see *La Bohème* at the Albert Hall. We had to leave you here with Maria from next door and she came round and heard me playing it and she thought it was beautiful.'

He said it happily, and Emma remembered a time when the house had been warm and clean and full, and the neighbours friendly enough to trust with a baby. All of those things resigned to memory now.

'It's gorgeous, Dad – thank you so much, what an amazing find.'

He nodded and took the box from her, winding it again and, placing it delicately on the table, he stared at it until he seemed to have completely switched off, then his attention returned to the room. 'So tell me about your writing, Emma – who is it for?'

'It's for a glossy magazine, probably a couple of hundred quid – not quite worth giving up the day job, but a step in the right direction.'

'Are you wanting to give up the day job, then?'

'I wouldn't mind being a writer proper, but I'm worried, I guess. It's risky.'

'Yes, well, it's not easy I suppose.'

She felt his shame with a pang of guilt.

'I'll be fine either way, Pops. I'm not going to do anything rash.'

She touched his hand, which was crinkled and bony.

'I nearly forgot the card!' he said, moving over to the sideboard. He opened a drawer and plucked out an envelope, which he handed to Emma.

She tore it open and smiled at the card. It had an illustration of a teenage girl in roller-skates and inside was printed 'To our Number 1 daughter'. He had signed it from 'Mum' as well. Inside, a twenty-pound note lay crumpled and soggy looking.

'Thanks, Dad, you don't have to give me this.'

'Don't be silly, Emma – it's your birthday, buy yourself something nice.' He patted her on the shoulder, went out the door, and walked slowly up the stairs.

Why so slowly? She worried about his health.

When she heard him shut the bathroom door, she got up and went over to the drawer where she knew he stashed his benefit money. The tattered brown envelope was the same one she had taken from as a teenager, in her short-lived stealing phase, when they'd had money to steal. She peeked in the envelope, and flinched when she saw just £15 remaining. She heard the toilet flush and slipped the twenty from her card back in, shutting the drawer quietly and sitting back in the seat.

'Are you hungry, Em? I've got beans, or some nice soup – they do a good tomato one in the corner shop.'

'I'm all right, thanks, Pops. I'll come over and cook soon though. I'm pretty good at it.'

'I don't know where you get that from, I've always been hopeless in the kitchen and your mum wasn't much better. She once wrecked a jacket potato.' He chuckled. 'I don't know how she managed it.'

He stared into the distance and Emma's heart twisted into a little knot.

'How did the film score go?'

He lit up briefly. 'They loved it! They used it in the main film as well – shall we watch it?'

She stayed as long as she could bear, and when she sensed he was itching to tune back into Radio 4 she got up and took their cups back to the kitchen. As she rinsed them out, she looked at the washing-up that was already there; it was congealed, the bits at the bottom more than a few days old.

'I'll be off then, Pops. I'll come round for dinner soon, or you can come over any time. There's parking at mine, it's a nice place.'

He got up and walked with her to the door.

'Do you need anything, Dad? You only have to ask. I could come over and clean up some time.'

He looked at her kindly. 'I'm fine, Emma. You let me know if you need anything.'

They hugged and she held him tightly, wishing there was something she could do. She wanted to buy him a nice house by the seaside, or pay for a cleaner or get him a decent car. She waved at the end of the road and watched him go back inside. She ran her fingers through her hair; the oil had set and it had matted her curls. She resolved to go back and clean up soon, and headed towards home.

24

Trump My Drama

Emma bundled into the flat laden with shopping bags; she'd gone organic to mark the occasion and had felt a pinch of guilt at the checkout when she remembered the envelope at her dad's house. Should she be donating her disposable income to him?

She pushed through to the kitchen, sweating and irritable.

Paul emerged from his room, helped her lift the shopping onto the counter and then plonked himself on the sofa.

Thanks a lot.

'What we 'avin'?'

'Broad bean and feta bruschetta and roast chicken with salad, and potatoes, maybe, if I can be arsed.'

'Ooh, bruschetta,' he mocked, rolling the 'r'. 'Fancy.'

'Yeah, if you think toast is fancy.'

As she said it she abandoned the bags and threw herself onto the sofa next to him, feeling her motivation to cook a three-course meal slipping away.

Shit. I forgot cake.

'No dessert,' she added.

'Good. Who needs dessert after a middle-class feast like that?'

'Clem will be here around eight. Is the toilet in a respectable condition?'

'I have no idea. I've been pissing out the window for weeks.'

'Good. Then it probably is.'

By 10.30 p.m. they were sitting at a table surrounded by empty wine bottles and dirty plates.

Clem was on fighting form, hot off the Drake Jones high: 'A toast! To you, Emma, to your first assignment – may it be upwards from here. To your masseuse – may you always be inspired by gift vouchers and nudity, and to your birthday – may you never wrinkle!'

They clinked glasses and Emma tapped a fork on the table. 'And to you, Twist! To your first agent – may he not be the glossy asshole he looks on the internet. To maid of honouring – may your cock straws be fruity and your dress be without puff. And to *Moonshiners* – may it be picked up and pay you a fortune.' She stopped shouting. 'Seriously on that bit, though.'

Paul held his glass in the air. 'And to me!' They both looked at him and he lowered his glass. 'That's it. I'm awesome.'

Emma drained her glass and refilled it. 'So how is wedding planning?'

'It's an endless stream of screeching phone calls, emails and appointments that all seem to be at 9 a.m. on Saturdays. As if Saturday at 9 a.m. is even a thing.'

'Is it not a thing?' Emma asked.

'Not when you're a writer who works in a bar.' Clem took a big gulp of wine and looked at them. 'So, what else is new? Can either of you trump my drama?'

She turned her drunken gaze to Paul. 'What's going on with you, DJ fit face?'

'Well, Clementine, I'm glad you ask, because my current drama is that I'm in love.'

Both women exclaimed in surprise.

'With who?' said Clementine.

'With Lucy,' said Paul quietly, plucking a piece of feta off the table and squeezing it between his fingers.

'In actual love?' Emma asked.

'I think so . . . yeah, in love. I love her.'

'Wow,' said Clem, glancing at Emma. 'Who would have thought it?'

'She's really nice,' Emma said, defensive on his behalf. 'I really like her. Does she feel the same?'

'We haven't said the L word yet, but I think so – she exhibits all the symptoms.'

'That's not miserable OR dramatic,' Clem said.

'I've been trying to find a way to break the news to you chronic singles, I am officially off the market. You'll have to resort to someone else for your back-up husbands now.'

They laughed sarcastically.

'What's your story?' Clem demanded of Emma.

'Well, I have to go on a company away day tomorrow, where my stalker will be expecting me to blow him. I am officially a junior copywriter . . . '

Clem rolled her eyes. Emma felt a stab of anger, realising only now that she had hoped to be congratulated.

'I spent the day getting mauled, burnt and fondled by a small Chinese lady who laughed at my bra. I'm perpetually broke, and there are at least five Mondays in my working week.'

Clem sighed and filled her glass up again. 'Well, Em, congratulations – you're officially a sell-out.'

Emma gave an empty laugh. 'Nice to know someone's buying, though.'

Clem glared at her. 'I dunno, Em. You just fucking—'

'All right, red wine, take it easy.' Emma was already exhausted and didn't feel like getting a bollocking for what, in normal circles, might be considered good news.

But Clem went on, 'You're so good at everything you do, but you never take responsibility for what happens to you. You know you're talented, but the only outlets you have are a blog you don't promote and a puff piece for a women's magazine. You're so close to being an actual writer but instead you're going to sell your talent in tiny pointless pieces, to those cretins at ARCP.'

'APRC,' Emma corrected absentmindedly.

'WHO GIVES A FUCK, EMMA!'

'All right, jeez, sorry. I'm still a writer though, sort of.'

'Oh, come on. Everything you produce for them is a disposable and single-serve. It's the Nespresso machine of writing jobs. Even if you actually produce something of worth, which doesn't seem likely, it's immediately sold to the highest bidder and nobody gets a share. It might be different at *Get Up* if you wrote something real, but at this rate they'll only ever ask you for work that women will digest with their vitamin supplements and shit out none the wiser.'

Emma didn't argue; she didn't disagree with what Clem

was saying and she knew better than to fight back when she was on a red-wine roll.

'You think you can justify spending your working week denying everything you believe in. The Emma I remember thought advertising was for talentless twats.'

'I do still think that. But I don't know what else to do. Better the devil you know, right?'

'No, Emma, definitely not.'

'Maybe I'm just a talentless twat too, Clem.' Emma wanted her to leave, wanted everyone to leave her alone, wanted to get under a duvet and stay there in the dark.

'You need to get a grip, Derringer, take some responsibility for yourself. What have you actually made since uni, apart from money?'

'She made dinner,' Paul interrupted.

Emma felt a roll of temper. 'I've already had this lecture from Hilary this week – I get it, I'm a loser, thanks.'

'Who the fresh fuck is Hilary and where does she step off lecturing my best mate?'

The conversation dropped a note of ferocity.

Emma rubbed her temples. 'I think I'm trapped in this now, this lifestyle; apart from weekdays, I like it, I like living here and going out and buying fucking feta for my friends. Sometimes I think it's enough – to tread water. I've got nothing to fall back on. You can be the successful one, I'm happy to watch.'

'I think you're trivialising your life, Emma. I know it's not easy, but you're putting way too much emphasis on the money. How bad do you think it will ever get for you? You can always be a temp, you will always have options, you have a degree and you're smart and you have a decade of admin to *fall back on*. You can do boring shit any time you like. I don't believe it's what you *want* to do that makes you who you are. It's what you actually do that forms the basis of your character, much as we would like to deny it. Wanting to be a writer isn't cutting it. You're trying to fit your real ambition into the cracks between shit you hate or don't care about. Drop the act, and do it soon, Emma, because I am bored of my best friend being a pseudo-creative marketing douchebag.'

Paul mouthed, *Yikes*.

'Yeah, well, at least I can help you develop your *personal brand*, Clem – and based on your tone of voice, you'll test really well with the judgemental bitch demographic.'

Paul sat wide-eyed and helpless.

Emma relented. 'I didn't mean that, but you have to admit you're in an industry that's just as packed full of arseholes as advertising is.'

'No, I won't admit that. It's a bit *finance* at times but at least cinema is an art form.'

'Oh yeah, it's true, *Grown Ups 2* was just showing at the Tate.'

'You're so right, Emma, and I've seen many a mind-expanding poster for fucking nougat sticks.'

'You're permanently skint though, Clem.'

With her voice lowered, Clem stared at Emma. 'Jesus, did you seriously just say that? What's happened to you?'

'You're making me take this side of the argument. I'm trying to do something else but I haven't got my parents' house to fall back on. I don't want to bankrupt myself trying to be a writer, I don't know if it's worth it. The publishing industry, the film industry ... all the creative shit, it's the same as advertising but without the pay cheque. It's all the dumbing down of ideas for money. If you're making films for the art of it, Clem, you're going to be broke and living at home for ever.'

They looked at each other. They never normally fought; there would be no winners and they knew it, but nobody wanted to stop.

'WHO ARE YOU, EMMA? When did you get so conformist? Have you completely given up on yourself? Have you been like this all along? A capitalist cock in an Emma suit?'

'Yeah, maybe I have. But now I've got this thing that resembles a career and I'm not sure I have the energy, the time or the talent to start a new one. I've been working my way up through this company and if I leave now I'll have to start at the bottom. I'm just trying to be realistic.'

'There's realistic and then there's just giving up. Fuck savings, Emma – save yourself. What you're doing is worse than moving home and having shit all to show for yourself by the time you hit thirty, take it from me.'

Emma did not agree, picturing her dad's crummy house. Clem wondered if Emma believed what she said. Then she remembered that she couldn't storm out without asking for the cab fare.

Paul looked alarmed and poured more wine in an ill-considered attempt to defuse the situation. Both girls drank big from their glasses. Paul realised his error and put the last of the bottle in his own glass.

'Is this an actual argument?' he asked.

'No,' Clem snapped at him but then mellowed and added, 'It's just a really aggressive compliment.'

The girls touched glasses gently. Emma was on the edge of tears. Clem was sorry, but they both knew she was right.

Clem tried to dial it down; the anger left her voice. 'Emma, you're a writer. It's so easy to change your headline, just stop telling people you work in advertising. Seriously, write the thing for *Get Up*, get the money and build from there. But do it now, before we're old and tired and there's nothing but babies and bills and an ice age to look forward to.'

They clinked glasses again and Paul moved to the sofa out of the firing line.

Emma booked a cab for Clem, who left with a stilted, 'Thanks, bye.' Paul shirked the washing-up by falling asleep on the sofa. Emma tidied away, feeling attacked. She opened a blog and started writing an entry she knew she wouldn't post called 'All Your Friends Are Better Than You'. Drunk and angry she marched around the house throwing random items into a duffel bag, ready for the away day she hadn't had time to start dreading, then fell asleep in her clothes hoping that by the next time her birthday came round, she would be celebrating, instead of furious at her best friend and lamenting her life choices in a handbag storage facility.

25

Away Day

Why, she thought as the District Line shook her throbbing brain, do I always insist on doing these things with a hangover?

She could see her reflection in the window opposite, her forehead stretched by the concave glass. Cone-headed, no make-up and teetering on green she gulped and pressed her eyes shut. *Fresh hell.*

She arrived at Earl's Court and had time to grab a Cherry Coke and a packet of Hula Hoops before heading to the meeting point. She hoped her sunglasses would disguise her bloodshot eyes and Hilary would be able to cover for her. Hilary looked relieved when Emma approached; she was standing alone a little way off from the rest of the group, the only PR person present.

'Hey, champ, you OK? I thought you might not make it.' She gave Emma a nudge on the shoulder. 'You texted me at 3 a.m.'

She held her phone up, showing Emma a message that said 'hadawodawod hermig never put.'

'Wow, I do not remember sending that,' said Emma, wondering who else she might have drunk messaged.

'Luckily I speak fluent nonsense so I assumed it said, "I am totally shitfaced and never put".'

They clambered onto the minibus and sat together at the back.

They were crawling through Earl's Court when Hilary yelped and rummaged through her bag. Emma had her cheek pressed against the glass of the window, enjoying the coldness and wishing she had brought iced water, a pillow and some aspirin.

'Look!' Hilary held up her phone to show the *Get Up* homepage.

'Oh god.'

Hilary looked at her, bemused. 'Come on now, it's your first paid piece, this is a monumental moment.' She scrolled down the page and read aloud, 'Emma Derringer's First Massage – Go Spa Yourself!'

'Jesus,' Emma muttered under her breath. 'What does that even mean?'

Hilary handed her the phone and leaned over her shoulder to continue reading. 'Feminist blogger Emma Derringer heads to London for her first ever massage! Find out what all the fuss is about!'

'Since when am I a *feminist* blogger?' said Emma.

'Since your blog isn't just about diets and shoes, I guess.'

'I'm not saying I'm *not* a feminist blogger, but that makes it sound like I write rape stats and angry book reviews. I would say I'm a narcissist blogger, if anything.'

'It's just for context – they pop you in a pigeonhole so everyone knows what to expect.'

Emma scanned the page. 'Yeah, I guess. I didn't realise posting a facetious blog about blowjobs was feminism.'

Ross had overheard the word 'blowjob' and was now peering over his seat.

Satirical narcissist feminist blogger. She tried it out for size and then let it go in favour of a wave of nausea and a blinding headache.

As she scanned the article her heart sank. Her first byline was followed by a 500-word advert for the spa, little more than a description of a massage. She found none of her punch-lines. Hilary peered over her shoulder. 'It's quite short, no?'

'They cut everything out.'

She handed the phone back and pressed her face back on the window.

Hilary sat silently next to her, tapping away on her phone and whistling intermittently. After a couple of miles she nudged Emma and said, 'You know what, it's your first time, it's good exposure. People will look you up. Don't be disap-pointed, Em. They put your blog in there at least – people will go there and find out you're properly funny. Yay, et cetera.'

Emma realised she was being ungracious. 'Thanks – yeah I know, totally. It's fine, it's a harmless article; I'm not upset, I'm violently hungover. I did enjoy the spa day.' She gave Hilary a little squeeze and smiled reassuringly. Hilary put her headphones on and stuck out her tongue.

The journey took over two hours, which Emma spent tentatively eating crisps and sipping Coke. Hilary was asleep, mouth open and head lolling, when Emma saw the first sign for Monkey Business. Her heart sank as the signs got closer together; she was horrible with heights.

*

They disembarked for their session. As they were being strapped into their harnesses, Drew, Adrian's second in command, noticed Emma's ashen face and stopped her as she went to join the line to be briefed on how best to avoid falling out of trees. 'Are you OK?' he asked, concerned.

'Smashing, thanks – love going up trees, nothing better.' Emma was shaking and if there had been a bar she would have bowed out. She could see that Adrian was listening and knew this was a day of judgement; quitting wasn't an option.

'You don't have to do anything you're uncomfortable with,' said Drew, reassuringly. 'You can stop at any time.'

Hilary stood behind them waiting, sniggering.

'I'll be all right, thanks.'

Drew moved on to the trial run, only 3 feet in the air, where the creative department were practising zip-lining to the ground.

Twenty minutes later, the rest of their group were up in the trees, suspended by their pants at 25 feet, making their way tentatively across the various cables that joined one enormous tree to the other.

Hilary and Emma stood at the bottom of the first net ladder, looking at the platform above.

'It's like *The Hunger Games*,' Emma moaned.

Hilary chuckled. 'It's really not.'

Behind them a group of pre-teen kids were on the trial run. Hilary looked at Emma. 'Do you want me to go first?' she offered, putting a foot on the net. 'We'll do it together.'

'Honestly, Hilary, I am shit scared of heights. I don't know if I can even get up there.'

She looked up and cringed; it seemed horribly high.

'Seriously,' she confided, 'I have trouble standing on chairs.'

Hilary attached herself to the ladder and shimmied easily up to the platform that circled the tree. She looked down at Emma. 'It's not that bad,' she said earnestly.

Oh god oh god oh god.

Emma reminded herself that this would be over in a couple of hours. She just had to nut up, climb a tree and dangle about for a while. Kids could do it, the Eds could do it, she could do it. Halfway up she stopped and took a breath. Hilary was still waiting. 'You're nearly there,' she yelled. Behind them the kids had gathered to watch Emma lumber up the net ladder. Hilary made her way across the first bridge easily and waited at the other end, saying nothing. Emma took her time, swearing all the way. She hooked herself with relief to the relative safety of the next tree. Behind them kids were streaming up the net ladder and waiting impatiently for Emma to get on with it. Emma hated them.

Hilary was halfway to the next platform, moving along a single line for her feet and another for her hands. Emma watched as she stepped, star-shaped, across the wire. Then she made the rookie mistake of looking down and groaned. She had a mental montage that documented all the bad decisions that had brought her to this point and inwardly cursed APRC and everyone who worked there. Gritting her teeth and taking deep breaths she waited for Hilary to get to the other side. Hilary hooked onto the next tree and turned to watch.

The rest of their group were three or four trees away by now, and noticing they had lost the two girls, most had stopped and were waiting for them to catch up. Emma was slowly and tentatively trying to hook her lines onto the next set of cables. Her hands were shaking uncontrollably.

She moved slowly out onto the line and wobbled horribly backwards. She had stopped about two metres along the cable, trying to right herself, when both cables started to shake. She managed to stand in the star shape required to stay upright.

'WHY IS IT SHAKING?' she yelled at Hilary.

'Don't worry, it's just you. Take deep breaths,' she replied.

Emma had these successive thoughts: that there was no way out of the situation, that the uncontrolled shaking was her arms and that she was having her first ever panic attack.

She was trying to breathe deeply and take control. She managed to inch along the cable by another couple of steps. She reeled forwards and found herself staring at the ground, which felt like a long way away.

She was hanging there, incapacitated, still holding the line with all her strength, when a bleach-blond instructor who had appeared below shouted at her in his Australian accent, 'Just sit down.' The kids that had gathered on the previous platform stifled laughter.

'Sorry, what?'

'Just sit into your harness!'

Emma wanted to cry. She tentatively leaned back into her harness, letting it take her weight. Dangling from the cable above, she used her arms to pull herself along. In that unflattering position she was able to get to the platform where Hilary helped her unhook and attach to the tree.

Their whole group had cheered and clapped, Adrian had called out, 'Go, Emma!' and the kids were whooping. Emma felt her jaw lock and her mouth fill with saliva. She tried to move around the tree and face out into the forest away from the audience, but her harness kept her strapped in place and there wasn't enough give to move. Instead she pulled against it and, suspended by her waist, leaned over the edge of the platform and vomited. An aquatic alien retch made its way out of her throat. The cheering petered out just before the lumpy brown liquid hit the ground. The splat was audible. The group paused in horror, the kids shouted, 'Ewwwwww!' in unison, and someone exclaimed, 'Good grief.' The instructor, thankfully, had stepped out from under it just in time.

'Jesus Christ, Emma,' Hilary said, convulsing with laughter and offering her a tissue.

Emma wiped her mouth and looked up sheepishly from where she was half kneeling, half suspended by the tree, aware for the first time that she had a sizeable audience.

'Did anyone *not* see that?'

'Nope.'

'Is there any way I can get down from here?'

'Nope.'

'How do I look?'

'You've never been sexier.'

Emma got to her feet, ignoring the running commentary from the kids, and turned to face the next bridge. It was a series of moving platforms. She looked at Hilary who squeezed her shoulder.

'Listen, kiddo. You can totally do it. I think after this you might be allowed to stay at ground level . . . and if it helps, that's the funniest thing I've ever seen.'

Surprisingly, it did help, as did getting rid of whatever insidious bile had been inside her. She went ahead of Hilary, who was finding it more difficult now that she had to operate her safety equipment with eyes tearing with laughter. Emma, who was being watched by her entire department, managed to cross the next three bridges, slowly, but without throwing up.

When she reached the zip line, the group had gathered at the bottom. She hooked herself to the cable and lowered herself into her harness. She shut her eyes and let go of the tree, feeling like she was making a bizarre entrance to a play. When she reached the ground she slid along her ass for the final few feet and department arms rushed over to unhook her, cheering and hugging her. Drew handed her a bottle of water and smiled sympathetically. Behind them Hilary landed gracefully, adopting a look of concern that was designed mostly to cover her ongoing amusement.

For the next couple of hours Emma sat on a bench with Ross, who told her she even looked hot vomiting off a tree. She watched as her colleagues teetered on the bridges and swung down the cables, Adrian and the Eds displaying rooster-like bravado that made Hilary roll her eyes at the spectators below.

When they had completed the course they all rallied around, whooping and comparing strategies. Adrian came over and threw his sweaty bear arm around Emma's shoulders. 'You win most spectacular exit, Emma.'

Everyone smiled supportively.

' . . . At least, your breakfast does.'

Jostling and energised from the exercise they clambered back onto the bus. Ross sat next to Emma and rubbed her back at intervals, proud to assume the role of caring friend. Hilary, now initiated, sat next to Adrian, who was grilling her about social network protocols. Emma shrugged Ross off and pretended to go to sleep.

After an hour of winding country lanes that had reawakened Emma's dodgy belly, they finally pulled into a driveway that led down to a large ornate Victorian hotel. Emma was the last off the bus, and rolled a cigarette while everyone else grabbed their things and trundled inside. She and Hilary stood, admiring the expansive view. Past the sculpted garden they could see hills rolling out towards the horizon. Cows or sheep were dotted about and clouds somersaulted over them.

'Well this is all right,' said Hilary.

'Not too shabby,' Emma agreed. She lit the cigarette but it made her stomach lurch. Stubbing it out she took some deep breaths, letting the soft, fresh country air clear her nausea.

They were standing there in meditative silence when a silver Mercedes prowled down the driveway and purred to a stop in front of them.

The driver of the Mercedes got out of the car; he was wearing a chauffeur's uniform. He nodded a polite hello at them and walked around to the passenger side, opening the door for the occupant. A young man stepped out onto the gravel and said something to him that they couldn't hear.

'Check out Mr Conglomerate,' Hilary whispered. 'Ooh la la.' She deliberately leaned over as if to admire his butt.

The driver handed him a receipt. Emma thought he seemed like someone with a company card, who signed for things instead of paying for them. Someone somewhere really valued his time. Whatever he did, he was good at it.

'He is hot,' she whispered.

He slammed the car door confidently as two boys from the hotel ran out to collect his small wheelie suitcase from the boot. Emma got the sense that the whole world ran like clockwork for him.

He walked past without noticing them until Hilary shouted, 'HI!' at him. He looked surprised and nodded, gliding past in a light cloud of Mercedes air.

Inside, their colleagues were collecting their room keys and gawping aimlessly at the antique furniture. When everyone had been assigned a room Adrian cleared his throat to make an announcement.

'We'll be having dinner at eight, so take half an hour and drop your things and enjoy your rooms. We'll meet in the gardens and take a small tour of the grounds and then meet for an hour or so to complete some exercises – nothing too strenuous, just who we are and what APRC means to us, all fun and games.' False enthusiasm swooped around the room. They turned to leave when Adrian called, 'Emma?'

She walked over, doing her best apology face.

'How are you feeling?'

'Still a bit dicey. Sorry if I spoiled it; I'm really bad with heights.'

'Not at all. It's making the effort that's APRC, not being quickest round the course,' he said, having been quickest round the course. 'If you're still feeling under the weather you can sit out the session.'

'Thank you so much, I really appreciate it. I'll see how I feel.'

Just walk away, she reminded herself, picking up her bag and trying not to look pleased.

All the perks and none of the PowerPoint? BONUS.

Upstairs she threw her stuff on a chair and sat on the four-poster bed. She'd never been in a real five-star hotel before. She turned on the taps of the massive bath and stared out of the window. The phone rang; it was Hilary. 'All right, vom-chops, are you coming to the meeting?'

'Nope, I'm off the hook – turns out barfing out of a tree means I don't have to do trust exercises.'

'You lucky schmuck.'

'Yep. I'm going to have a bath with the door open and watch my flatscreen TV.'

'All for a damn hangover. By the way, I just saw Mr Conglomerate again – he is dammmmn hot.'

'The boy from the big bad city?'

'Tank fly boss walk damn nitty gritty,' Hilary rapped back. 'Anyway,' she went on, 'I think you should come to the meeting ...'

'Ah, what? No. Why?'

'Because you just got promoted, you're the writer and you had a hangover. Play the game, Derringer.'

'Jeez, guilt trip much?'

'Ah, but that was my professionalism pitch. The guilt trip is next.'

'OK, I'm braced, give it your best shot.'

'It was your idea to have Adrian bring me on this ridiculous trip so it's your fault I'm not at home making babies with my husband. So get your drunken ass out the bath and come look at PowerPoints. You're the brains, kid.'

'But H, Adrian said I didn't have to. I am so close to getting away with it.'

Hilary's voice dropped a tone.

'That just means you get double points for attending. It's up to you, just saying.'

'Fine. I'll see how the bath pans out and let you know.'

She hung up the phone and cursed her friend.

Sitting in the bath she used all of the free cosmetics, shaving her legs and washing her hair. In spite of herself she wondered what was going on downstairs.

She got out the bath and dried quickly.

She was half an hour late for the meeting so at least she'd skipped the Nougat Stick section of the agenda.

The team were sitting around a large boardroom table and Adrian was talking. When she pushed open the door to the meeting room everyone cheered. She made a theatrical bow and pulled up the chair at the front.

A slide appeared on the screen: 'What APRC means to us.'

Emma's heart sank. *Bullshit.*

Adrian clicked the presentation to show an image of a massive pipe surrounded by construction equipment and forest. Various charts and photographs of grey-faced men wearing suits and yellow hard hats, looking serious, but pleased with themselves.

As if doing an impersonation Adrian stood in front of the image looking serious, but pleased with himself.

'This next task is about a new era for APRC. I want you all to think about your role in creative, and try to apply it to work within the energy sector, particularly one area of it that is so divisive in this country. We're going to be at the forefront of a new era of home-grown energy, and where certain groups' – he put 'groups' in air quotes – 'might oppose it now, it will be our job to show them the benefits and get as many people as possible on board.'

What fresh hell is this?

He clicked another slide and showed more smug white men milling about, this time wearing overalls instead of suits, one with a smear of soot next to his too-handsome-for-manual-labour smile.

'Love or hate it, shale gas is the closest thing this country has to a stable energy future. Hydraulics are the exciting new frontier for this country.'

Emma's heart sank. *A new low.*

'What I want to know is, if we land this client, what can you bring to the table? What, on a personal level, as well as a professional one, will you add to the project? We want a nation of fracking advocates. The potential scale for this project is enormous, in terms of the level of influence we can have.'

He puffed his chest out proudly.

'Think about how best APRC can help the client – the whole industry, in fact – achieve their goals and overcome their own internal challenges.'

Good grief.

She tried to think of manufacturers and industries she would more object to pitching to: there was the tobacco industry, nuclear ...

'Professionally, I suppose, I could probably soften their copy and inject the appearance of empathy, or sincerity, or whatever, to their "message",' she stammered.

'And on a personal level?' Adrian prompted.

She shrugged. 'To be honest, on a personal level I have strong objections to working in the sector ...'

Nonfrontational

'Objections? Do you object to a century of secure energy, Emma?'

It's the end of the world, Adrian.

She tried to adopt an expression somewhere between humble and weary.

'Well, yeah, kind of, I . . . '

His cheeks, chest and arms all waggled about like an inflatable tube man outside a used-car lot. 'What sensible objection can you possibly have to the UK being self-sufficient, Emma?'

'I don't object to the outcome, I object to the means.'

'Go on then, expand on that for us all.' His face wore an expression that was both furious and deeply patronising.

'I think it's a short-sighted solution that diverts investment from renewables. I get why it's a branding challenge, but on a personal level, I am not on their side.'

'And don't you think that might be a problem? In terms of producing your best work for them?'

Emma stopped. She was in a corner.

'I can see why you might think that.'

'Isn't it important to you, Emma? That you really believe in the product?'

Emma's brain boat did a quick lap of the products she had worked on in the past – Nougat Sticks, whisky, tyres, an online shopping system, a short-term loans company . . . She had once spent a week editing the small print on a snack for cats . . .

But fracking upgrades the work from pointless to poisonous.

'I have faith in my ability as a writer; the product doesn't have any bearing on that ability.'

The room was silent and everyone looked from Emma to Adrian; his had been a valid question, hers a good answer.

'Sorry, it's not the client per se, it's just fracking is something I find it hard to get excited about. I'd rather work for a wind farm, you know, being a hippy and all that.' She mentally slammed her face on the table. *I'm not a hippy, I'm just not a dick.*

'You don't have to be sorry, that's your opinion. I've always known you were a bit of a tree-hugger, Emma, but you have to realise that energy is the life-blood of capitalism, and supply must meet demand.' Adrian's tone, although probably intended to be understanding, was gruff and betrayed the sense of hurt he clearly felt that she wasn't immediately and unquestioningly on board. Emma could feel all the eyes in the room watching her.

'I understand; they think it's a necessary evil.'

Backtrack, play the game, quit when you're winning.

'All I really mean is that I don't know how much I could bring to the client, on a personal level.'

Adrian guffawed and patted his belly. 'Well nobody's asking *you* to deal with them personally, Emma.' He laughed and everyone joined in, taking sides in order to defuse the situation. Emma was glad they had, because not getting a laugh at that moment would have been adding insult to injury, and she had done enough damage.

I should have stayed in the bath.

Adrian moved around the room, but Emma had knocked his confidence and whenever the opportunity to defend the shale gas industry arose, he took it with gusto and directed his ferocity in Emma's direction. As far as he was concerned the industry was the pinnacle of client challenges. Emma sat through the rest of the meeting in despair. As long as she could justify the work she did as, at best, harmless, she could continue the charade. This was the first project that would require a complete subjugation of her beliefs and she wondered if it was the final straw. She thought back to the meeting where she should have quit and realised that her moment had passed, and she should at least try and play along. For now.

At the end of the meeting everyone gathered up their things and filed out. Emma hung back.

'Adrian?'

He looked up from his seat as if surprised to see her. 'Oh, hi Em, what's up?'

I can't do this and I won't.

'I didn't mean to cast a shadow over a new client. I realise it's a great opportunity for you.'

'That's exactly the problem, Emma. It's a great opportunity for *us*, not for *me*. We're a team at APRC – what's good for one is good for all.'

'Yeah, for us. Great opportunity; I'm totally on board.'

'That's the spirit!' He clapped her on the shoulder, satisfied, and veered off towards the bar.

She watched his massive ass walk away. He was a glutton, a consumer, everything about humankind she hated.

She stood in the doorway of the hotel by herself, shaking her head and playing the meeting over in her mind; had he actually bought that massive backtrack? Hilary found her there.

'All right, you little rebel?'

'I'm starving, man. All I've had today is a packet of crisps and they're currently drying out under a tree.'

'You might have got yourself off the project,' Hilary said.

'That would be a massive bonus.'

'It is all a bit depressing, isn't it, in corporate? I think I've developed mild racism towards old craggy-faced white men in suits.'

'Welcome to my world.'

'You know you'll just be editing a website and producing some soft copy? It's not like they're asking you to arrest protestors or something, is it?'

'It's all part of the same stupid shit machine though, isn't it? The only difference is the size of the cog; being a little cog is only slightly better than being a big one. It all makes the machine go round.'

'I thought money made the machine go round?'

'Same thing.'

'You need the money though, don't you, Emma? Isn't that why you do it?'

'I don't want to do it for them. It's the principle of the thing.'

Hilary stared out over the garden. 'Principles can be expensive, Emma.' She headed back into the hotel and away towards her room.

'Principles are priceless,' Emma muttered angrily.

She was still stewing over the sentiment when Mr Conglomerate appeared from the garden. Emma pulled her phone out of her pocket and pretended to send a text.

He said 'Hi' to Emma as he approached, and she looked up as though surprised to have seen him.

'Hi,' she replied, smiling politely. She found gorgeous men deliciously intimidating.

'Having fun?' he asked, rhetorically. His accent was musical.

'Nope.' She popped the 'p' as he passed and he smiled with mild surprise.

She took a deep breath of country air and went upstairs to find out what, if anything, she had packed while totally bozo'd the night before.

26

Hotel Dude

Between the starter and the main course, when the volume crept up to 'lightly sloshed', Emma got up and stepped outside, taking her large glass of wine with her and avoiding eye contact with the fair-weather smokers around the table.

She nodded a greeting at the receptionist as she passed, enjoying the sensation of wearing heels. She had been relieved to find an actual dress in her bag, along with some shiny tights and matching shoes. She retrospectively thanked pissed Emma for packing well, despite having been birthday drunk. Her hangover had dissipated and the wine had rid her of its last traces. She felt good.

Around the door, creeping roses created an archway over the carved stone. The security light threw an unappealing glare over her so she moved past the door and out into the garden. She placed her glass on a small white garden table and lit her roll-up, enjoying the head rush.

The moon was bright and the warm orange glow from the hotel threw a tan onto the black grass. The shift in volume was as nice as the change in temperature. The business guffaws sounded distant and separate.

She followed the sound of running water further into the garden. Someone was standing on the ornamental bridge. She could smell a cigar and make out the chubby glow of its tip. His back was turned but moonlight was bouncing off a curly-haired head. She chugged a gulp of wine and spoke, not wanting to make him jump.

'Hi.'

He turned around and she recognised Mercedes man. He had shiny eyes and long dark lashes. She stepped onto the bridge. He smelled expensive.

'Good evening,' he purred, bowing very slightly.

HELLO, she thought, but smiled instead.

The smoke from his cigar seemed to politely avoid touching his plush navy overcoat. He looked about thirty and he had rich people's skin. He was what Paul would call 'lintless'.

'Fancy seeing you here,' he said in a soft Middle Eastern accent. His voice was chocolatey. She did her best girly laugh.

'A girl like me, in a place like this.'

'Of all the gardens in all the world . . .' he added.

Jesus.

She wondered if this was the single most exciting thing that had ever happened to her. She wished Clem were witness to it, and thought of Raymond Chandler. Her spine tingled and she tried not to smirk.

'Do you come here often?'

He nodded over to the lawn where his briefcase was on a white garden chair next to his drink. His voice relaxed. 'One night only. And you?'

He leaned an elbow on the edge of the bridge. He looked like he should be on a movie poster from the '40s; he just needed a fancy hat. She took a nervous pull of her cigarette.

'Same here. Well, kind of a business and pleasure combo. It's an away day.'

Why am I talking in PowerPoint?

'Nice place to go for work.'

'Yeah, I guess, except we had to go and climb trees this morning.' She decided to keep the barfing story to herself, for now.

'Is climbing trees a part of your job?'

She laughed and didn't answer until she noticed he looked serious. 'Oh, no, just one of the perks.'

'What kind of business are you in?'

She was hypnotised by the silky tone of his voice and just looked at him until she realised he'd asked a question. She didn't want to say 'marketing'; it was too mundane for the conversation. *It's too mundane for any conversation.*

'I'm a writer.'

He nodded. 'Would you like to join me for a drink?'

YES.

'Actually we're in the middle of dinner, but ... maybe later, if you're around, I'll be in the bar.'

'I have some work to do this evening but I'll be in the bar later too. Or my room number is 120 – if you like, you can call.' He held out a tanned, manicured hand and she wished for the thousandth time that she had beautiful nails.

'I'm in 102.' She smiled, embarrassed.

'Karim,' he said. She noticed his manly, authoritative handshake, adding points each time he did something sexy.

'Emma.'

'Emma,' he said, as though he were kissing the word. She could feel his smile, and where their shoulders were almost, very nearly touching, it felt electric.

He went to pick up his briefcase and glass, smiling more broadly as he walked away. It was a kind smile that made him seem younger than thirty.

She let out a deep breath that she hadn't known she was holding. Her heart was pounding and it sent an email to her thighs, subject: YES. Her thighs forwarded it to her mouth and she licked her lips.

The away day just got good.

When Emma returned to her seat Adrian was holding court and Hilary looked bored. Hilary leaned over, whispering, 'I just saw Mr Conglomerate come in. You should 100 per cent hit that.'

'Ah, come on dude, give it a rest.'

'Just saying,' Hilary replied defensively. 'You've got to represent. Someone has to and you're the only sorry-ass singleton here.'

'I am not sorry-assed . . . and for the record, he's in room 120 and his name is Karim.'

'Yeah it is,' she said lasciviously, then stopped. 'Are you serious?'

'I am.'

'Good work, kid.' She saluted and turned her attention back to Adrian who was telling, for the thousandth time, the story about the time he shot a rhino in Kenya.

Dinner was long and relaxed. When the main course arrived the room was quieted by the sounds of eating. When dessert was over the group was thoroughly pooped (Adrian's phrase) and most of them went straight to their rooms.

Emma and Hilary headed to the bar with Drew, Ross and both of the Eds in tow. Emma did a discreet scan for Karim but he wasn't there. She was a bit disappointed but also a bit relieved.

The Eds were drunk and talking at a volume that implied they were the most deeply fascinating people in the world. They were telling anyone in hearing range (which was most of the hotel) about the corporate retreat where they'd met. They had been the only attendees wearing suits and had bonded over a mutual appreciation of Porsche Boxsters. At the tops of their voices they were telling Drew about the mimicking exercise during which they had cemented their friendship. Emma and Hilary were ordering large glasses of brandy as the Eds circled about, aping one another.

'I don't think I can handle much more of this,' said Hilary, leaning against the bar watching her colleagues with a look of undisguised contempt. 'Do you mind if I bail? I want to get involved with the huge tub in my room.'

'No sweat, I'm taking this upstairs as well.'

Without saying goodnight to the group they left the bar. At the top of the stairs they said their goodnights and went in opposite directions.

Emma entered her room and clicked on the bedside lamp, slid out of her shoes and threw herself on the bed. She was composing a text to Paul, trying to figure out the funniest way to deliver the puke story, when she heard a light knock on the door. Excited, she got up, calling out, 'Just a sec,' and checking her reflection. Pleased to find her hair and make-up in good condition she went to the door. She hadn't seriously expected him to call on her. She slipped back into her heels, adopted her most seductive smile and opened the door. In the hallway stood Ross, looking greedy and drunk, his hands shoved in his pockets.

'Oh, it's you,' she said, leaning, by way of a barrier, against the frame.

He looked her up and down and she thought for a moment that he was going to grab her but he just grinned.

'Who were you expecting?' he said, pushing the door open further and walking into her room.

She let the door close and stood just inside, watching as he sat on the edge of the bed, moving her phone out of the way and dropping it clumsily on the table.

'I've come to collect,' he said. She supposed he was trying to be cute but was appalled at his lecherous grin. He patted the bed next to him and she laughed nervously.

'Are you serious?'

'A deal's a deal,' he replied. He wasn't intimidating but she felt suddenly vulnerable. She moved further into the room.

'I was kind of hoping you might let that slide,' she said, laughing lightly, trying to take the tension out of the room.

He responded with a fake laugh and leaned back on his elbows. His groin was pressing against his suit trousers and he kicked his shoe against the edge of the bed.

'Nope, I always honour my bets,' he said, with a hint of accusation; *I* always honour *my* bets.

'Yeah, well, I should probably have thought about it before I said it. But I'm not into you, not like that, and you're, like, totally married.'

'Yeah, well . . .' he said, looking around. For a moment

she thought he was going to undo his fly, but he just shifted position slightly.

'Do you mind, though, if I say no? I really don't think it's appropriate.'

'It's *so* appropriate,' he said, looking cross. 'We're in a hotel, we've got wine, there's a bed. A deal's a deal, Emma, what could be more appropriate?'

What indeed? The mention of wine gave her an idea.

'Umm, well, let me just run to the bar and get us some drinks.'

'Great.' He looked pleased. 'I'll have a double Scotch, on the rocks.'

She picked up the hotel key card from the bedside table and opened the door. He jumped up and pushed it shut before she could leave. He leaned into her; she could smell wine and cheese on his breath.

'Don't be long,' he said, right into her face.

'I'll be right back,' she said reassuringly, ducking out of the path of his kiss.

She pulled the door open against his weight and slipped out into the hallway.

Yikes.

She stood for a moment outside the door. She realised with a pang of regret that her phone was on the table and she didn't know which room Hilary was in. On the wall directly opposite, a hotel sign pointed to rooms 100–110 and the bar to the right, and 120–130 to the left.

She went left.

The next morning when Emma woke up, Karim had just stepped out of the shower and stood with a towel around his waist, glistening from the belly up. His hair was wet, shining and spiky. Her opening thought for the day was, fit fit fit.

He was standing in the doorway of the bathroom. She hoped that against all odds, for just this one morning, her hair had formed a beautiful halo around her sleeping head. She sat up, naked, and the mirror opposite confirmed that it had not.

'You slept well?' he said cheekily, sitting on the edge of the bed, cupping her boob and kissing her on the neck. She felt a double dose of relief that he wasn't going to turn into a one-night weirdo and hide or look embarrassed until she left.

'I did. I had an amazing sexy dream about a guy I met in a garden.' He laughed and moved over to the dresser where the hotel people had brought coffee and the *Financial Times*, which to Emma, for that instant, became a deeply sexy paper to read.

'Shall we order breakfast in here and stay in bed a while?' The question gave her ego a well-needed rub, and she wondered what she had done to deserve such graciousness from someone so handsome. Her mind flashed to the night before and she allowed herself a chuckle.

Oh yeah, that.

Glancing at the clock she realised she was late for breakfast and hoped nobody would see the walk of shame she would have to do back to her room. She remembered with a jolt that she had left Ross in there last night. *Shit.*

'I have to go have breakfast with my company, sorry. Thank you for last night, though, it was ... ' She blushed. She left the sentence unfinished, but thought, *insert adjective*.

She got out of bed, pleased with her belly for being flat in the morning but feeling gently hungover and slightly sick. She dashed into the shower while he checked his emails, frowning and becoming Mr Conglomerate once more. She kissed him goodbye and ran, clutching her shoes, tights and bra, back to her room. It was empty, but the staff had brought coffee and placed it on the dresser. The bed was ruffled but still made, and she wondered how long Ross had waited there. She poured the coffee, cleaning her teeth and dashing around, changing out of her dress and into jeans and a T-shirt. She was ready with five minutes to spare, and lay hugging a pillow; she could feel the remnants of pleasure moving around her system. She was still lying there when she noticed her phone. She had a message from Ross: 'Thanks for nothing.' He had sent it at 3 a.m. She deleted the message, ran some water through her hair and took a large gulp of coffee.

In the dining room, Hilary was at the breakfast bar pouring muesli into a bowl. 'Here she is, conquering hero.'

Emma shot her a look and Hilary clamped her mouth shut. She waited until Emma had poured a coffee and an orange juice and they sat together on the table adjacent to the others.

Adrian looked up from his paper. 'How are you feeling today, Emma? You certainly look a lot better.'

'Yeah, good, thanks,' she replied. From where she sat she could see Ross scowling at a piece of bacon.

'So ... I called your room last night and Ross answered,' said Hilary. 'It sounded like I had woken him up. Did you guys, you know ... ' She whistled, the universal, two-toned tune for 'doing it'.

'Ross? God no, gross.' She studied the menu.

Hilary looked confused and was about to speak when the waitress approached. 'Would you like a hot breakfast?'

'Yes please, one of everything,' said Emma, grinning, putting the menu on the table and turning to Hilary.

'I deserve a hot breakfast after the crazy hot night I had.'

Hilary's face lit up.

'No way! Mr Conglomerate? Tell me right now.' Hilary's fist pumped the air.

'OK, give it a rest. I went to his room last night; I left this morning.'

'Awesome. Good work. So, like, what does he do?'

Emma started to answer and then snapped her mouth shut. 'Dude, seriously, what kind of a question is that? I have no idea what he does. Chin-ups, probably. Who cares?'

'I know, right – what the hell happened to me? That is such a married person question. My follow-ups were how old is he, does he have kids and when are you seeing him again?'

'Yikes.'

Hilary rested her head on her hand and regrouped. 'Sorry, what I meant to say was, how was it?'

'Oh god. So good. He ordered room service and played dulcet French tunes. He ordered champagne and a fruit plate, H, with strawberries. It was like a movie. He had a fireplace in his room. Everything looks fit by firelight.'

Hilary purred.

Emma closed her eyes, bit her lip and nodded languorously.

'We fucked like it was 2008.'

'I have no idea what that means. Was that a good year?'

'It was.'

Hilary squealed with laughter and everyone looked over. 'Shut. The front door.'

Emma looked at her to shush her and went on quietly, 'You know those guys who are having a dialogue with your hoo-ha, and all the rest of you can do is eavesdrop?'

'God, I don't even know if I do,' said Hilary mournfully, stirring her coffee.

'Well, it's almost an out-of-body experience for your brain, but your vagina is just pleased that someone's finally talking to her like she's an adult.'

Hilary nodded and didn't quite take a sip of the coffee that was right on the edge of her lip.

'Mr Conglomerate and Ms Yes had a long conversation. And he's strong, he made me feel tiny, he could literally pick me up with one arm.'

'Jesus.'

'Yes ma'am, it was religious.'

'You lucky bastard.' Hilary took a deep breath. 'God I miss being young.'

'I'm not young.'

'God I miss being younger.'

'Don't we all.'

'Good work, Emma D, you know how to get the job done.'

'I got several jobs done.'

'Shut up.'

'It's true; I can't have slept more than an hour. It was like a competition ... I haven't had competitive sex for ages, I recommend it.'

Hilary watched as the waitress put down Emma's

breakfast. Emma stabbed a sausage and held it up for examination. They both cackled.

'Married sex is the opposite of competitive sex.'

Emma crumpled up her nose. 'Sounds boring.'

'Yeah, I guess, but it's quite nice really – no one has to make an effort, no one has to do any discovering, you know what you like and you get it.'

'I know what I like, and I got it, I got it good.'

'Slut,' Hilary said happily.

After breakfast everyone dispersed to pack up their things. They met at the bus and headed for London. Emma felt like they'd been on an epic holiday. She felt good, despite the lack of sleep. Adrian was deep in conversation with Hilary when they boarded the bus so Emma took a seat on her own at the back. Ross was the last to board and sat next to her, reluctantly, avoiding eye contact, avoiding any kind of contact at all.

She smiled at him, hoping to defuse the situation although not feeling she should apologise for it. When the bus set off and the roads rolled away under them, Emma felt her heart sink. Every time she left London she felt like anything was possible and nothing would ever be the same again, and when she returned and inevitably nothing had changed, she felt like she was being sucked back in.

After a few miles she started to doze against the window, enjoying flashbacks of Karim's body, the light bouncing off his muscles, all the soft and warm turned damp and hot. Ross leaned over and whispered her name.

'Hmm?' she murmured, turning to him.

'I'm really sorry about last night. I had an argument with

my wife and I just thought ... ' He was bright red and looked genuinely mortified.

'I was drunk. Do you hate me? I'm so sorry, Em.' He sounded sincere to Emma.

She thought about making him suffer but didn't feel angry about it any more.

'Don't worry about it. No harm done.' She turned away and opened *Get Up* on her phone, wanting to change the subject. He looked relieved.

She was reading her article when he noticed her name. 'Since when are you a feminist blogger?'

'Since *Get Up* decided I was, I guess.'

Ross plucked the phone from her hand and read aloud, '"The masseuse rubbed my neck forcefully, and the tension of the week evaporated. Why hadn't I done this before?"'

The others on the bus turned and looked at him and he waved the phone at them. 'Emma's famous.'

Adrian stood up and looked over the bus. 'What's this, Emma?'

'Nothing.'

'Emma's a feminist blogger for *Get Up* in her secret life.'

Adrian walked to the back of the bus and took the phone from Ross, scanning the article. Then he looked at Emma.

'Well, it seems we have a feminist in our midst ... as well as a tree-hugger. This is great, Em.'

'It's really not that great; the piece I wrote was funny, that's just advertising.'

'Thanks for nothing,' Emma said to Ross, inadvertently quoting his text. He looked embarrassed and Emma felt guilty and watched the cars zip by.

*

When she got home Paul was on the sofa waiting for a pizza. Emma ate a carrot, sat down next to him and opened her computer.

'So, how was it?' he asked, lighting a joint.

'Good, thanks – just writing a blog about the super fit guy I slept with last night.'

'Sexy times. Did you blow the stalker?'

'I did not, although he got quite rapey about it.'

'Jesus, really? What happened?'

'You can read all about it in the blog I am currently writing.'

'I can't read, silly, I'm a DJ. Give me the short version.'

'Stalker came to my room, I went to fit dude's room. Went for and got.'

She raised her hand solemnly and Paul obliged her with a slow, sturdy high five.

'But what do you mean *quite* rapey? Is that a thing?'

'He kept saying "a deal's a deal", which I know is true, but seriously, do you think I had to do it? When it comes to sexual favours there's room for discretion, right?'

'What the hell, Emma? That's a bit much.'

'Yeah, but if he hadn't turned up demanding oral, I wouldn't have ended up in hot dude's room so, you know, totally worth it.'

The doorbell rang and Paul went downstairs to retrieve his dinner. While he was gone Emma thought about her first weeks at APRC. She had just got back from three months in the States, a road trip with Clem. She had arrived in London feeling like she had the world in her pocket, but spent three desperate months sleeping on sofas and getting turned down for jobs she thought she was too good for. Eventually, and after some serious re-jigging of her CV, she had been hired at APRC on a temp contract. When the three months was up she was indoctrinated and invited to stay and couldn't face going back on the job market which had dried up and turned nasty.

When Paul came back she headed off to bed, glum and not wanting to wallow in cheese. 'Do you think I should quit APRC?'

'I dunno. Yeah, if you want to.'

'But what will I do instead?'

'Don't ask me, I've never had a proper job.' He pressed pause to pick up a slab of melted, doughy mess. It smelled delicious. Emma's mouth watered as she watched him take a big, sloppy bite.

'Maybe I'll have one slice . . . '

'Get lost, this is my dinner.'

'That's a 16-inch pizza, Paul, you can no way eat the whole thing.'

'Challenge accepted.'

Emma left him to his saturated meal and went to her room, pondering the night she'd met Paul. He hadn't changed even slightly since then. He had made no concessions to adulthood, he didn't eat well or get stressed or go to bed early. He was the same boy at twenty-nine as he'd been at nineteen. He had better clothes now, and a better haircut, and better skin and teeth, but his mind had frozen in the zenith of his youth, his career had taken off without him ever needing to make a decision about it.

She turned on the light in her room. It was immaculately tidy, as always, her bed made with hospital corners, her bed-side table practically curated, alarm clock, novels and water glass arranged deliberately. She wasn't jealous of Paul's lifestyle, the thought of it was exhausting and she had already started to feel the rumblings of the two-day hangovers that women over thirty bang on about. She liked the slowed pace of her late twenties. She enjoyed going for dinner and good lighting; she wanted to hear herself think.

Oh my god did I just say that?

She pushed her shoes off and lay on the bed thinking about Karim.

27

A Clementine Twist

Clementine shoved her phone, lipstick and shoes in a bag and went into the kitchen to say goodnight to her mum. Malcolm was wearing a thick pair of glasses and peering at a magazine that had foliage on the cover.

'Not staying for supper, Clementine?' Malcolm asked, without looking up.

Who says 'supper' any more? she thought, irritated by the word and instantly wanting to punch him in the face.

'Oh Clementine, before you go, have a look at this,' her mum said.

She moved over to the sideboard where a local newspaper lay open. From where she stood in the doorway Clem could see a big red circle and stifled a groan. She was already running late for her shift.

Clutching the page, her mum waddled slowly over to her daughter. The wanted ad said 'Receptionist, full time, competitive rates'.

'Mum, I've got a job, and it's only a temporary measure, I promise.'

'But it's so late, Clemmy – you're only just leaving now and it's nearly nine at night. Wouldn't you like a lovely day job?' She had an expression that anyone but a grown daughter would find endearing. Clementine clenched her teeth through a wave of irritation.

She kissed her mum on the side of her head and took the paper from her. 'I'll check out the rest on the bus, OK?'

She walked out of the house wondering why it was so hard for them to grasp that she was a screenwriter. For some reason she couldn't fathom, they considered her entire career to be some childish hobby that she would eventually have to grow out of in order to get a 'real' job. Even when she had told them that Drake wanted to sign her, shown them the agency website and given them a copy of the script, they had just looked at her like she was five, and being cute. She wondered what it would take to convince them she was doing well, and thought, reasonably, that it would probably take her getting her own house, a husband and a dog. She hadn't heard from Drake since their meeting and was starting to doubt that he'd been being sincere. The initial excitement she had felt after meeting him had given way to scouring the internet for other agents who would have seen her work when Columbia had sent it out to their alums and connections.

The club took forty-five minutes to get to; a bus into Ealing and the Central Line to Tottenham Court Road, then a five-minute walk. She berated herself for only ever allowing twenty minutes to do it.

Her Oyster card beeped negative when she got on the bus. 'Ah, come on,' she muttered under her breath. It rejected her twice more before the bus driver tapped the ticket machine.

She tried two further cards before one worked. An old woman sitting at the front tutted and Clem tutted back. She had a long night of dealing with impatient knob-heads ahead of her.

When Clem reached the door of the club she pressed the button that rang through to the reception desk and stuck her tongue out at the camera. The door opened with a satisfying clunk. The reception area was behind a black, shiny marble surface surrounded by a thick velvet cloth. The whole place teetered precariously on the classy side of kitsch. When customers, (whom she was required to refer to as clientele) entered they were greeted in the first instance by Clementine's forehead and eyes, peeping up over the edge of the counter. As they approached they would get an eyeful of boob and if they were lucky and she stood, they were treated to a glimpse of her entire body. She tried to stand as little as possible, but she didn't object to the occasional high-tipping oligarch ogling her tits.

In her absence, her boss, Alan, lounged like a mafia overlord, spinning slightly on the leather office chair. 'Clementine. You very pretty, darling, but you late every day, no?'

'Sorry Alan, train was late.'

'Train is late every day, no? You come from countryside or something?'

Clem smiled her best flirtatious smile. She wasn't afraid of Alan but she was well versed in hospitality services hierarchy and knew better than to show him anything but the utmost respect. She knew he thought she was devastatingly beautiful and although she was late every day, her legs, lips and tits were worth the wait.

'I give you warning today, Clementine. Tomorrow you arrive on time, OK?'

'Sure thing, Alan. Abso-fucking-lutely.'

The Ionian specialised in serving enormously expensive but suitably well-made drinks. The bar staff were a tight team but Tina had ensured they welcomed Clementine into the fold; they admired her because of her regard for fine cocktails and her ability to put them away and hold her own.

They split their tips with her and kept her fully loaded on their best creations for the duration of her shifts, and often long beyond them. Clem's inherent contempt for the punters meant she was entertaining, and her rapport with Alan made all their lives easier.

Clem enjoyed the backstage part of the job. She had quickly discovered that London bartenders occupy an inner circle, leading to cheap nights out and glamorous ways to feel like a million dollars. She knew she should be trying to make more money, but she would only spend it on drinks anyway; at the Ionian she was simply cutting out the middleman.

Leaving Alan manning the reception she went upstairs, past the Lounge – designed to make the punters feel, and pay, like high rollers – and into the storeroom where the staff kept their things. Here the walls were smeared with a hostile yellow gunk, the lockers hung on their hinges and they had fashioned benches out of old buckets of cooking oil.

The single staff toilet lurked behind a broken door. It always smelled of dirty socks and miscellaneous filth.

Clementine took her phone out of her bag and put it in her pocket. Kicking off her tattered, flat-bottomed shoes she pulled from her bag a pair of tall, black, suede stilettos and dropped them on the floor. She winced as she stepped into them. A busboy leaned against the door and watched.

She turned to the small, cracked mirror that had been stuck to the wall with Blu Tack, and applied a generous dose of deep red lipstick. She bunched the rest of her things into her weathered excuse for a handbag and threw it into a locker. Transformation complete.

'Ay Clementine, you sexy, yeah?' He whistled his appreciation.

'Thanks babe,' she said huskily, heading out of the dingy room and into the relative freshness of the club. Her shoes hurt, but she enjoyed the feeling of wearing heels; they made her walk with her shoulders back and swing her hips, and those two extra inches did a lot for her ego.

Downstairs Alan was checking football scores on the reception computer. He looked up when he heard her footsteps behind him and smiled at her tits.

'You undo top button for clientele, yes?'

'I don't get paid enough.'

'You get paid too much for that button, I think.'

He pressed the top button of her fitted black shirt and when she looked down he bonked her nose with his finger.

'I get you again.'

She smiled at him and undid the top button. This routine was familiar and she had pre-emptively buttoned her shirt to the collar.

Clementine's main role at the Ionian was to make the clientele feel important. She buzzed them in, checked her booking forms, had them sign on a clipboard and assigned a waiter to lead them around the bar to their tables. The signatures meant nothing but Alan said they added a sense of officiousness that the punters loved.

As her shift got underway, Ferocious T sent her a tall, pink Porn Star martini; it was going to do the trick. Clementine's busiest part of the night was usually between eleven and twelve when non-members who'd read about the club on some poorly informed London listings website would turn up in drunken droves, demanding Jägerbombs and lager tops. Clementine had become adept at turning them away without causing a ruckus or insulting their pride. In one of her initial shifts her snide remarks had led to some manhandling on Alan's part and some tears on the part of a roughed-up suit with a little penis who couldn't take being put down by girls or picked up by the lapels by tall Albanians. She laughed at the memory, but did her best from then on to keep everything civilised. She had seen a side of Alan in that tussle that she did not want to unleash on anyone undeserving.

She had just seated a group of women, at least two of whom were models, when the buzzer went again. She glanced at her booking sheet and at a name that rang a vague bell. Clem was under strict instructions to turn away anyone from a reality show, but didn't know enough about reality shows to enforce it.

She buzzed the group in and froze as Jordan entered, surrounded by an entourage of suited-up agents, press guys, accountants and yes-men. He was in conversation so she had time to compose herself, or at least enough to clamp her mouth shut, before he saw her. She looked down at the booking sheet as if in deep concentration. She was having a heartquake, a judder of shock that had pounded her heart and was now doing a handbrake turn in her belly. Her skin felt as if she'd passed through a sheet of ice, and then her face, hands and ears burned.

She sat in the chair and tried to lean forward far enough to obscure herself from his view. From there she looked up only enough to catch the eye of the man at the front of the pack. 'Please sign here,' she said, pointing the pen at the dotted line. She pressed the intercom for a waiter to come and collect them and when the busboy answered, Clem spoke as quietly as she could: 'Table for six, upstairs, quick as you can.'

'OK, Clem-en-tinnne,' he said, not picking up on the urgency she was trying to convey through gritted teeth. She could feel the group watching her and resisted the temptation to look up. Alongside the embarrassment, dread and anger, she felt heavily tempted to look at him, to stare at him, to swim in his stupid beautiful bastard eyes. She wanted to scream.

'Are there any wait staff around?' she asked the busboy.

'Yeah I get, I send, don warrry Clementine.'

She hung up and looked at the leader. 'Someone will be right with you, your table is upstairs in the Lounge.'

'Clem?'

She kept her eyes still for a moment, thinking game face game face game face, and then looked up with her best 'fuck you' smile.

'Hi, Jordan.'

Their eyes met and she felt everything he'd ever made her feel in one hot shot of emotions. He pushed through the huddle of guys in suits and took off his glasses. He seemed taller, shinier and more confident.

She stood up and clenched everything she could – belly in, boobs out, slight pout. Leaning over the counter they kissed lightly on both cheeks. She thought she felt him smell her. She hoped to convey exactly none of the things she felt.

'How's it going?' she asked. She checked over her shoulder for a waiter, and wished there was an emergency exit button, an ejector seat under her desk or a shutter she could slam up between them.

He leaned on the counter and stared at her with an expression she knew he thought was cute. He was right. The accent she hadn't heard in real life for months took her straight back to his apartment in New York.

'I came to London to promote my new film.'

'Yeah, *Mind Games*.'

He laughed his deep, delicate New York laugh.

'*Mind Games*, uh huh – you've seen it?' He looked her up and down. She felt like sending her hardest right hook across his face.

'I saw the poster.'

'Well, it should be pretty good, hopefully. I was going to call you when I got here ...'

'My number's changed.'

There was a heavy pause where he didn't ask, and she didn't offer it. He looked around the bar and then back at her, adopting, again, his photo face. 'Nice place.'

'Yeah. I'm the receptionist.'

'It suits you.'

She could feel anger starting to rise in her belly.

She wanted to tell him to say something real, Jordan, or fuck off. Instead she said, 'Well, good luck with the film, it looks ... thrilling.'

A waiter appeared to guide them up and away from her.

'Guess I'll see you in a bit, Twist.'

'Have a great night, Jordan.'

He headed with his group of suits up the stairs, leading the way. As they passed, each of them eyed her curiously and she felt the awful sensation of being an artefact, an exhibit in the museum of Jordan Guillermo. When they were safely obscured from view she groaned and flumped in her seat, pressing her head on the desk. The panic had subsided and left an empty space in her mind for old resentments to swirl and spin and make her feel sick.

He had to be the only person in the world who could do this to her. She wanted to text Emma but didn't know if they were supposed to be cross with each other. She picked up the intercom phone. 'Get Ferocious T to make me something strong – tell her my ex is upstairs and I need sedation.'

An hour later Clementine should have been brilliantly drunk, but the knowledge that Jordan was in the building wasn't letting the alcohol do its business and so she sat, forlorn.

'I made this for you.' Ferocious T leaned on the counter, watching Clem's pain with mild interest. 'It's called a Clementine Twist,' she said proudly, pushing the glass towards Clem.

'How does he look? Please don't be impressed by him.' Clem took a sip. 'Jesus, T, that's a bit serious – what's in it?'

'It's equal parts clementine-peel-infused gin, Campari and Italian vermouth. It's your own personal Negroni. It's a journey drink.' She held Clem's chin in her hand. 'And that ridiculous specimen upstairs looks like an *utter* penis. He's wearing fucking sunglasses indoors, Clem, at night. And he's drinking a French martini. He's clearly a tosspot of the highest order.'

Clem took another sip. 'What's a journey drink?'

'It starts strong and bitter, then hits a sweet spot of refreshing. Just like you, sugar tits.'

Clem downed it. 'I love it. Please may I have another?'

Upstairs Jordan had extended his entourage to include the models that had arrived earlier, probably with a budget that only extended as far as the nearest table of men.

Clementine didn't know what to do. Nothing, was the most obvious move. She wanted to want to do nothing, but what she actually wanted to do was to throw herself at him, sleep with him, scream at him, she wanted to fuck the pain away, and beat the shit out of it. What she really wanted, she reasoned, was for the pain to just go away of its own accord. She had a flutter of a heart attack every time she heard footsteps on the stairs behind her so had positioned her screen and turned the image off so that she could see the reflection and brace herself for his reappearance.

Things must have happened for the rest of her shift, people must have come and gone; she drank enough to floor a weightlifter but felt nothing. She could only feel the pressure emanating from the Lounge. She was trapped in a vortex of Jordan thoughts, memories, stories that she had tinted sepia and put in storage somewhere deep in her brain.

When they had published his cover with her arm in he had jokingly framed it, signing it 'your first cover' and drawing a big arrow over his own face to the small piece of her arm that hadn't been 'shopped out. He'd installed it as her screen saver for a joke, so that when they'd gone to class and she'd opened her laptop he'd been grinning out at them from her screen. He'd yelled, 'Whoa, stalker!' over the lecture theatre and when everyone laughed, kissed her generously.

She nearly smiled, but now, looking back, all she could see was Elise, the *other* woman, sitting a couple of rows back, laughing harder than anyone else, because as far as she was concerned, 'stalker' was right.

'Hey. Pssst. Lady.' Alan peered out through a curtain that hid the doorway to his office. 'You busy? You wanna cocaine?' He pronounced it 'co-cay-eena'.

She followed him through the curtain into his office where two boss-sized lines were waiting. Alan lit a cheroot and handed her a silver straw. Clementine leaned over and schnarfed a line gratefully.

'What's wrong with my darling Clementine?' Alan asked, lowering his nose onto the remaining line and immediately reaching into his top pocket to replenish them.

Clementine told him the short version of the story while Alan listened.

'You want me to chuck him out? His money is no good here, I tell him – you get out of here, Yankee scum?'

'He's a celebrity though, he's good for business – anyway we can't chuck out all the dickheads, can we? It'd be empty.'

Alan nodded, distracted by the enormous line he was about to inhale. Outside the office the door buzzed.

It took about two minutes for the coke to work on

Clementine's insides and her stomach knotted, sending an urgent memo that she should get to the bathroom. The joy of coke, she remembered – all it does is make you shit and want more.

She asked a waitress to cover the counter and headed upstairs, keeping her head down as she passed the Lounge. The bathrooms at the Ionian were designed for corporate cokeheads. The communal sinks area was outfitted with a chaise longue, large gilt-framed mirrors and padded walls. Three bulky doors were marked for men, women and disabled, furnished with chrome fittings that were usually covered in traces of powder by midnight.

The women's door was locked and she could hear the high-pitched giggles of more than one occupant. She opted for the disabled cubicle and closed the door gratefully.

When she emerged, Jordan was standing right outside, waiting.

'Hi, Clem.'

'Hi, Jordan, everything OK?' she asked, headed for the sinks. She washed her hands and made to leave but he stood in her way. She wondered if he was going to kiss her; she wanted him to. Somewhere just under the surface of her love, self-respect was definitely trying to get a word in ...

He leaned in and she held her breath.

'I just wanted to make sure you don't hate me.'

It was like being slapped.

What a huge surprise that this is about you, she thought.

'I know it didn't end well with us, Clem, but I would really like it if we could be friends ... while I'm here.'

He touched her arm.

'I don't really know what to say, Jordan.'

'Just say you don't hate me, Clem. Say we can be friends.'
He stepped closer. He was going to embrace her; her core
wished he would, but her brain got back in touch to remind
her that she did hate him.

'I don't hate you, Jordan. I really don't care either way.'

She watched his expression carefully and even through
the drunkenness could see that her not caring hurt. 'Good
luck with this whole . . . ' she gestured towards him, making
a circle with both hands '. . . thing.'

She left the room with her mind racing, knowing that in
ten minutes she would think of a million things she should
have said.

She knew he wanted her to hate him, because that would
mean she loved him. She didn't want to shout or scream any
more, she just wanted, with all her heart, for him to get out
of her club.

'Clem?'

'What?'

He looked genuinely pained, rooted to the spot where he
stood, in the stinky Soho bathroom. She knew this would be
the last conversation they'd ever have.

'I'm sorry.'

Words caught in her throat, and tears waited on the
sidelines for their cue. She rolled her eyes, made a sound
somewhere between a laugh, a sigh and a sneer and left the
bathroom, letting the door shut behind her.

At her desk she felt better, kind of. It had been cathartic –
she could totally have fucked him in the toilet if she had
wanted to. She had nothing to say to him. He had broken
her but she would fix herself – he wasn't the glue, he was a
useless B-list actor. She went online and looked up Elise.

Fuck you, Elise, she thought. Your boyfriend is a cheating dick. The venom she felt for her former friend had never abated. She stared at a page of pictures of Elise and Jordan together; they were definitely still an item.

Elise's profile picture was of them both and her most recent update mentioned his trip to London and how much she missed him. Clem shut the window. Fuck them both.

At the end of the night the team sat at the bar. Clementine stirred another of her eponymous cocktails; the bartenders clinked solemnly. 'To the end of an era,' said Clementine. 'Jordan is dead – long live handsome bastards.' She winked at Santiago, a tall drink of water behind the bar, who blew her a kiss.

28

Bang

The meeting, even by Emma's standards, was not going well. Adrian was sweating with dissatisfaction, one of the Eds had loosened his tie in a cartoon-esque display of stress and the other was furiously making notes on his phone.

Emma's current chain of thought had begun, innocuously, with what to have for dinner but had segued into a detailed fantasy about blowing her brains out with a .357 Magnum. She was trying to decide which angle she would favour. If she shot from the right-hand side, through her skull, she would splatter Ross and Gemma with brains, and while that would be visually satisfying, it would ruin their clothes and possibly their lives. She thought about sticking the barrel in her mouth and firing backwards into the wall. Her ex-head would leave a stain that would haunt the room, seeping slowly through each new layer of paint, lest anyone forget how bad this meeting had really been. She felt that a mere spattering of blood was copping out, though; she also thought the metallic taste of the gun, as her last sensation, would be depressing. She decided the best option was to do it left handed, splurting her skull over the Eds. She pictured the moment: Eds covered in brain, Adrian frozen mid-sentence, Gemma's look of deep incomprehension, Ross's inscrutable blankness. She wondered if the bang from the gun would be loud enough to pause Soho, a millisecond that belonged to her dramatic demise; one ferocious blast and she'd be gone and this meeting would be officially the most over a meeting had ever been.

Outside, summer was dressed up as autumn and rain hammered at the windows. The sky was a mute, apocalyptic grey and the room was too warm. It felt like nap time in an old people's home. The room, the building, the city was having a bad day; London's collective consciousness wanted a cup of tea and a blanket.

Adrian was looking at her; she blinked the room back into focus.

'Hello? Earth to Emma? Are you in the slightest bit interested in any of this?'

Nope.

'Sorry, Adrian – I was thinking about the client. Do we know how they communicate internally? Because that seems like a natural starting point.'

She paused as if in thought; a classic blag. 'The language they use does not represent a company who's trying to reach a mass market. These are executive-level people.'

She went on more confidently: 'I think if we go in there with a normal presentation, they're going to think we're small fry; let's get them to do the ideation, while we oversee the process.' She was paraphrasing; remixing words that Adrian had used himself on the away day. She was a clever parrot.

One of the Eds turned and sneered in her direction. 'That's all well and good, Emma.' She put the barrel of the gun against his forehead, and pulled the trigger. 'But we can't just go in empty-handed, can we?'

Emma chewed the top of her pencil and then paused, going for the slow build and picturing brain-soaked Ed . . .

'Let's make them pitch to us.'

Adrian laughed so loudly everyone jumped. 'She's absolutely right! Let's go in and make them tell us what they're going to pay us to do. It's exactly what we should do.'

Emma kept the look of surprise at bay. She let the vision of the gun fade away. Probably just PMT, she thought; wanting to spray skull over her colleagues was a bit extreme, especially for a Friday.

As they left the meeting room Adrian caught up with Emma. 'You're really getting the hang of this now,' he said proudly. 'I really feel like you're becoming part of the team.' Emma felt an intriguing mix of pride and despair.

It was a familiar process, she thought, as she sat and sulked at her desk. She knew that the week-long build-up to the client meeting would mean the atmosphere in the office would incrementally tighten until everyone, from the security guy to the size 4 secretary in corporate would be so highly strung they were collectively the Philharmonic. To Adrian's ears they produced a beautiful melody, to everyone else it was a torturously high-pitched wail.

Adrian's façade of patience, which was tissue-thin on a good day, would crumple and tear under the strain and he would march from desk to desk, not actually working but instead peering over shoulders, wringing his hands and sweating into the pits of his shirt.

Other guaranteed highlights would be the inevitable demise of the printer at the crucial hour. Gemma would be reduced to tears, the only visible sign that she was taking part at all. Adrian would demand tedious and ill-conceived design changes to their company presentation and be increasingly incredulous that such things took more than a matter of seconds to action. He would become an unbearable sack of noise to be humoured by Emma, who would coddle him and encourage him and tell him he was right.

The process would hit fever pitch the day before the meeting and everyone would work late, complaining and texting cancellations to plans they should have known better than to make. It was, in short, fresh hell.

Adrian passed Emma's desk just as she let slip a long, agonised sigh. He frowned and shouted over the creative department, 'This is a great opportunity for you guys to really flex those creative muscles. Looking forward to seeing what you come up with.' He moved into his office and shut the door while Emma rested her head on her hands and tried not to cry.

Outside the rain stopped as abruptly as it had started, the storm moving over to some other part of London to drench ill-advised cyclists and horrified tourists who would stand in doorways and look incredulously at the sky.

29

Winters-Gould

Clementine was sitting in a small, stuffy room above Wardour Street waiting for Caroline Winters-Gould. The room was a classic Soho attic space; the address was the sole source of glamour. Clem looked at the dead flowers in a vase on the windowsill. The glass of the window was brown and dusty; in fact, she noticed, everything was dusty. Stacks of paper, books and an ashtray littered the desk. The phone in reception had been ringing non-stop since she'd arrived, ten minutes previously. The receptionist was a surly teenager and Clem had decided she must be a relative of Caroline's – an unruly niece, perhaps, sent to London from Wolverhampton to do work experience for her big-shot aunty. Twice while Clem waited in reception she had answered the phone with a 'Wot?'

When Caroline appeared, however, she sat up straight and used a fist to wipe some of the greasy fringe out of her eyes.

Caroline managed to be small and mousy, whilst pro-jecting an enviable sense of power. Clementine liked her immediately. She was clumsy but confident, charming but humble; she was the kind of woman Clem liked.

'So, Ms Twist . . .'

'You can call me Clem, or Clementine, or whatever, if you prefer.'

'Clem. Thank you so much for meeting me – it was a bit naughty of me to ask you, really.' She smiled cheekily and poured two coffees from the mini-cafetière on the desk, spilling it into both saucers.

'I know you're in talks with Drake Jones, and that you don't *need* to be here, but . . . well . . . Basically I want to steal you away from him and keep you for myself.'

Clem was surprised.

'It's *Drake Jones*, though,' she said in Drake's own nasal, self-important voice.

Caroline threw her head back and laughed loudly. 'God I know, he's just *so Drake*, isn't he?' she mimicked his accent. 'I do realise that he might be a bit irresistible for you, Clem. But before you sign a contract with them, will you have a little listen to my pitch?'

Clementine couldn't think of anything she'd rather hear. Already the relationship had been more fulfilling than the months she had spent chasing one email from Drake, who'd had her script and two treatments for several, silent weeks. Caroline had contacted her from her tiny agency of three, having read not just *Moonshiners*, but everything Clem had ever produced, including her entry essay to film school, which she had quoted in her introduction email.

'OK, Clem, so, here we go. I used to work with Drake at The Agency, I was there for ten years and I know what they do. I will be honest; they can offer you a global reach, that much is true. But what I can promise you, Clem, is that I'm not going to let your work sit on a shelf and gather dust while you hope that someone comes along and decides to read it. That's not how I operate. If you'll let me, I'm going to be shoving your scripts in faces day and night. I'm going to get you into rooms, and onto desks, and that's going to get your script optioned and get you paid. Clementine Twist . . .' She broke off for a moment and changed tone, adding quietly, 'God, it's such a great name already – *Clementine Twist*, you're going to be such an easy sell . . .'

Clem felt a bit coy. Caroline was pitching like a pro.

'Now if you were already established, and had studio people breaking down your door, then Drake would be the right guy for you and we wouldn't be having this conversation, because when it comes to big players that man is at the top of his game. But Clem, he's not the kind of guy that takes an unknown and builds them up; he's not going to risk putting your scripts on desks when he has producers on speed dial chasing him for his biggest clients. I know how it feels, when you get a guy like Drake Jones asking you to sign a contract, and I'm glad he did because he's right, you are going to be a gold mine and you deserve to have him make you feel like a million dollars. And Clem, in five years' time when you're worth more than a million dollars, you'd be right to call him and say sorry.'

Clem took a sip of coffee. 'Why am I saying sorry?'

'You're saying sorry I turned you down five years ago for Caroline, but now she's made me rich and famous, I'll take that meeting you've been begging me for.'

Clem pictured the scene, in which she was wearing a power suit and carrying an Oscar.

Caroline took off her glasses. 'The thing about agencies like them, Clem, is that they cast their net pretty wide. We all heard about you when you left Columbia; you're already being talked about and so naturally, The Agency want you on their books. But they want you *in case* you become the next big thing; they're not going to work that hard to make sure of it. Someone has to put in the hours and, well, I'm not saying they definitely won't, but I can promise you that I definitely will.'

Clem was recollecting the number of times she'd contacted Drake trying to get that first brief and unsatisfying meeting. Caroline looked at her calmly.

'So, what do you think?'

'I think I love you.'

Caroline laughed big. 'Brilliant. So, shall we do this?'

'Definitely.'

'Oh that's so great, Clementine. You're so talented, we're going to have a lot of fun together, you and I.'

She thrust a hand at Clementine, who shook it. 'Now, do you want to break it to Drake, or can I?'

As Clem closed the door to the office, she saw Wardour Street with new eyes. The film companies and post-production houses were her future. The execs marching up and down and celebrities walking eyes to the ground were her colleagues. She put on her shades and walked, back arched, towards the bus stop, hoping she had enough on her Oyster card to get home. She could picture Caroline on the phone to Drake, and hoped she'd tell him where to shove his cappuccino.

30

Crying in the Toilet

Blonk.

It was an IM from Hilary that connected the dots.

Have you got a tampon?

Emma checked her desk drawer and replied:

Nup, sorry, you'll have to ask one of the hens if they're layin.

Then she looked at the date. A wave of dread worked its way over her body. Suddenly she had complete clarity about the last couple of weeks. A relentless hunger, shattering insomnia, sick every time she lit a cigarette.

She googled 'first signs of pregnancy' and scrolled through the search results with a sinking heart. She tried to remember when her last period had been but only knew it was worryingly long ago. Denial stuck around for a few more minutes before acceptance and stress joined the meeting.

She felt light and cold as she walked to Boots at lunchtime, in a trance. The own-brand test was £3.99.

As Emma walked back to work, slowly, her phone rang. It was Paul.

'What you up to tonight? Do you want to come and get messed up at Shaggy May's?'

She answered with a ghostly 'No,' and he asked her what was wrong. She murmured that she would talk to him later and hung up while he was still speaking.

The five-minute walk lasted thirty; the sun on her face felt accusing. She could hear, on a loop, a selection of the snide remarks she had made about accidental pregnancies over the years. She could hear with abject clarity the sound of her own voice berating Clem for her multiple pregnancy scares. She could see herself shaking her head in mock disgust at her friend's immaturity.

At work she went into the disabled cubicle and locked the door. She knew, she absolutely knew. She stood and stared in the mirror, but as the test lines appeared, two for positive, she slid down the wall and onto the floor.

Hotel dude had been careful, super careful, and she didn't even think there had been time for a baby to form since him. That only left Lee Freeman and she counted the weeks since that ill-fated night feeling like a terrible slut for not knowing the date by heart.

Her mind raced with unforgiving regret. Lee Freeman, that bastard, in her life, again. Fury rose and fell like a tide. She felt heavy and unclean.

Emma stayed in the toilet for fifteen minutes, trying to adjust to her new reality, contemplating the next steps. When she could stand, she looked in the mirror. Her face was grey. She realised with a sense of finality that the cause of her strangeness for the last few weeks was a tiny baby that she was going to have removed and thrown away. She felt appalling.

She walked back to her desk with her mind screaming. *You idiot, you cliché, you're supposed to be a grown-up, you're supposed to know better, why did you let this happen?*

She sat and stared at the beach scene on her screen. Tears streamed down her face and she tried to take deep breaths but they caught in her throat.

Gemma looked around her screen. 'You all right?' she said, but when she saw Emma's face she looked quickly away. Emma felt Ross staring at her and turned to him, imploringly, but he turned away, stared at his screen and pretended not to notice.

Blonk.

An IM from Gemma.

What's wrong? Can I help?

Gemma leaned around the screens again, looking deeply nervous. 'Do you want tea?' she whispered, eyes wide with worry. Emma thought she seemed so sweet, so totally useless, and she nodded yes.

In the kitchen Gemma found Hilary swearing at the coffee machine. She whispered to her and Hilary slammed her cup down and marched over to Emma, followed by Gemma holding the empty kettle. Hilary sat in an empty swivel chair and moved in closely. 'What's wrong?'

Emma took a deep breath, and said it aloud for the first time.

'I'm pregnant,' and as she whispered it, it became truer still and the sob that had stuck in her throat was released.

223

Gemma's hand covered her mouth and her eyes widened. Hilary took her elbow and guided her gently to the small meeting room. They sat looking at each other.

'It's going to be OK, honey,' Hilary said, sounding more like a grown-up than she ever had before.

'I need to have it out, I don't even have a doctor.' A surge of panic rose up without warning and Emma looked earnestly at Hilary. 'I'm not even registered with a doctor, H – what am I going to do?'

'It's OK, Emma, it's going to be fine.'

Hilary took out her phone and made a call. 'It's Hilary Hassuc, I need an appointment this afternoon. Can I please speak to Eliot?' She stepped out of the room, shutting the door gently behind her. Emma watched her; she had her corporate face on. Whatever she was doing was about to get done.

Through the glass Emma watched Gemma knock on Adrian's office door. She entered and started talking, then in unison they looked over, directly at Emma.

Oh my god, what has she done?

Emma looked away, disbelieving. A fresh wave of horror flashed through her. *The intern has just told the boss.* Hilary came back in and saw the expression, looking over her shoulder for the source of Emma's angst.

'Oh shit, do you think she just told him?'

They looked at each other, horrified.

At the end of the room Gemma sat down, blushing in her chair, and Adrian made his way, grim-faced, towards the meeting room.

Gemma, you massive little bastard.

Emma looked at Hilary, who whispered under her breath, 'Deep breaths, Em.'

Adrian pushed the door open gently and stuck his big pink head through the gap.

This is so personal, she thought. He knows things about my uterus. This is not suitable for work.

Adrian coughed; his discomfort would have been funny at any other time.

'Gemma's just let me know the situation,' he said. Emma groaned and put her face on the table. 'And if you need to leave it's fine, just let me know what you need. Don't worry about anything here, OK?'

Emma's eyes filled up, the kindness tipping her over the edge. She nodded, not able to speak. He stood for a moment longer and Emma sensed the solidarity that he was projecting. She knew his instinct was to hug her and he was stopping himself. They watched him leave and for that second she loved him.

Hilary turned to her. 'Right, so, James and I are seeing this consultant. He is A. Mazing. He's my bitch until he can get me knocked up, so to speak.' She stopped, realising she'd been insensitive but also that she'd just blurted out a secret. Emma felt a fresh wave of guilt; she and Hilary occupied opposite ends of the pregnancy spectrum.

'I'm so sorry,' Emma said miserably, the revelation adding another layer of regret to the rapidly growing pile.

'God, no, *I'm* sorry,' said Hilary. They sat quietly, letting the moment pass. 'Anyway,' she went on, 'he is really good, I consider him a friend. They'll count it as an appointment for me and just make sure you're OK. OK? They'll see you at four. It's in Tottenham, is the only thing. Bleak as hell.'

Back at her desk, Emma's phone rang. She looked, saw it was Yasmin and clicked it to silent. Gemma brought her a cup of tea and touched her lightly on the back. It was a supportive gesture and she appreciated it. She had already forgiven her for telling Adrian; someone needed to and she was glad she didn't have to say it herself. Yasmin had left her a voicemail saying she was in Soho and asking if Emma could pop out for a coffee.

Emma sat and stared at her screen, unable to focus. She texted Yasmin. She knew she'd rather see Clem, or Paul, or a long list of people that, if she were being honest with herself, was headed up by her mum, but at that stage anyone would be better than watching Adrian shifting uncomfortably in his glass box or Gemma shuffling about in embarrassed silence.

She shut down her computer and collected her things together. When her screen was black she turned again to Ross, who didn't look up. She made a mental note to never forgive him.

She poked her head through a gap in Adrian's doorway. 'Hey, Adrian, I'm going to go, I've got a doctor's appointment. I'll update you when I know what's happening. I'll see you in a few days anyway, for sure. I'm ... I'm sorry – all a bit embarrassing, really.'

'You take care of yourself, Emma. Like I said, if you need anything at all you just say, OK? Lots of love.'

This nearly tipped her into tears again so she nodded her thanks and left. For once the PR department was quiet – or, she thought, maybe pregnant ears block out high frequencies. As she passed the big meeting room she could see Hilary, who made a phone with her hand, mouthing, *call me*.

Emma was all the way outside the building when she remembered she had left the pregnancy test in the bin at work.

Free drama for the PRs.

*

Yasmin was outside a coffee shop a couple of streets away, smoking an e-cigarette. She was perky as ever, but when Emma got within hearing distance her smile dropped and a look of concern shaded her face. She rushed over and any chance of playing it cool left Emma for the day. 'What's wrong with you?' she said, pulling her in for a hug.

Emma wanted to be matter-of-fact, she wanted to be an adult about it; it was a mishap, a technicality, an untoward happenstance. Instead her nose turned red and ran, her cheeks flushed and she cried. Every time she said it made it worse. Yasmin, naturally, made it worse.

'Oh my god, who have you told?'

'Only you and Hilary, but the intern told my boss.'

'Jeez, Em, this isn't supposed to happen to us. We're so too old for abortions.'

It was the first time anyone had said the 'A' word, and it made Emma's insides clench.

'I know.'

'What are you going to do? How long has it been? You have to go to the doctors, like, now.'

'Yeah, thanks, I know. I've got an appointment at four.'

'They're expensive, you know.'

'What are?'

'Abortions. You have to go private, you can't get it on the NHS. Apparently they just give you this pill and it can go really badly wrong – my mate had it and—'

'What the hell, Yasmin? Can you just ... Can you just give it a rest for a minute?'

'Sorry,' she said defensively.

They pulled up chairs at a table outside the café.

'But you'd better sort it sooner rather than later.'

'Yeah. I get it.'

'Have you spoken to Clem?'

'No, I haven't seen her . . . '

'Well you know she saw Jordan?'

'What? No. When?'

'Yeah, he came to her work, he saw her sitting there on reception. It must have been so embarrassing.'

'Oh shit, I can't believe she didn't call me. Is she OK?'

'I don't know, really. I think so.'

Yasmin clicked another drag of the e-cigarette and offered it to Emma, who shook her head.

'I guess you shouldn't, in your condition.'

She blew the vapour at Emma and looked at her. She seemed outlandishly happy – awash with gossip and loving it. Emma wished she had stayed at work.

'Do you want me to come with you? To the doctors?'

'It's fine, thanks. I can handle it, I think . . . and it's in Tottenham.'

'Oh, well, I have a thing at seven. How long will it take?'

'I don't know, but it's fine, I can go by myself.'

'So . . . whose is it?'

Emma's instinct was to lie, but all the possible untruths that surfaced sounded much worse than the reality. She put her head in her hands, muttering through her fingers, 'Lee Freeman.'

'No. Way. From that night at Cotton? Oh my god. I told you not to go home with him.'

'Yeah, you did. I should've listened.'

'I knew it.'

Emma was silent and fighting the urge to kick Yasmin in the shin.

'Are you going to tell him? Do you even have his number?'

'I actually haven't thought about it.'

'I don't think you should tell him.'

Emma wanted to ignore any advice that came out of Yasmin's mouth so immediately thought she should tell him, although the idea appalled her. She shrugged. 'Maybe I would if he was a nicer guy, or if he had been nicer to me. But he's such a child, what can he do to help?'

'Nothing. That guy is a dick.'

They sat in silence until a waitress came over and asked for their order.

Yasmin touched Emma's arm. 'I'll get these.' Turning to the waitress but not making eye contact she said, 'Two cappuccinos.' And turned back to Emma who muttered, 'Please,' under her breath.

'PLEASE!' shouted Yasmin at the waitress, which was somehow ruder than not saying it at all.

Emma, tied in to the chat for at least a cup of coffee, tried to change the subject.

'So, how's the wedding planning?'

'Oh my god. So, Adam's parents are like, so happy for us. They totally love me; they offered to pay for the honeymoon. Guess where?'

'France?'

'No. Better. Much better.'

'Germany?'

'How is Germany better than France? Silly. No, sod Europe – we're going to Hawaii. For two weeks.'

She waggled two fingers at Emma, who tried to muster a smile.

'Yay.'

'Yeah, YAY! You should be happy for me, Emma.'

'I am. I'm thrilled for you. Well done. *Mahalo*.'

Emma sat in the Birth Place centre, staring at a poster of a woman holding a baby.

The reception was far more upmarket than anywhere Emma had been before. Medical journals lined the walls where there would normally be flyers for stopping smoking, or flu jabs. Everything was shiny and clean and not at all like the doctors she was used to, which were plastic, filthy and full of angry ill people.

Two leather sofas away from her a father sat holding a tiny baby, while trying to keep a toddler entertained. The toddler was picking various items up and throwing them on the floor. When Emma made eye contact she toddled over and stood with her hands on Emma's knees.

'Hi there, little one, how are you?'

'Ooodabaaaa,' the kid replied.

'What are you up to today?'

'Dubababa roobaba,' she said, flinging a plastic truck over her head and then looking with surprise at her empty hand.

'Oh, really? Me too!'

The kid wandered away, burbling happily. I do not want one of them, thought Emma, wondering if it was true. Did kids find her more appealing now? Could they sense it?

A handsome doctor in a striped shirt called her name from a clipboard and she got up and followed him down the hallway. The kid sat on the floor, waving a leaflet at the baby on her dad's lap.

They sat down in his office and looked at each other.

'So, Hilary sent you to me. It's a bit naughty of her but she's my favourite patient, so ... How can I help?'

'I'm pregnant, but I don't want to be, I guess is the short story.'

'Are you late?'

'Yeah, at least a week. Maybe two.'

'Do you know when you finished your last period?'

'It's been about eight weeks I guess, maybe more. I don't keep tabs properly,' she said.

What grown woman doesn't know when her period is? This one.

'Have you done a test?'

'Yeah, it was positive.' She could feel her eyes filling up. She urged herself not to cry.

'OK, well, if you're late and you've done a test I don't need to do another one. I'll do an ultrasound to find out how far along you are. Have you thought about your options?'

'I don't want it.'

'And you're sure about that?'

'I don't want it; it's an accident from a one-night stand. It's not a difficult decision.'

He looked at her sympathetically and tears rushed down her face. He handed her a small square tissue.

'If you hop up on the table we can have a look and see how far along it is, then we'll have a better idea of the best way to proceed. Ignore the stirrups, by the way – we won't be doing anything invasive.'

The doctor stood up. She found his presence deeply comforting; he smelled nice and he looked very clean – even his soul seemed clean, she thought, like he sweats kindness.

She got up on the table and pulled her T-shirt up to her boobs. She instinctively sucked her belly in and a rush of regret sucked up with it. He splurted some jelly onto her stomach and pulled up a stool next to where she lay.

'Certain procedures can only take place after seven weeks. Before that the foetus is too small and there's a risk that the surgical team won't be able to locate it. This will be a bit cold.'

He pressed the sensor against her stomach and moved it around, squidging jelly on her skin. It doesn't look pregnant, she thought, experiencing a moment of pleasure that she was still skinny, until regret took centre stage once more.

The doctor moved the ultrasound screen so that she couldn't see it. He clicked a few buttons and pressed harder on the softness of her stomach. Part of her enjoyed the pain; she felt she deserved it.

He clicked a few more buttons. 'This looks around seven weeks.'

'Can I see?'

He turned the screen towards her, pointing to the area of pulsing cloud that looked like a bunch of nothing.

'How big is it?'

'Around the size of a peanut.'

Awwww.

A peanut.

My peanut.

I've got me a peanut.

She knew what she was doing and stopped herself. She also knew that if at any point anyone referred to it as 'him' or 'her' it would be over and she'd be a single mum with half a Freeman for the rest of her life. All of her hormones were telling her that was a good idea. Her brain was in staunch opposition.

She felt her palms start to sweat and turned away from the screen, her eyes filling up.

The doctor clicked it off and gently wiped her belly with a handful of blue tissue. She wished he would give her a hug and instead took a deep breath of his adult man cologne.

He went and sat back at his desk and waited for her to join him. She looked at the blank screen where the smudges of her mistake had been. A peanut.

'Are you OK?'

'Yeah I'm fine, thanks. I think my hormones are going mental but I don't want it, I really don't. I barely know the guy who did it. He's an ex, it was a totally pointless replay and there's no way I want it. Honestly I don't know if I want kids at all, but I definitely don't want one like this.'

'OK, Emma, try not to be too hard on yourself, these things happen. There are a lot of options and they're all very safe and simple. I'm going to talk you through them, is that OK? Are you up to it?'

She nodded.

'So you can take a pill, this induces a miscarriage. You will usually be out of action for a couple of days while it takes effect. It's not unlike having a very heavy period. There are mixed reports about how painful it is but everybody's different and so we can only tell you what to expect, not precisely how it will be. Are you familiar with any of this?'

Emma nodded. She had googled it.

'The benefits of this are that you can do it right away, it will be over in a couple of days, and it has the lowest cost implications. The downside is that you are likely to experience some quite severe discomfort. Is that clear?'

She nodded again.

'The other options are surgical – we can offer a local procedure or you can have a general anaesthetic. Do you have any idea what you'd prefer at this stage?'

'Surgical, definitely.'

'General or no?'

'No anaesthetic.'

'You're sure? It can be quite a painful procedure.'

'I feel like I should feel it happen.'

He looked at her dubiously. 'Why?'

'Because it's my fault and I should feel it.'

She felt like he was talking to a version of herself that she had never met. 'That's not a good reason, Emma; you don't need to punish yourself. People usually only opt for a local anaesthetic when there's some medical reason they shouldn't be put under. Don't do it because you're hurting yourself. I can see you're upset. Do you want to take some time to think about it?'

'No, surgical.'

'I'm going to recommend you have a general anaesthetic, what do you think?'

'Yeah, OK. Thanks.'

'So, since you're around seven weeks, I can refer you to a clinic we partner with in Richmond. You probably know we don't actually conduct terminations here, but we do have a great relationship with the clinic. It's private so there will be a cost, but I am able to apply a discount that we have in place with them. OK?' He handed her a set of leaflets.

She nodded.

Termination. Terminate. Kill the peanut, kill it dead and flick it in the bin.

Her hands were shaking. Her peanut was getting ter-minated. Her heart was badly bruised and on the way to breaking.

'I'm going to make the appointment for as soon as pos-sible but it will still give you a couple of days to think about it. If at any point you need to talk to someone or you want to change your mind or ask any questions, these are support numbers, and this is my number. Do you have any questions now?'

Will you give me a hug?

'No, thanks. Thank you for being so nice about it.'

Doctor Eliot had a wedding ring and she thought how lucky Mrs Eliot was. He looked at her with an expression of warmth and concern.

'Emma, I really want you to understand that you shouldn't punish yourself. I can see you feel terrible but you need to give yourself a break. I don't want to trivialise this, because I know it's a serious situation, but you're the only person who's going to suffer and you're the only person who can stop it. OK? I know it's difficult, but you have every right to make this decision. Do you understand? It's your right as a woman to have control over this.'

They stood up and she left the office, walking through reception and out into a sun-soaked traffic jam. She looked around, and realised she had nowhere to go. Clem was still being evasive and Emma didn't want to have to explain it all to anyone else. She just wanted it over with. She stood looking at nothing. In the distance she could see a huge blue warehouse. Ikea.

She walked in that direction. Ikea had clean furniture and cactus plants; it had tape measures and little pencils and rugs and cupboards. Ikea was a big blue and yellow haven of nowhere-ness.

Emma's tray was full. Twenty meatballs, fries and pale brown sauce and a blob of jam, a salad bowl heaped high with coleslaw and sweet corn and a slab of Daim bar cheesecake. The woman behind the counter had instinctively looked her up and down and Emma had practically spat 'WHAT?' She carried the load to a table by the window. It seemed everyone had brought their kids to Ikea for the day – babies screamed, toddlers toddled and mums looked harassed.

She pushed a meatball around the plate; suddenly the smell of it brought on a wave of nausea. She took out the set of leaflets the doctor had handed her, and turned decisively to the fees page. The surgical procedure with general anaesthetic was going to cost £707. With the discount from the Birth Place it would be £565.

It was almost exactly the amount she had been in credit by on the last payday. She nodded at the predictability of it, looking out over Tottenham. She watched cars full of families and furniture swing around the roundabout and pull out onto the road. Big dollop tears fell from her face onto the meatballs below. She picked at the cheesecake, which was overwhelmingly sweet, and wondered what to do next. She sat there for an hour, ignoring strange looks from people and wishing she were elsewhere. At 5.45 her phone rang and Hilary was ordering her out of Ikea and into a cab to her house.

When she arrived at Hilary's place, a gorgeous Georgian townhouse in Highbury, she felt dulled inside. Hilary answered the door and for the first time since they'd met, seemed much older than Emma.

Bundling her indoors, Hilary announced, 'I've got all the Pixar films, a couple of *Harry Potters*, a tub of popcorn, two steaks, a bag of crisps and more chocolate than you can shake a love handle at. How does that sound?'

It sounded spot on.

Hilary gave her a tour of the house; they had a spare room, her husband was away on a trip for the weekend and she had cancelled her plans.

They were watching *Finding Nemo* when Hilary looked over and noticed that Emma was staring into space.

'Hey, it's going to be OK. I can lend you the money, if you're worried about it?'

'I have it; it just feels like a shame to spend it on this. I wanted an iPad,' she joked.

Hilary tried to smile but it was downcast. She wanted a peanut so badly. Emma read the expression.

'I didn't know you were seeing a baby doctor.'

'We've only been going for a few months. It's probably fine, we're just getting all the help we can. Nobody's firing blanks, we're just impatient.'

Hilary turned the volume down on the film neither of them was watching and turned to Emma. 'Have you thought about telling the guy? Like, asking him to pay? Shouldn't he have to contribute at least?'

'He is so good at making me feel like shit, and since I feel like shit already, his role is redundant.'

'But he could front some cash.'

'I don't even want to start the conversation. I don't

really know what happened that night. He'd just say it was my own fault. That's pretty much what he said when he cheated on me, back in the day ... He said, and this is a direct quote, "You never said I couldn't sleep with other people – I thought you were cool." Who knows what ridiculous comeback he'd have to this? He's a capital bastard.'

Hilary turned back to the TV.

'Do you think he has a right to know?' Emma asked. She had spent the last few hours trying to mentally re-categorise the situation. It was an illness, not a baby. A problem, not a person.

'You're the only one whose rights I care about. I only asked because of the money; I'm not sure your ovaries are anyone else's business.'

They watched films until midnight, then went to bed. Emma shut the door to her room. It smelled like a grown-up's house, all laundry and carpet shampoo; her own house smelled of weed and boys and pizza boxes. She lay on her back and looked at the ceiling, her mind jangling. She pressed her belly and tried to detect any abnormality – it hurt her to think that there was a peanut of potential in there. The line of thought depressed her beyond measure and she turned on her side, humming Britney Spears, '*hit me baby one more time*'. She lay awake for a long time.

The next morning Emma woke up and rushed to the bathroom to puke. She could hear Hilary downstairs and made a decision to buck up, splashed some water on her face and gargled with mouthwash.

'How you feeling?' Hilary was dressed and making breakfast.

'Fresh hell.'

'You look pale. Do you want to eat?'

'No, I'm OK. Thanks so much for last night. I'm going to go home.'

'Is there anyone there, though? Or do you want to be alone?'

'My flatmate is there, he'll look after me. Or at least take the piss.'

Hilary put a cup of coffee in front of Emma. 'So ... I realise this might sound inappropriate ...'

Emma looked interested. 'Go for it.'

'I was thinking last night, that you should write this up. You could produce something really powerful. It might seem a bit raw now but it would be an interesting change of pace for your blog, to have something weightier. Tell me if I'm being totally tactless.'

Emma sipped the coffee. 'No, it's a good idea. I will.'

After a shower Emma set off across London towards the flat. It was a grey day, overcast, and neither warm nor cold. The world felt quiet.

When she got back to her flat Paul was mopping the floor. 'Whoa, you look rough. Hangover?'

'It's you I'm worried about. There's a mop in your hand. Are you having a stroke?'

'You're almost funny, Em. Lucy's coming for dinner.'

'Actually, not to be a dick, but could she not?'

He stopped mopping. 'Seriously?'

'Yeah, sorry. I feel really weird ... I got knocked up. I'm having it out next week.'

Paul rushed over. 'What the hell, Em? Why didn't you call me?'

'I'm fine. I stayed at Hilary's last night. It's all fine, I've been to the doctor and everything. I'll have it out.'

'I'll tell Lucy not to come,' he said, heading to his room. He stopped in the doorway.

'But I'm not cleaning again when she does.'

She flipped the TV on and listened to the muffled sounds of his phone call. She wondered if he would tell her outright, Gemma-style, and knew instinctively that he wouldn't.

She got her own phone out of her bag and scrolled through her contacts, wondering when so many people had become just acquaintances. She paused at Yasmin and considered calling. She knew she just wanted to ring Clem but she didn't want their first conversation since her birthday to be so needy and lame. She put the phone back on the table and stared at an advert for a stairlift.

Paul came back and sat on the sofa.

'Breakfast wine?' he asked.

'Yeah, what the hell, why not.'

'I bought it for Lucy so it's a nice one as well.'

'Ah, man, sorry to ruin it.'

'No, don't worry, you're a worthy recipient. So listen, don't get cross ...'

'Why? What about?'

'I called Clem, she's on her way.'

'What? Why?' Emma felt a bit betrayed but largely relieved.

'Because she's your best friend, you muppet, and I am not equipped to handle this alone. I have one of these.' He stuck his hand in his jeans and poked his finger out through his fly, waggling it around.

'The sense of humour of an eight-year-old?'

'Yeah, exactly, I'm out of my depth.'

Clementine arrived in a whirlwind of products and quips. She had carrier bags full of junk she'd lifted from her mum, and booze she couldn't afford. She hugged Emma and whatever animosity there had been was immediately dispensed with.

'So,' she announced when the table was loaded with magazines, junk food and wine bottles, 'did you talk to Yas?'

Emma nodded. 'She basically said, "I told you so".'

'Jesus,' Clem shook her head, 'bang on brand. Is it hotel dude's?'

'Lee Freeman.'

'Eww, that prick. Definitely have it out then. I was thinking if it's a gorgeous international-man-of-mystery kid we could share it.'

'Alas, it'd be at least half dickhead.'

Both girls made a face and laughed. Emma felt better.

'How do you know about hotel dude?'

'I read your blog religiously, obviously. And Yasmin told me about it, although I think her version was embellished – did you actually get attacked by a colleague and run into this guy's arms?'

'No.'

Clem was unsurprised.

'How are you?' Emma asked, ashamed she hadn't been in touch.

'I am awesome. I had a meeting with an agent who isn't a wanker!'

Emma yelped. 'What happened to Drake?'

'I don't really know. I sent him a load of work and he said he loved it all and was going to send me a contract. But then he just didn't. I was starting to feel like a stalker until Caroline got in touch.'

'And what's her deal?'

'She's one of the old-school ones – she seems to actually give a shit. Caroline Winters-Gould. She's read *Moonshiners*. It was the best meeting ever, and I signed with her. She says she's going to make me rich and famous.'

Emma stood up and hugged Clem. 'I'm so proud of you, you starlet. Congratulations!'

Clem grinned. 'It might be starting, Em. Something real.'

31

Pram Marathon

Emma was in her room having an interesting chain of thought about what one wears to have an abortion. She had decided that Hilary's idea to write it up was a good one and so was noting any elements that made it more interesting than the frankly horrific abortion posts she had seen online.

She wasn't supposed to eat before the procedure so she left the house hungry, wearing a floaty white shirt that had a hint of maternity about it. She put a ribbon in her hair to try and be cheery.

The District Line trundled clumsily towards Richmond. Emma was edgy, but had made peace with the idea. She'd had moments of hormone-induced indecision but Clem had pointed out that she had been drinking all weekend so it'd be born with webbed feet and, she'd added, Lee Freeman's stupid face. Still, her instincts wanted her to keep it.

Clem said, 'Tell your instincts to fuck off.'

Richmond seemed to be hosting a fancy pram marathon. Outside the station Emma was surrounded by the unchecked wailing of a thousand toddlers, and a beatbox of tuts from crop-haired mums pushing prams that cost more than a second-hand car, wearing ballet flats and sun hats and glaring smugly at each other. The street should have been littered with dummies and single socks. Emma looked around and soaked it in.

Fuck. That. Noise.

She made her way past upmarket shops and cafés, glad to be an outsider. Everywhere she looked there was another pram, another screaming infant, another distended, alien-containing belly. It started to feel like a bad dream and she was relieved when the crowd of the high street thinned out and she was walking along a tree-lined avenue.

The clinic was in a tall Victorian building that could have been anything from a nursing home to a lawyer's office. As she approached it occurred to her that there might be pro-life clowns outside, so she was practising potential rebuttals when the building loomed large ahead of her. She was equally pleased and disappointed that there were no protestors. *Maybe they're off duty today.*

Inside the clinic Emma sat, waiting for her turn. The rest of the patients were a motley crew: there was a teenage couple that checked all the stereotype boxes and a few much older women. Emma was surprised to find that she was probably in the exact centre of the age range in the room. Evidently there was no such thing as too old for an abortion.

Sitting directly opposite her, an older woman sat with her daughter. The girl seemed to suffer from a mental deficiency, although Emma couldn't tell exactly what was wrong with her. She had thick glasses and greasy hair and stared around the room with her mouth open and her tongue hanging unchecked over her lip. The mother was fierce-looking and bundled up in a big fur coat; her hair and make-up were professionally finished and it was obvious she hated being there. It would have been funny if it hadn't been so sad.

When Emma was called, led by a small Indian lady into a cubicle and given another ultrasound, she didn't look at the screen and tried to think happy thoughts that didn't involve any legumes. The lady placed a plastic wristband on her arm. Then she was asked to go upstairs and into a changing room that was like being in a swimming pool. She put on a hospital gown and stuffed all of her belongings in a locker. Then she sat on a bench in a corridor with some of the women from downstairs. The girl with the tongue looked thoroughly alarmed and Emma felt like she was on a conveyor belt of sadness.

They called her into an operating theatre and she lay while people with bad attitudes plugged her veins into various machines. She was clutching the end of the wristband, nervous and tense. The doctor prised her fingers open, demanding to know what she was holding, and then dropped her hand on the bed, tutting. What's your problem? she thought, and then realised he had one of the worst jobs in medicine.

They asked her to count down from ten. When she got to eight she felt a surge of panic that she had made a mistake, and blacked out into nothing.

The recovery room she awoke in was surprisingly jovial. Eight of the women from the waiting room sat up in beds around her. The lady in the bed next to her said, 'You all right, darling?'

Emma nodded yes.

Two of them were talking about the procedure: 'I didn't even think I could still have kids,' one was saying. 'I thought I was too old. I've got two teenagers, there's no way I'm doing all that nonsense again.'

'Too right,' said the other. 'I got my little girl at home too.'

The girl with the tongue woke up and cried woefully. Everyone looked at her and a brusque-looking nurse came in and told her to pipe down.

'It hurts,' she wailed. 'It hurts.'

Everyone else sat quietly. Emma wasn't in any pain and felt sorry for the girl who didn't seem to know what was happening.

They were required to sign some forms and wait for at least an hour for the anaesthetic to wear off. Emma felt better than she had done for weeks. While she changed back into her clothes she noticed the colour had returned to her cheeks. She had an appetite and she felt, she admitted guiltily, pretty good.

The final stage of the process was an interview with a rat-faced nurse who scolded her for being careless, and forced her to take a handful of condoms. Emma joked, 'I won't be needing them,' and the nurse took the opportunity to tell her that she definitely would need them, if she didn't want to come back. Her tone was deeply condescending and it was the first time someone had been cruel about what had happened. She knew the nurse had a point but she didn't stop herself telling her to mind her own business. The nurse sneered at her and said, 'That will be all.'

*

As Emma walked through Richmond, the baby paraphernalia took on a new significance. She knew she had made the right decision, and she felt physically better than she had done for weeks, but she also knew that she would never forget. That she would think about the kid that wasn't, about how old it wasn't as each year passed, until she was old and it never was. She knew this was one of the moments that would haunt her as a split in time, a life junction; and that there was a parallel universe, where she had the kid and never regretted it, because, if you believed all those soft focus, dewy-eyed mums in the nappy adverts, nobody ever regretted having a baby. In that universe she would love it, and nurture it and be glad of it.

But in this universe, she wouldn't make the same mistake again and she would produce a piece of writing about it and put it all behind her. The relief was palpable; the baby parade that was the high street made her feel young and free and powerful again.

She named the blog post 'The Lost Peanut' and spent hours writing and re-writing it. Once it was published she watched the stats exceed those of any other post she had ever written. Within an hour it'd had 500 views, by the end of the day close to 2000. She watched as it got shared, then went global, and pride mingled with the traces of sadness still in her system.

Despite the fact that she felt her health immediately return to normal, Emma took the rest of the week off, escaping the meeting preparation panic. She spent it playing writer. Drinking black coffee at her desk and updating her blog, riding the wave of popularity. On days when he was home, Paul, Lucy and Emma had lunch together. Emma was invariably grateful that Paul and Lucy were not saccharine to be around, and Lucy's enthusiasm for pretty much everything was a welcome modification to the mood of their house.

By the time Sunday came round, her work had been seen by 40,000 people, and shared in nineteen countries. Abortion was a hot topic and a lot of people had something to say and agreed with her decision and the subsequent relief she had felt. So many that she felt vindicated. It wasn't until she was about to go to sleep that the dread of another Monday at APRC hit her and the gloom descended to drag her back into the monotonous depths.

32

Title Studios

Clem was lying on her back staring at the ceiling, not sure how to approach her day. She couldn't stay in because she felt the glaring pressure of Mum and Malcolm quietly admonishing her for 'never doing anything'.

Clem closed her eyes through a surge of resentment. Malcolm's idea of 'doing something' was building a wall or mending a radio. He was old school, he was sheds and cogs and whistles and spanners. Clementine was MP3s and live streaming and Google docs.

Motherfucker.

They weren't willing to count her job at the Ionian amongst her accomplishments because it occupied the same hours as her party lifestyle. Regardless of when she got home (3 a.m. on a good day, 7 a.m. on a reckless one), they thought she should get up before 9 and do something productive with her day.

Without rolling over she fumbled about on the floor for her phone. It was 12.15; hopefully Malcolm had had to go to the office today and wasn't downstairs waiting for someone to talk to. She had a new message from Caroline:

Clementine. Title Studios. Call me.

She sat up. She didn't want to call Caroline with sleep in her voice, but she didn't want to delay a conversation that had Title Studios in it.

She did ten star jumps and called.

'Hi, this is Clementine Twist calling for Caroline.'

While she waited she pictured the opening credits for *Moonshiners* . . .

'Clementine, darling, how are you?'

'Good, thanks – how's Title Studios?'

Caroline laughed her loud, agent's laugh.

'They love your script, they want a meeting.'

'Well that's the best news I've had all week.'

'I know it is. So I told them you have other people interested, but to be honest, Clem, I think they're the right company.'

'Me too – they're Title Studios.'

She laughed again. Clem pictured her wide smile and glasses.

'Great, so I'll set up the meeting for early next week and let you know . . . '

'Cool.'

'Clem?'

'Yeah?'

'I'm excited. I think you should be too. Just keep working, keep putting ideas together, this is going to happen for you, OK? You're a massive talent, Clementine Twist.'

Part of her knew this was standard agent shtick; the rest wanted to squeal.

'Thanks, that means a lot.'

'Ciao, sweetie.'

Clementine took a deep breath.

Then she did squeal, and clenched her arms and fists and teeth in a muscular hurrah. Then she took another deep breath, had a shower, put on a shirt, skirt and shoes and made a coffee, greeting Malcolm with a cordial smile and a polite 'good morning'.

She marched though to the 'study', which was a sectioned-off part of a corridor where they kept their ancient Dell and dial-up internet box, and opened the script that was currently on some exec's desk at Title Studios. She stared at the first page.

Moonshiners
By Clementine Twist

Although this had been the main piece of work to come out of New York, and so was the most familiar, she was looking at it for the first time. She was looking at it with eyes that knew someone else was looking at it. She could edit it now with a renewed passion, with an invested sense that other people would see the mistakes that she hadn't been able to see any more from having read it so many times.

Malcolm came upstairs to ask if she'd like a cup of tea – in a whisper, as if not wanting to interrupt her work.

She leaned back on his black leather executive chair. 'Yeah, lovely, thanks. Do you need the computer? I can move.'

'No no, I don't want to disturb you, just being your secretary.' He winked at her. 'How's it going?'

He wasn't the obvious first person to tell, but he was the only one there. 'I just got a call from my agent – she's setting up a meeting for my script to be optioned.'

'Wow, Clementine, that's great. What does being optioned mean?'

'It means they pay me to work on the script until it's ready to produce.'

'Clem! That is great news.'

'I know! Thanks!'

'It's so nice to see you excited, Clem. I'll go and play secretary. Maybe you'll have a real secretary soon!'

He pottered off down the stairs and Clementine watched him go, pleased to have told someone about the call. She wondered how long it took from setting up a meeting to moving into a house of her own.

33

Shit Wizard

Adrian fiddled with the buttons in the door of the cab. Emma sat up straight, clenching her body to avoid touching his knees with hers.

Adrian was trying to get Emma up to speed after her week off. He was treating her absence as some controversial unmentionable. He was anxious about the meeting and it was making him belligerent.

Emma watched the suits marching up and down Monument Street. They were the chardonnay drinkers and holiday bookers, alarm-clock setters and Polo drivers. They had in-laws and diaries and insurance. They sat in meetings and were interested in the things being said in them. They weren't winging it; they were working it. They were living it. They knew what a balance sheet was. They got the Central Line, swaying and sighing and moving in shoals. They drank coffee at seminars and went shopping for pleasure. They got building work done on the houses they owned. They went camping on purpose, wearing North Face anoraks and packing blinis for breakfast. They didn't tip waitresses or have time for music. Their weekends were dominated by children and gardening and sports.

They were the grown-ups.

Adrian was still talking when they pulled up outside a futuristic glass building by St Paul's. An immaculate receptionist with a spine of diamonds directed them to the fourteenth floor. They were led to a boardroom that was the stuff of Adrian's wet dreams. He whistled his appreciation. The view spread out over London. Emma could see all the millions of windows, a million people in a million meetings. Creating work to fill the time and space of a million brains.

If they downed pens and walked out right now, nothing would happen. In fact, the world would probably be slightly better off.

Two expensive-smelling men walked into the room and the requisite hands were shaken and small talk made. Emma felt suitably childish next to them.

They took their seats, APRC on one side of the long mahogany table, ICF on the other. While they waited, Adrian continued to wax lyrical about the office.

Another immaculately dressed assistant brought in a pot of coffee and worked around the table, serving each person in turn. None of them said thank you. For a moment Emma envied the simplicity of her role.

They sat for a few minutes longer before a woman with her hair pinned impossibly tightly to her head, an enviable tan and 4-inch heels appeared.

Emma's initial reaction was, *That girl looks just like Yasmin.* Followed swiftly by *Holy fuck!*

In the absence of hyperactivity and a flurry of shopping, Emma barely recognised her.

This Yasmin was severe. She wore a charcoal blazer over the cleanest shirt Emma had ever seen. It looked like her collar was starched. Her hair and make-up were perfect.

She was in full work mode; she looked calm, serious and impressive. When her eyes met Emma's she smiled, a fake, saccharine smile that made no suggestion of their relationship. Emma had no idea how to play it.

Yasmin turned and moved decisively over to the coffee where she poured herself a cup. Then she put her things and cup in front of the chair furthest from Emma and tapped around on her iPad.

I didn't know she had an iPad.

Adrian kicked things off by introducing APRC. He spent the first fifteen minutes talking about himself and why he'd started the company; it was the ten-year speech and she'd heard it before. When Adrian had finished a decade's worth of self-congratulation he put a hand on Emma's shoulder.

'Emma is the latest addition to our creative team. She's a junior copywriter but her specialism, and the reason we brought her along today, is that she has tremendous insight.'

All eyes turned to Emma, who pasted on her best professional smile.

'Why don't you tell them more about yourself, Emma?' said Adrian. Yasmin looked up for a beat, then back at her iPad. She hadn't made eye contact with Emma since she'd walked in.

'Hi – thanks, Adrian. Hi everyone, I'm Emma. As Adrian mentioned, I'm a writer, but my task for today is simply to observe, listen and monitor.

'At APRC we know that it's not always what *is* said that gives us the most valuable insight, it's also how those things are said, and what isn't said. My job is simply to listen, to learn more about you guys, to try and pick up any underlying themes or ideas that might not be explicit, but are nonetheless relevant.'

Adrian beamed at her like a proud father and everyone else nodded except Yasmin, whose sneer Emma interpreted as *You're a secretary with a pencil.*

When the one of the expensive-smelling men took charge of the conversation he introduced Yasmin with an air of reverence. For the first time since they had met, over a decade before, someone described at length what Yasmin did for a living.

It turned out that she was an ICF senior project manager in charge of their special projects department and had, most recently, been working on a contract that outsourced parts of the major UK fracking contracts to a Dubai-based equipment company, which would dramatically reduce the cost implications for the UK taxpayer. She was, he said proudly, their most valued consultant. Emma narrowly avoided snorting water across the table. Yasmin sat impassively at the other end of the table.

Using her iPad as a remote, Yasmin took control of the meeting, opening a presentation on the huge screen.

Adrian made no attempt to disguise his awe and exclaimed at intervals as graphics swooped about and camera angles changed rapidly. At one point he actually yelped. It reminded Emma of *Iron Man*.

ICF, Yasmin explained, was strongly focused on emerging markets in the Middle East, including but not limited to the energy sector and the financial markets. They were heading up the delivery of contracts and needed a brand that the public could really 'get behind'. Emma watched her dominate the room, sitting in the background alternately scribbling notes and thinking of the text she couldn't wait to send Clem about their friend's alter ego as a shit-hot executive.

When the meeting was adjourned and they stood up to leave, Yasmin shook her hand and winked at Emma on the way out of the door.

She resisted the urge to goose Yasmin on the butt.

In the cab on the way back Adrian was sweating with corporate excitement. It glistened in his hair and made his eyes shine.

'That girl, Yasmin, wasn't she something? What a knockout.'

What a knockout.

Adrian babbled excitedly for a few more minutes. 'What did you make of it, Em?'

'Yeah, interesting . . . ' she murmured without enthusiasm. Something about her week off had reduced her ability to feign enthusiasm to practically nil.

'Did you get any valuable insight?'

Emma tried to put her corporate smile back on. 'Well, that presentation was super tight. I thought they seemed unusually guarded – don't you think? Like we only learned about them what we could get from Companies House or something. Maybe I'm being paranoid.'

Adrian pursed his lips and seemed disappointed.

'I was really hoping you would pick up something we could use, Emma.'

His tone and expression transported her back to school. Little Emma, eager to impress, afraid of everything, desperate to get it right.

'I might have something useful . . . '

Adrian looked at her with a puppy-like eagerness.

'I know Yasmin quite well.'

'*That* Yasmin?'

'I went to college with her. Actually I introduced her to her fiancé.'

Adrian looked out of the window and muttered, 'Bloody hell,' before turning to her suspiciously. 'You must have known she would be there, then? Why didn't she acknowledge you?'

'I don't know, it didn't seem appropriate somehow. The Yasmin I know in real life is, well, she's not like that. I had no idea she was so high profile, actually – I thought she was a PA or something. It's a running joke that she never talks about her job. I don't think I've ever heard her mention the company name.'

'So what's she like in *real* life?' said Adrian.

'She comes across as scatty, I guess. I don't even know which one is the act.'

'Do you think she's going to want to work with you?' he asked as he turned his gaze to the street.

Emma resisted the urge to laugh at him; she had his financial future in her hands. Her phone buzzed. It was a text from Yasmin that said: 'That was SO weird. SO excited we might work together – shall we go for a drink tonight?'

Emma looked at Adrian. 'She wants to go for a drink.'

The journey was starting to feel pleasantly like espionage.

'Go for a drink and tell her how amazing we are.' Adrian's tone made it almost an order.

Emma toyed briefly with the notion of refusing but couldn't find the nuts.

'Yeah, OK.'

When they arrived back at the office Adrian marched through ahead of everyone and shut his office door. At her desk Emma texted Clem:

> Dude, Yasmin is an actual fucking exec – she turned up to a meeting just now in a power suit.

Clem didn't miss a beat.

> *Does this mean we can put drinks on your company card if she's with us?*
> Yep.
> *Win.*

Over a bottle of chardonnay, Yasmin and Emma sat in a bar in Soho.

'So *that's* your boss . . . ' Yasmin tittered over her glass. 'He didn't seem so bad. My guys thought he was pretty sharp but—'

'I know I've slagged him off a bit . . . '

'A bit? Emma! I once heard you refer to him as a shit wizard.'

Emma laughed; this was going to be a hard sell. 'Honestly, on a philosophical level, he and I will never be on the same page. But he is good at what he does. I respect him, he's got skills, I just think he's misguided, philosophically.

Professionally I can't criticise him. If you're uncomfortable working with me then I can bow out of the project – I don't want to work in the energy sector anyway, if it's not green.'

Yasmin surveyed the bar; her expression was serious, austere. Emma could see in her the woman who had been in the meeting. She could see it in her make-up and her nails, in the way she held the wine glass and looked around. An expression that Emma would once have called vapid now seemed to disguise a serious, calculating adult. Emma speculated that maybe Yasmin's expression had always contained these things. She felt a tiny bit intimidated by this new version of her friend. What was she capable of?

'Did you tell them? That you know me?' Yasmin asked.

Emma quickly weighed up her responses and found her loyalty divided. 'No.'

'Good. It's not that I'm embarrassed, it's just that I need it to be separate.'

'I figured, since you're a total hard-ass apparently.'

'Yeah, well, none of you ever asked.'

'We ask you all the time.'

'Not sincerely, you just take the piss. What did you think? That I was a PA or something? I'm good at what I do, Emma.'

'But you do it for the fracking industry.'

'Yeah, well as of next week, so do you.'

They clinked glasses. Yasmin shot her a look that Emma thought was hilariously Disney wicked queen. Then she practically evil laughed and added, 'This is so exciting – I'm going to be your boss.'

34

Bank of Cal

Clementine was sitting at a bus stop waiting for her brother to say he would lend her yet more money. Callum was on the other end of the phone, making it as boring and difficult as possible.

'The thing is, Clem, if I keep bailing you out, you're never going to stand on your own two feet.'

'Come on, Cal, don't act like I'm a child. I am trying to stand on my own two feet. I just need a little leg-up, a little shove. I can't even get to work – I'm literally sitting at the bus stop because my card won't work. I don't know what to do.'

She heard Callum cover the mic on his phone and say something to his wife. Realising they were being listened to compounded Clem's embarrassment. The loan was going through the approvals system of Mrs Callum and all the little Callums.

The phone un-muffled. 'I'm sorry, Clem, I have to say no. I can't keep adding to your debts. I don't mind holding off asking for the money you owe me, but I just can't keep giving it to you.'

'Oh fuck, Cal, seriously. Can you just skim me a tenner so I can get to work and back?'

'Sorry, Clem.'

He hung up and Clem stared at the phone, devastated. Were the shoe on the other foot, she thought, she would never hesitate to help him out. It hadn't actually occurred to her that he might say no. She got up off the bench and started the walk to the Ionian. At least it's a nice day, she thought.

The walk took an hour and forty-five minutes and she arrived sweaty and knackered. Ferocious T was leaning against the bar talking to a waitress who was covering Clem's post. They both watched Clem huff in.

'What's wrong with you?' Ferocious T asked.

'Had to walk, my fucking card got declined.'

Both Tina and the waitress nodded; this was not an unusual occurrence for any of them.

Clem got changed and took her seat on reception. There were hardly any bookings – the club was never as busy when the weather was good, because of the lack of windows and outside space. Clem would normally have been glad, but fewer punters meant fewer tips.

Tina had abandoned the bar and pulled up a chair by Clem, while Alan was leaning on the reception counter watching the few people in the bar nursing their drinks.

'Why they take so long?' he asked. 'They got smallest drink in the world.'

'Give them some peanuts, Al, help speed them along,' Tina suggested.

'Pssh – for free? What is this? No nuts.'

He went back to his office, muttering about profits. Tina turned to Clem. 'So I've just exchanged on a house in Walthamstow.'

'Holy shit, Tina – congratulations!' Clem wondered how this was possible on a bartender's salary, but it didn't seem polite to ask.

'Yeah, my parents gave me the deposit so I thought I'd best actually buy something, rather than drink, smoke and snort it.'

'That's awesome.'

'When you're back on your feet, there's a spare room with your name on it. I mean, I'm gonna paint over your name, but it's there nonetheless.'

Clem scowled at the feet phrase. 'That's the third time I've been told to get on my feet today.'

Tina held her hands up defensively. 'Sorry, kitten, no offence intended – but, well, it's a long walk from Walthamstow.' She backed away and returned to the bar and Clem felt guilty for snapping at her, hoping the offer of the room would still stand when she actually had got on her stupid feet.

They shut at twelve since it was so quiet. The bartenders approached Clem cautiously, as if she were a dangerous animal.

'Hey, Clem,' Tina said. 'We're not splitting tips tonight, you get the pot.' She pushed a plastic change bag over the reception desk.

Clem's eyes filled with tears and she shook her head, trying to stop herself sobbing. 'You guys don't have to do that.' Her voice cracked.

'It's no problem, woman. We need never mention it again.'

Clem hugged them and slung her bag over her shoulder, leaving the building and heading for the tube and feeling more than ever like London was winning.

35

Hen Night

Emma was still in her pyjamas when Clem arrived at the flat fully loaded with bags that spewed black feather boas, cock straws and various disposable tools for gender-specific organised 'fun'.

She threw down the bags in a stressy huff and perched on a chair, then immediately plucked her phone from her bag and tapped away at it, aghast.

'So, three of them still haven't replied, five of them haven't paid and from what I can gather from the several billion emails I've received, none of them can spell.'

Emma put the kettle on and poured tots of rum into two cups. 'What time does it kick off?'

'Oh god, Emma. I had to plan it all with the bridesmaids. They are so completely peach. It's like arranging a party with a box of cupcakes.'

Emma stared out of the kitchen window over the roofs of east London; below the window lay the APRC values books that Paul had thrown out. They had turned grey and were starting to bond irrevocably with the tarmac surface.

'Sounds hellish.'

'Anyway, let's celebrate – I've got a meeting with Title Studios next week,' Clem said.

'Really? Congratulations! That's so amazing, right? You're officially a professional screenwriter! Yay! No?'

Clem sighed. 'It will be good, but until someone sends me a cheque I'm still urchin skint, the bank are all over my case and Callum is chiming in with brotherly advice. That total bozo.'

'Chin up, treasure, I'll shout you tonight. It's double celebrating now – or triple, if you count my unoccupied uterus . . .'

'Yay!' Clem came over to where Emma stood and put her hands on her belly.

'Congratulations? Is that the right word?'

'Not really.'

Emma and Clem both looked at her belly and Clem pulled her in for a hug.

'How do you feel about it?'

'Equal parts relieved and gutted, I guess.'

They allowed a moment to pass; a moment's silence for the lost peanut. Emma loved Clem for the way she could acknowledge a feeling and help without saying a word.

'So, the plan . . .' said Clementine, sitting back down and reaching into her bag for a folder full of papers. 'This, I hope you can appreciate, is an Excel spreadsheet that Dorothy, the *head* bridesmaid has made. Colour-coded, Em, in a range of pinks.'

'Yikes.' Emma smirked, adding coffee to the rum and sitting at the table amongst the spreadsheets.

'Dorothy has done most of this so don't blame me for the sheer mundanity of it, OK?'

Emma nodded and sipped the coffee, trying not to laugh at Clementine's rising fury. 'What's a *head* bridesmaid?'

'Well I gather from her insistence on being referred to as the head bridesmaid that she feels she should have been maid of honour, so instead wants to make sure she has the appropriate authority over the other, non-head bridesmaid. Seriously, Emma – candyfloss, the pair of them.'

'Who is she? I've never even heard of a Dorothy.'

'Get this: Dorothy is Yasmin's PA.'

'Ah, that kind of makes sense, I guess, to have your PA on your crew.'

'Yeah, and Dorothy is good at it, from what I can gather. She made a spreadsheet, didn't she?'

Emma chuckled at Clementine's obvious disgust.

'So Dorothy is at the venue right now dressing everything up in black and white, as per the dress code. She's got all the usual bollocks: gifts and a photo album and a Mr & Mrs game, all that shit. My job ... Our job, is just to get Yas there on time. Dorothy wants us to blindfold her so she doesn't know where we're going.'

'Where are we going?'

'To a restaurant in Swiss Cottage, about five minutes from Yasmin's house. Dorothy says it's her favourite.'

'Won't she know, if we get her in a cab that stops five minutes later?'

'That's what I said, so Dorothy reckons we have to go round the block a bunch of times.'

'What's the point?'

'I have no idea, Em. I really don't. But Dorothy knows best so don't argue.'

At 6 p.m. they arrived at Yasmin's house. On the doorstep Clementine turned to Emma, reaching up to press the doorbell and said, 'Game face.'

Emma nodded. 'Game face.'

Yasmin answered the door in a dressing gown, her hair bundled on top of her head. She ushered them in and led them to the kitchen where she popped a bottle of champagne.

'I'm so glad you guys are here, I've been drinking alone for an hour!'

She beckoned them both to join her. Pouring three glasses they clinked ceremoniously. 'Before we go I want to ask you both something.'

Clementine caught Emma's eye and then grinned at Yasmin. 'Shoot.'

'Do you think I should marry him?'

They were caught off guard and Clementine choked on the sip of champagne she had taken. Emma looked at her glass and said with gravitas, 'Yasmin, if you have any doubts, you shouldn't. But you don't. Do you?'

'I don't. But do you?' She looked from one to the other.

'We just want you to be happy, Yas,' said Clem.

'Do you like him?' she challenged them.

Emma and Clementine nodded. 'He seems nice,' said Clementine.

Yasmin got up from the table, carrying her glass. 'You don't even *know* him,' she said accusingly. 'I want you both to promise me something.'

'What?'

'When he's back from the stag, you have to take him for dinner, and get to know him properly.'

'That sounds nice,' Emma said quietly.

'Promise,' Yasmin demanded.

'OK, yeah,' they replied in unison.

'Yay. OK. Good. I've got to go and finish getting ready.'

She went over to the stereo and cranked up what could only be described as gym pop. They heard her rush up the stairs and into her bedroom.

Clem and Emma sat in silence listening in awe to the chorus, which kicked in with 'I like to party' and included the words 'I'm a rich-ass bitch but I ain't too pretty to slap a ho, so all you girls getting shitty best kiss my toes, I like to party . . .'

'Good grief,' Emma muttered.

'I wish we'd got some Xanax,' said Clem.

Clementine necked the rest of the booze in her glass and leaned over to fill it up. Emma followed suit.

'Who'll pay?' asked Clem.

'Pay for what?'

'Pay for dinner. If we have to take him out and get to know him that sounds like our treat, doesn't it?'

'If he's marrying Yas, he'll be used to paying for dinner.'

Clem fiddled with a Jasper Conran salt shaker, turning it upside down to inspect it and depositing a small pile of granules on the table. 'I don't mind going for dinner. Let's set it up, and encourage him to go Dutch.'

They were most of the way through the bottle when Yasmin reappeared, and they wolf-whistled and applauded. She was wearing a deep red dress, a low-cut number that hung, shimmering, under her ass and showed off her long, tanned and waxed legs. She clutched her black handbag and rushed around the kitchen. Clem and Emma watched her calmly.

The cab ride was a one-way-system nightmare of squeals from the blindfolded Yasmin. 'This is so exciting!' she screeched, alarming the driver who was taking every opportunity to stare at her tits in his rear-view mirror. 'We could be going anywhere!'

We're not, though, we're literally not going anywhere. Emma stared out of the window and tried to brace herself for the onslaught of the evening.

When they finally pulled up, twenty-five minutes and twenty quid later, they led a tentative Yasmin through the busy restaurant, guiding her past tables full of noodles and sizzling plates.

The restaurant had prepared a back room that had its own small bar and several cocktail-style tables dotted about. Yasmin sensed the change of scene and wailed excitedly. In the room fifteen women sat looking pensively at each other and speaking in hushed tones. When Yasmin entered they gathered in the centre. The waiter closed the door behind them, shutting them off from the normal punters outside.

Emma moved round to join the others and Clem whipped off the blindfold with a flourish.

'SURPRISE!'

Yasmin screamed with delight and some hapless member of the group pressed play on Tom Jones's 'Sex Bomb' while Yasmin moved around the room, doling out hugs and kisses. Emma edged out of the way and headed to the table loaded with the makings of all the girliest cocktails. She slowly poured three cosmopolitans and turned to watch, sipping gratefully at the sour pink cliché.

After lots of high-pitched noise, more shots than is wise for a room full of women who've eaten nothing but canapés, and several dozen cocktails, they gathered in a circle to play 'Mr & Mrs'. Dorothy ('Darling, call me Dot') took the floor, and Emma had to hand it to her, she had presence. Before long everyone present knew Adam's favourite sex position (Clementine had screamed 'Missionary!' with delight), they knew what he liked Yasmin to cook (cheese on toast) and what her favourite thing about him was (his smile). Dot hushed the room for the next question.

'Which of Yasmin's friends once had a love tussle with Adam?'

What. The. Fuck.

Everyone chuckled and 'oohed' except Emma and Clem, who sat with their mouths hanging open.

'How do you know about that?' Clem asked loudly, drunk, as Emma turned crimson.

'About whom?' said Dot seductively, waiting for the big answer.

'About Adam and Emm ... ' Clem said, trailing off but not in time to save herself.

The room fell silent. They could hear the mumble of diners outside carrying on their evening blissfully unaware of the unfolding drama in the back room. Someone made a POP sound with their lips.

'Sorry, what?' Yasmin aimed the question at Emma. Emma stared at the floor.

In an attempt to diffuse the tension, quizmaster Dot laughed too loudly.

'WRONG answer. It was Abigail!'

Clem and Emma both looked at her. 'What?'

'The correct answer was Abigail.' She turned the card over and read the back.

'When Abigail and Adam were in little school, Adam asked Abi to sit next to him and they held hands for a whole story time.'

Fuuuuck.

Yasmin was glaring at Emma, who was trying to suffocate herself on her boa.

'I want to know what love tussle Emma's had with my fiancé,' said Yasmin.

All eyes pinged to Emma, who wished she could evaporate. Clem had her head in her hands and was looking at her through gaps in her fingers.

'Well, Emma? Let's hear it.'

Emma took a deep breath and tried to adopt an expression that suggested silly indifference. Instead she went bright red and stammered, 'Well, I mean, it's no big deal. The night we met him, at Cotton Club, I was totally off my face. We snogged for like, five seconds, it wasn't anything at all, then you came over and the rest is history. Seriously Yas, it wasn't anything. It didn't even seem worth mentioning.' She shot the last sentence at Clementine. The hens were spitting ocular daggers at Emma.

'You know what, EMMA?'

Oh god.

'He told me about it on our first date. I've been waiting for over a year for you to be honest with me.'

The room was hushed. Emma thought she heard someone hiss.

'He told you? And you didn't say anything?'

'*You* should have said something, Emma. And yeah, obviously he told me. We're getting married, he's my best friend, he wouldn't lie to me – not about anything and definitely not about you.'

'I'm sorry, Yasmin. I am really sorry.'

'Yeah, well, you know what, you should be.'

She turned and looked back at the girl asking the questions who was, along with everyone else, staring, horrified, at Emma.

'Keep going then,' she said to Dot. 'What else can we find out about my friends?'

When Emma saw Yasmin slip outside she joined her in the doorway.

Yasmin turned and saw her approaching. She folded her arms, expectant.

'I'm so sorry, Yas.'

'You get what I'm angry about, right? You had so many opportunities, Emma. I assumed you had just forgotten, because I know you black out sometimes, but you didn't, and you've told Clem and that really hurts. He's such a nice guy and you're always so horrible about him, and you know what? He told me to forgive you and forget about it. He's the one who said, don't hold it against her – it's only because of him we're even still friends.'

'Honestly, I didn't know it would last.'

'Yeah? Brilliant – thanks for the vote of confidence, Emma.'

'It's not like that. Obviously if I'd known that he was the one for you, I would never have ... I just, I figured you'd break up eventually and then we could laugh about it, but then it got serious and it seemed so much worse.'

'It was a snog in a club, when we were all strangers – who gives a shit? Seriously. You thinking it's a big deal makes it worse.'

'I wish you had said something. I've felt wretched about it this whole time.'

'Yeah, well. So have I. I thought we were best friends, Emma.'

'We were. We Are. I love you, man. I couldn't be more pleased that he's the one for you.'

'Yeah right.'

Yasmin took an angry drag of her e-cigarette and blew the vapour out into the street.

'Is that why I'm not in the wedding?'

Yasmin softened. 'Don't be daft, Em, I'm not that petty. You're not in the wedding because you hate girly stuff. Do you even want to be a bridesmaid?'

'Huh, no, not really.'

'You know what, Em, you're right. It's history.'

Emma didn't know if the snog was history, or she was.

'Your face. In there. That was pretty funny.' Yasmin looked at Emma fondly. 'Tell me something else.'

'What?'

'Why did we sit in a cab for half an hour, to come to a restaurant we could have walked to in fifteen minutes?'

Emma laughed. 'It was Dot's idea – she wanted it to be a surprise.'

'It was.'

'So, are we good?' Emma ventured. 'Friends?'

Yasmin linked arms with Emma and led her back into the restaurant. 'Friends. But you owe me a drink.'

Emma's relief was palpable. They entered the room and everyone looked up at them, expectant, poised for drama.

'We're back, everything is FIIIINE, everyone can be nice to Emma again,' shouted Yasmin, and everyone cheered.

'Shots for everyone!' Emma added, with instant regret. She went to the bar and ordered sixteen Jägers; it felt like a hundred quid well spent.

Clem went over and stood next to her at the bar. 'Mate, I am so sorry, I've got total foot-in-mouth disease at the moment.'

'No, it's good – maybe not the best timing, but at least it's out.'

Clem gave her a friendly nudge and took the tray of Jägers to the table in the middle of the room.

Part 3

36

Adam

'Shall we fuck with him?' Clem said quietly.

'No, dude.'

'Ah come on, let's mess with him a bit.'

'He's marrying Yasmin, he's getting messed with enough.'

They hushed as Adam returned from the men's room and took his seat at the table.

Emma, Clementine and Adam sat in a restaurant in West Hampstead. The tinkle of cutlery and low murmur of people having actual conversations seemed, to Emma, to really emphasise that the three of them were sitting in silence.

Clementine was staring to her left at a wall, disengaged. Emma wondered whose responsibility it was to lead the conversation. Then she wondered what they were supposed to talk about. She thought she should probably give it a pop.

'So, are you excited for the big day?'

'Jesus Christ, Emma,' Clementine said. 'Is that the best you can do?'

Emma giggled nervously and Adam, about to reply,

clamped his mouth shut and stared, wide-eyed, at his empty glass.

The next time a waiter walked past Adam signalled to him decisively and ordered the second most expensive bottle of red. Emma sensed Clem warm up a bit.

'Do you know why we're here, Adam?' Clem asked, as if it were his fault.

Adam seemed to look around for an exit. Emma felt sorry for him.

'Yas said she doesn't want you guys to be strangers at the wedding. She was like' – he broke into Yasmin's accent – '"I know everyone on your side of the aisle and you don't know Clem from Em."'

His impression was spot on and he visibly savoured the reaction when they laughed. He seemed by a notch, to relax.

'I do think it's strange of her not to join us. But she said she wanted you to get to know me as an individual, not me as her husband, although honestly I hope the two are not that different.'

'Why do you look so scared?' Clem asked.

Emma punched her in the arm. 'Ignore her; she's being deliberately obtuse. It's a good idea – we want to get to know you, we're interested to find out more about the lucky guy that tamed Yasmin.' She didn't mean it to sound sarcastic but it unmistakably did. When the waiter returned with the wine everyone was relieved.

'Do you guys know what you're having?' Adam asked, studying the menu.

Clem huffed her chest up and over the table so she was all boob, and pouted. 'I'm not eating, I'm on a diet. I've got to be *so skinny* for the *wedding*.' She was doing an impression of

Yasmin and watching Adam closely. He kept his head bent over the menu; he didn't react at all, but they could clearly see his ears burn.

'Stop being a dick, Clem,' Emma said. Clementine rolled her eyes and resumed her staring contest with the wall.

Adam put his menu down. The wine he had gulped greedily was already working on him and it was clear he had resolved to take some control of the situation.

'So I heard the hen was a great success.' He smiled at them, shooting Clem a look that said simultaneously 'please love me' and 'go fuck yourself'. He went on: 'Thank you for making Yasmin feel so special. The stag do was good. We went clay-pigeon shooting in Wales.'

'Is Yas being a bridezilla about the big day?' asked Emma.

'She's surprisingly calm about it all actually. We got really lucky with the venue, and she has the dress and flowers sorted now and that's what she was most worried about getting right. Everything seems to be going remarkably smoothly, thanks largely to the girls.' He nodded generously at Clem, who yawned.

Adam continued undeterred. 'Sorry, it must be so boring for you guys. I bet it's all she talks about.'

'No, it's not boring at all, we're really looking forward to it,' said Emma. 'And she must have mentioned that we might be working together?'

'She mentioned you had a meeting. I've been reading your blog, by the way – it's very funny. You're a great writer.'

'Thanks.' Emma was surprised; he didn't seem the reading type.

'I sent it to a friend of mine, actually. We used to work together. She's just joined an exciting little start-up and she asked me to let you know she'd like to meet you, if you're willing?'

He refilled all three glasses. 'Yasmin suggested it, in fact, getting you two in a room. She mentioned you're not really happy at APRC?'

Clem snorted into her glass.

'Her name's Erica – we put you guys on the same table at the wedding, so you'll meet there if not before. She came round recently actually, Yasmin tried to set her up with Timmy . . .'

'*That* guy. How did it go?' Clem said.

'Not well – though possibly better than it went with you, which is doubly impressive because I'm pretty sure Erica is gay.'

All three laughed and the tension was broken. Clem, evidently, had decided to stop trying to get a rise out of Adam. The wine was lubricating the conversation and making everything easier and more fun. Good old wine.

Clem turned round and joined in properly for the first time that evening. 'Sorry if I came across as obnoxious that night. Timmy was a total spring job.'

Adam shook his head. 'I know. It was a bit painful, wasn't it? I told her to give you a heads-up. For some reason she's decided Timmy is her pet project. She likes a challenge but honestly, he's single for a reason.'

'What's the reason?' asked Emma.

'He's enormously boring.'

'Right?' Clem exclaimed. 'I'm so glad you said that, I thought it was just me.'

'You and all the other women in the world.' The laughter diffused any remaining tension and the rest of the night was all the way fun. Adam was engaging, interesting and quick. Every time he made them laugh he seemed to enjoy himself more. Soon they forgot the Yasmin connection altogether.

When the bill arrived Adam took control, thanking the waitress and sliding the leather fold to his side of the table, peeping at it and pushing his card in simultaneously, in a move that he must have known was smooth.

Clementine and Emma made polite objections but he laughed gently, holding up a hand.

'Really, I insist. I'm sure you both had better things to do than humour my future wife tonight,' he said knowingly.

'Well, thanks, Adam,' said Clementine. 'It's actually been really nice – it wasn't a chore at all. Yasmin was right to make this happen; it's going to be good getting to know you.'

Emma thought he looked so sweet and happy in that moment. Both girls knew why Yasmin was marrying him, and that she was lucky. Emma raised her glass, still half full, and proposed a toast: 'To you guys, and no one else.'

They drained their glasses.

On the street outside, Emma and Clem watched Adam hail a cab and step in like a proper executive. They linked arms as they wound their way towards the Underground.

'Well that was a bit perfectly charming, wasn't it?' Clem said.

'I know, right? I feel thoroughly warmed by the whole affair.'

'Maybe that's the difference between house red and proper wine.' Clem was waving her other arm about. 'Proper wine makes you have a good time, and shit wine makes you angry.'

'Makes *you* angry,' Emma corrected.

'Yeah, makes me angry, makes you cry.'

'True. Let's try and only drink expensive wine from now on.'

'Deal.'

37

The Cat

Emma stood with her dad in the small, cemented backyard of his house. They were staring at the ivy. At some point it had been an elegant climber; now it was a monster, threatening to swallow the wall completely.

'I haven't seen him for at least a week.'

Emma had been summoned. The cat, Tumnus, was missing.

'Well yeah, Pops, but the house is a wreck. He probably has another family now.'

'Treacherous bastard. After everything we've been through.'

'What have you been through?'

'A fortune in cat food for a start.'

They went inside and Emma stopped in the doorway. The kitchen was much worse than the last time.

'Dad, this isn't OK. You're like one of those people off the TV. You're a hoarder.'

Daniel sat at the table, turning the radio off. He scanned the room. It was shambolic.

'You're right, Emma. It's just that it's got to that point where I don't know what to do any more.'

'Yeah, I know the feeling.' She picked up a pair of rubber gloves and went under the stairs for a bucket and any cleaning products she could find. She dragged out mops and a broom. 'But we do know what to do. And we're going to do it right now.'

It took hours. Emma left her dad in the kitchen with the washing-up while she tackled the upstairs bedrooms, bathroom and hallway. They hoovered and mopped and dusted everything in sight. The only room they left was the music room. They stood in the doorway and peered into the gloom. Instruments were everywhere.

'I'll do you a deal, Dad.'

'Go on,' he said.

'You can keep this room however you like, I won't clean it or throw anything out. But you have to promise you'll wash up every day and hoover every week. Like, at least. Please.'

'I'll need some sort of reminder system.'

'I'll remind you.'

'You're too busy for that, Emma. I'll set an alarm.'

They went through to the kitchen, exhausted by the effort. Emma put the kettle on and made them drinks. 'It looks so much better.'

Daniel nodded. 'Thank you so much, Em. You're so good at this stuff – you should be a life coach.'

'Yeah right.'

'How's work going?'

'It's a total nightmare. I hate every day more than the last. We're working with a fracking company.'

'Good grief, Emma – surely you have to leave?'

She joined him at the table. 'What? Are you serious? What about the bills and the rent?'

'There are more important things in life than bills. Did I not teach you that?'

'Well yeah, but—'

'But what? But fracking? No way, Emma. Really. I thought you were doing well there. I bet you can find something else without too much trouble.'

'Maybe, Pops. Maybe.'

'You could always be a cleaner. You're brilliant at it.'

They touched cups.

'Cheers.'

38

Executive Mode

Clem sat in a cool office, drinking cooled cucumber water and listening to cool people tell her she was their new favourite writer. She was letting the kindness glaze her like she was a doughnut – every sentence seemed to plaster over one of the cracks that had formed in her ego since Jordan had thrown her off the roof.

Caroline had warned her that this meeting would be a schmooze, that she should take a pinch of salt in her pocket, but she was falling for it, every lovely bit of it.

'The thing I love most about *Moonshiners*,' said Kirsty, the development executive, a woman in her early forties with a kind face, a designer jacket and no shoes on, 'is the depth of the characters. It's so refreshing to have that combination of a modern, female voice and these brutal historical male characters.'

Everything she said had the long 'a's of the super posh: *marrle chaaraacters*. Clem had to remember not to mimic the accent when she spoke – which she hadn't, for some time.

'What was your inspiration? Where does this amaaaarzing story come from?'

'I've always loved history, especially the history of London, and what I was really writing about is the fact that London will never change. You could literally base this story right now, on the same streets, with the same characters, and it would ring true.'

Next to the development executive sat the executive producer, nodding enthusiastically. 'That's why it's so epic – we could set it any time.'

Clem's heart lurched happily. *We could set it* . . . rang in her ears. They were going to set it.

'We'd really like to progress the project with you. We think you've got something here.'

'Great, thank you.' Clem wasn't sure what else to say. There was a light knock and a young woman poked her head round the door. 'Kirsty, sorry to interrupt but apparently Artichoke's had an accident.'

'Oh for god's sake!' Kirsty stood in a huff. 'That little bastard. Clementine, you'll have to excuse me. It was wonderful to meet you and we'll be in touch with Caroline to discuss the details.' She kissed Clem and gave her a media hug – touched both her shoulders – and left the room.

'Her dog's in the office today, probably done a poo on the carpet,' said the executive producer, chuckling.

'Ah, I thought it was her kid.'

The executive producer stood up and shook Clem's hand firmly, leading her towards the door. 'Thanks for coming in today, Clementine, it's a real treat to meet you. I am very much looking forward to working together. We'll be in touch.'

Clem left the office and walked a polite distance before calling Caroline.

'What does it mean, Caroline?'

'They're going to call me with an offer this afternoon, probably around the 10k mark. And I'm going to turn it down and ask for 20.'

Clem did some quick maths: twenty thousand pounds would get her most of the way out of debt, and all the way out of Malcolm's house.

'Holy shit, that's amazing.'

'Well don't go giddy, Clem, we'll likely stick on 15, maybe less. Still, it's a start. I'll call you when we've got a solid offer. Congratulations, darling.'

She hung up and Clem sat for a moment on a wall, savouring this new feeling. She felt relieved, elated, and for the first time in a very long time, she felt safe.

She got up and checked her pockets to see if she had enough money for the Tube to work. It was hard not to appreciate the irony of having to walk, again, and she set off, smiling.

39

Friday Feeling

The office felt particularly oppressive today. Emma was keeping count of the number of times she heard the phrase 'Friday feeling'. Ross was staring anxiously at a presentation. Gemma's usual abject lack of interest came with a side of youthful hysteria. The accounts department were having an actual party. They had a selection of snacks on paper plates and someone had brought in a guitar – they were going mental. In his office Adrian was shouting down the phone, enjoying a brag about the weekend. He was smacking the table and squealing at intervals. Emma was sullen, exhausted and hungry.

The only thing she could find to be positive about was that it was Friday, and tomorrow was Yasmin's wedding.

She knew that at this very moment, Yasmin, Clem and Dot the wonder PA were being styled and massaged and were watching Yasmin transform into a princess all ready for the rehearsal dinner.

Who needs to rehearse having dinner?

Emma scowled. Beneath the layers of jealousy, resentment and rejection there lay the blind, unsophisticated rage of PMT. The knowledge was both a relief and an irritation.

'Emma, can I grab you for a sec?'

'Sure thing, Adrian,' she said brightly, minimising Etsy and pushing her chair back.

In his office Emma listened while Adrian spoke at length about his weekend plans, which included golf, supporting Chelsea and a Michelin-starred blah blah blah. Emma's brain filtered out information that she didn't expressly need, and thought instead about hats.

Since her week off, Emma's attitude towards APRC had been gradually rotting. It was a sagging balloon of ambivalence. She saw in Adrian and ICF everything that was wrong with humanity. She longed to tell him to shut his pie-hole and shove fracking up his arse.

Eventually after his long gloat, he nodded to the sideboard behind her, on which stood a pink gift bag. It contained a bottle of champagne and a card. Adrian asked that she take it to the wedding and hand it to Yasmin on his, and all at APRC's behalf. Emma agreed, cooed appropriately and slunk back to her desk.

Eventually Adrian left for the weekend, and as the double doors clicked closed, a palpable change in atmospheric pressure swept through the office. Nobody was doing any more work today.

The email itself, by Emma's standards, was largely innocuous, but retrospect wreaks havoc with reason. The subject was 'Stupid Shit Machine'.

Hey honey, I wrote a new blog about selling out called
'We're All Fracked' – have a look.
In other news, Adrian's left for his capitalist paradise
for the day (it's like gangster's paradise but for fathead
white men in stupid socks). Shall we sack this off and
go on a booze binge? I need to spend all the money
I don't get from my 'promotion'. And I wanna do
Yasmin's wedding with a f*cking massive hangover.
xx

She even starred the 'fuck' because she thought it was funny.

At the same moment as she pressed send, a boulder was released from a great height directly above her head. It slipped gently off the precipice of her consciousness and began a steady, heavy plummet. As it gained speed the colour in her cheeks rose up in a bright vermilion. Her lips parted, and her lungs paused their good work to see what all the fuss was about. Time stopped, her skin froze and the room turned 360 degrees, *Matrix*-style. She felt the air conditioning jeer at her.

Whaaaaaaathaveyouuuuuuuuduuuuuuunnnnn?

Emma shut her eyes. Disbelief was in a fistfight with denial. The boulder hit Emma in the throat; she gasped, then her eyes snapped open and focused on the message she had just sent, irretrievably, to Adrian.

She stared, agape, at the message, the keywords throbbing, bold and brazen. She rushed past Gemma and into Adrian's office; he would have left his computer on, a token 'fuck you' to the environment. She shook his mouse to wake it up – could she get into his email and delete it? Or was he already looking at it on his phone? Maybe he was on the tube and she had time. She looked at his emails. It had been opened. For a moment she had an overwhelming urge to put her things in her bag and simply walk away, no looking back. A rush of anger tried to replace the rock, which had landed right in the middle of guilt city.

She felt faint as she returned to her desk. An email from Adrian blonked into her inbox. She felt her skin burn and her hands shake. She closed her eyes. This was a nightmare.

The reply from Adrian said simply:

Let's talk on Monday.

She hit reply and stared at the screen for eleven minutes. Then she reached around the screen and without clicking save on any of the open documents, she held the power button for five seconds, so that the whole sorry mess powered down with a gentle but final humph.

She picked up her things in slow motion and stood.

'Hey, you guys.'

Everyone looked up.

'I'm going to go now, I don't think I . . . I don't feel . . . '

She didn't feel like lying and she didn't feel like telling the truth.

'I'll see you on Monday.'

She could hear Gemma saying something about the time but all she could see was the exit.

Her journey home was careless to the point of suicidal and it was largely luck that got her there in one piece. Once at her front door she called Clem, who answered with a cheer that was the vocal equivalent of pink prosecco.

'Emmmmma! I can't really talk – I've got a face covered in mud, and cucumber in my eyes! People actually do this shit! Oops, sorry. You're on speakerphone, Em, so be polite.'

Emma considered just hanging up, but with as much enthusiasm as she could manage to project, she said, 'Yay, good for you guys! Just checking in, making sure you're having a great day.'

She heard Yasmin say something in the background and Clem giggled. 'Em, I have to go, we're getting our nails did! Mine are going to have patterns!'

She sounded happy and Emma wasn't so self-absorbed that she was going to spoil it, but she urgently needed to tell the email story; she needed to hear it out loud.

'Have a great day you guys, lots of love, see you tomorrow.'

She hung up before they could rub it in any further.

Emma tried to force herself to have a cry as she stomped up the stairs, but she didn't feel tearful, it was deeper and more placid than that. It was a resignation, a whole body funk.

Oh

God

Oh

God.

She peeked in the big cardboard boxes full of handbags as she passed, hoping she might find an elegant number that would mean at least one of the pieces of her wedding outfit would be new. But they were the pink cowboy hat of handbag designs and all she found was studs, leopard print and pleather. In the flat she found Paul, sitting at the kitchen table, on his computer and singing along to Al Green.

Then she remembered the bottle of champagne on Adrian's sideboard.

Then she cried.

40

Your Mum

Clem and Yasmin sat in beige leather chairs, wearing thick white dressing gowns, with pale green gloop on their faces, cucumber on their eyes and pink prosecco in their hands.

'How's Emma?' Yasmin asked gleefully.

'She sounds miserable,' Clem answered, taking a happy sip from the ice-cold flute.

'She *always* sounds miserable,' Yasmin pouted through her avocado face.

Clementine, her loyalty firmly elsewhere, murmured by way of response. Yasmin took her lack of solidarity as a slight.

'Is it because she's not in the wedding?'

'No, it's because she hates her life.'

Yasmin rolled her eyes, conveying it even through her cucumber shades.

Yasmin's mum, Gloria Attali, was swaddled in several sheep worth of woollen robe when she directed her face masseuse to wheel her over to the girls. She sat beaming at them from under a head full of rollers.

'So, Clementine, when are you going to find yourself a lovely husband, then?'

'When there's a sale on at the lovely husband warehouse, Mrs A.'

'Mum, don't be so presumptuous. What if Clem's a lesbian?'

'Lesbians can have husbands, too, Yasmin – haven't you read the news?' She gave a big, wobbly-chinned pout to Clem. 'You're allowed to wed nowadays.'

'I'm not a lesbian, Mrs A. I just haven't met Mr Right.'

She conceded to the cliché. Yasmin gave her mum enough beef; Clem could live without asserting herself on this one.

'Yasmin says you've got a film star for a boyfriend anyway, Clemmy? She showed me a picture – he's good-looking and rich and famous and everything.'

'Maybe on the outside, Mrs A, but he's a horrid little troll under the skin.'

Yasmin's mum leaned forward, gut all over the place. 'Well, it's not like it was in our day – who needs men any more? You girls have got it so good, you can do anything you like, darling. You got your jobs and your own money and your own cars, why would you have a man take that from you? No one gets married any more, according to *Loose Women* anyway.'

'Mum, leave her alone, come and sit by me.'

The long-suffering Mrs A picked up her skirts and plunked herself down by Yasmin with thinly veiled disdain. 'I'm not paying for your stylist so you can look like a salad, Yasmin.'

'Mum, stop being such a pain. Go and get a pedicure or something.'

Gloria pouted. 'No, I'm waiting for you two. After tomorrow I think I will never see you again.' She turned her attention to Clementine, talking directly past Yasmin's face. 'You'll visit, won't you, Clemmy? When this one is too busy being married and important and clever for her old mum.'

'Stop being so dramatic, Mum.'

'I'll probably still be living round the corner, Mrs A.'

Gloria dismissed the notion with a wave. 'Psh. Not you, Clemmy, you mark my words. Beautiful, clever girl like you.'

Clem smiled and Yasmin tutted loudly. 'Shut. Up. Mum.'

'No, you shut up Yasmin, be nice for once in your life,' Gloria snapped back.

Clem knew the drill. 'Hey, both you princesses play nice. Let's get our nails done together. Mrs A, of course I'll visit – we both will, and you can come to my mansion in LA any time you like.'

Gloria grinned and kissed Yasmin on the side of her head, taking a big piece of avocado with her chin. 'You're both good girls.'

She bobbled off to some other area of the salon and began shouting cheerfully at some hapless teenager.

Clem watched her go. 'Does Adam know that's what you're going to turn into?'

Yasmin laughed and shook her head, saying fondly, 'I'm trying to keep them apart, at least until after the wedding.'

41

Stupid Shit Machine

Emma woke up with a headache and a sharp pang of angst when she remembered the email. She listened to Paul making coffee. Adrian had played a blinder. 'Let's talk on Monday' was genius. He'd know that Emma would spend the weekend stewing. It was a punishment that required absolutely no effort on his part.

She grudgingly gave credit where it was due. She also resolved to absolutely not fall for it. When she had arrived home the night before her tears had been met with laughter. Paul had cheered when she'd read aloud the email. The more she'd cried the harder he'd laughed until she couldn't help but join in. Over a bottle of red he'd convinced her it only mattered if she cared about it. 'Fuck that clown,' he had yelled happily, spinning her round. 'If you get fired you're a legend. If you don't, nothing happened. Either way, who gives a shit?' He agreed that the punishment was the purgatory of the weekend and they had drunk to ignoring it. 'Fuck Mondays!'

Paul knocked on the door with a cup of coffee, which he put on the bedside table and waved the wedding invite at her.

Emma sat up. 'You're cheery.'

'Free booze, dancing and girls in heels. What's not to like?'

'What's Lucy up to today? Speaking of girls.'

'She's on a research trip.' He perched on the edge of the bed. 'Did you dream about Adrian?'

'No. But I did have a brainwave and texted the night security dude who has hidden the champagne in my desk, so Adrian need never know I added insult to injury. Or petty larceny to insult or whatever.'

'Clever Emma.'

'Damn straight.'

They spent the morning doing laps between the bathroom and the full-length mirror in Emma's room. Paul was trying to get the perfect ruffle in his hair and Emma was staring, panic-stricken, at a plastic storage box full of shoes. She picked up a pair of mint green stilettos and held them up next to the blue dress she had draped over her head.

'I could power clash, right?'

'If anyone can power clash, Em, it's you,' Paul said without taking his eyes off his hair.

Emma slipped the shoes on and looked around Paul at her reflection. 'I don't remember ever in my life buying a pair of mint green stilettos.'

'Maybe one of your more exuberant lovers left them here.'

'Or I got drunk and bought them on eBay.'

'Or you've had them since you last went pants shopping, in 2005.'

She kicked the shoes to the side.

'Or I could go blue and yellow?' She held up a bright yellow belt and waited for his attention. He looked past his reflection in the mirror and shook his head.

'It's a bit Ikea.'

Emma slung the belt back in the accessories area of the cupboard (she called it the accessories area, a stranger might call it a jumble of tat). She bit her lip and searched for something else mint green. The pre-party tension that went with getting ready was jangling her nerves. Also she'd had three cups of coffee.

'I'm weirdly nervous.'

'Shall we smoke a joint?' Paul asked.

Emma shook her head. 'It's hard enough trying to do this sober. Tell me though, green shoes? I'll be able to walk in them for exactly forty-five minutes by the way. Or this leafy thing, glittery thing, flowers fascinator, blue brooch, yellow hat?' She held up each item in turn and looked up at him imploringly.

'Em, you're just listing things I don't care about.'

'Just tell me what looks nice,' she said, exasperated.

He turned from the mirror and surveyed the various items strewn over the bed. He pointed. 'Green shoes, orange thing in hair, whatever that fancy thing is. Call it a primary-colour palette. Bang. Done.'

Emma screwed up her face. 'They don't go. Also, green and orange aren't primary colours.'

Paul shrugged, left the room and put on his pre-party playlist.

Emma loved living with Paul but in these rare moments she really wished there were a girl in the house, preferably a stylist with a shitload of accessories. When her make-up was as good as she could get it, she slipped into the shoes and went into the lounge. Paul greeted her with a long slow wolf whistle.

'Daymn gurrl, you fine,' he said.

'Thanks, buddy. Shall we go?'

'Yeah, maybe we can get a pre-ordeal drink on the way.' He glanced at her small bag. 'Haven't we got them a present?'

'Who's we? There's a bottle of champagne in my desk drawer with their names on.'

Emma plunked down one step at a time, and her shoes hurt by the time they got to street level. She started to totter towards the tube station but Paul stopped her.

'You are rubbish at being a girl, you know that?' He hailed a cab.

'You're really good at it,' she giggled as they plunged into the taxi.

They arrived at the hotel in good time and made a beeline for the bar. The guests were milling about in their finery and from her vantage point Emma spotted Adam, red-eared and looking nervous. He wore a traditional tuxedo and was surrounded by groomsmen. Emma never tired of the penguin-ness of a group of men in matching suits. The hotel was a large ornate homage to cigar smoking, dealmakers and women who walk elegantly in expensive heels. Emma was surprised by the number of proper grown-ups in the room and wondered if they constituted Adam's family or if, as a couple, Yasmin and Adam preferred the company of serious, grey-haired people who she imagined knew terms like 'hedge fund'.

Paul and Emma stayed rooted to the bar, greeting people as they came over for drinks. Emma loyally introduced Paul to anyone she knew and by the time they were called through for the ceremony they were two bloody marys and a gin and tonic more relaxed.

They took seats near the back, surrounded by chandeliers, lilies, the whole bit. French doors opened onto a large courtyard garden and the chairs had big bows on the back. Paul scanned the room. 'This is well kitsch.'

'It's a wedding, idiot, that's the point.'

Adam waited and whispered nervously to the groomsmen. Emma made a note to dance with the tall one when she was drunk enough to ask.

The music swelled and the room hushed. They stood up and Emma peered up the aisle along with everyone else. When Yasmin appeared there was an appreciative gasp. Emma bit her lip; Yasmin looked the most beautiful she ever had and stepped slowly down the aisle surrounded by flower girls throwing rose petals before her.

Clementine followed, looking gorgeous if slightly green. The make-up artist had done her best and coated her hangover in a thick foundation that had since developed a patina of sweat. She smiled wanly at Emma and Paul as she passed. The flowers in her hair made her look a bit like she'd been at a festival for two days. Emma struggled not to laugh. Dot the PA and Adam's sister (who looked exactly like him if he were tubby and dressed in drag) walked in unison behind Clementine, taking the whole process seriously enough for the lot of them. Dot, on noticing Emma, turned her smile sour for half a beat. An expression that Emma caught and returned.

The ceremony was short and sincere and Paul sighed romantically and rested his head on Emma's shoulder while the couple *I do'd*. Emma got surprisingly close to tears. Adam and Yasmin walked up the aisle, kissing guests and adopting well-practised photo faces. When they got to Emma and Paul, Yas dropped the pose long enough to comedy roll her eyes and leaned over to give them both a kiss.

'Thanks for coming,' she said, and as Adam tugged gently on her arm to follow him, she whispered, 'Love you guys,' and put the photo face firmly back on.

They emerged in a hallway where Adam and Yasmin stood on ceremony, receiving their guests like royal dignitaries. Paul and Emma stood at the back where the canapés were likely to come from and drank.

The call for dinner went up and Paul and Emma were distraught to find they'd been split up and put on tables with strangers. Paul's table consisted entirely of women.

'What the hell, Em?' he asked. 'Am I being *Four Wedding*ed . . . ? Have I slept with any of these girls? Emma?! Help meeeeeeee!' he called in mock desperation as a small tide of people swept him away.

Emma took her seat next to a woman with an afro. She wore a tropical dress and impossibly high heels, a bunch of flowers complete with nesting bird balanced delicately amongst her curls. As soon as she sat down the woman turned to her and with excitement yelled, 'Emma? I'm Erica. I'm so excited to meet you! Finally!'

Emma was surprised and flattered at the enthusiasm and shook her hand firmly.

'You too,' she replied, trying not to sound surprised.

'I LOVE your blog. When Adam sent it to me I nearly wee'd. I've been looking for exactly you for so long. I love that guy, he's a genius.' Not noticing that Emma hadn't agreed she went on, 'You might not think it, to look at him, but that guy knows his shit.' She leaned across to the bottles in the centre, completely ignoring the rest of the guests pulling up chairs around the table. 'Red?' Erica said and Emma held up her glass. 'Did he tell you anything about me?'

'Only that you work in publishing and you would be on my table.'

'Yes I do, and here I am,' she said, cheerfully.

They were interrupted by the announcement that Mr and Mrs Adam Harley were entering the room. Everyone stood and cheered as Yasmin, looking positively thrilled, and Adam walked through the crowd to the top table. As they took their seats Erica turned back, in full flow.

'So, my company is just a start-up at the moment, but it's growing fast. I'm in charge of commissioning development, which is fancy chat for finding talent and making them rich.'

'Sounds nice.'

'It is, it really is. So I love your work and I want you to come and meet a team I'm putting together. We're changing the way women consume media. How would you feel about joining a features department?'

'I would feel warm and fuzzy about it,' said Emma, feeling the red wine join the gin and vodka party in her belly.

'I reckon with your voice and my team, it could be the new frontier for women's media. I mean really, magazines are so ridiculously old-fashioned, don't you think?'

'Definitely.'

'The way we use technology now means there's a gap in the market, or so I have a bunch of market research goons all telling me. We could carve out a little niche for someone with your style.'

Erica sipped her wine and went on, with seemingly unstoppable enthusiasm.

'Women don't want to be told that they should be thin and have shiny hair any more, you know? I don't think *women* ever really were interested in that stuff; I think it's been shoved down our gullets for so long that we forgot we couldn't give a damn what other people look like – or at least, we shouldn't.'

Emma agreed. 'Hear hear!'

'We're so much more cerebral than that, don't you think? And I love your sardonic undertone; what you produce is so much more interesting than usual women's media, but still completely feminine. I love it.'

Emma was so delighted she could have cried. She felt like this was the first conversation she had ever had. She wanted to kiss this beautiful woman on her gorgeous glossy lips. She looked across the room at the top table, trying to catch Clem's eye. Clem was deep in conversation with the tall groomsman and Adam was staring lovingly at Yasmin. Emma felt a rush of love for them all.

'What are you doing at the moment, work-wise?' Erica asked, breaking a hunk of bread off the artisan loaf in the centre of the table.

'I'm currently extracting myself from corporate advertising,' she replied.

'Good grief, how awful. How long will it take to shake that nightmare?'

Emma smiled. 'I reckon around thirty days from Monday, actually.'

'Perfect. I'm setting up the meetings right now. This is going to be so outrageously brilliant.'

Emma's favourite parts of a wedding were the ceremony and the speeches. They were the elements with the most personality; everything else was just the budget.

Adam stood up and tapped his fork on his glass. The room hushed. He said all the requisite thank yous and then kicked in to the good bit. Emma loved him for looking scared but delivering his speech like a pro.

'The first time I knew I loved her, she was driving through Kensington listening to the radio. They were playing 'Sweet Like Chocolate' and she sang along at the top of her voice. She knew all the words. I was staring at her, realising that I was completely in love with this woman, when she turned to me and said, "Oh, sorry, I forgot you were in the car."'

He paused while the crowd laughed.

'I know it might sound like an odd moment to fall in love, but once she'd noticed I was there, she dedicated the rest of the track to me. She even missed a set of lights because she was using her hand for a mic and wasn't in gear.'

He looked at her and placed a hand on her shoulder; she put her hand on his. Emma's heart did an involuntary squeal.

'Naturally it's not her taste in music that makes me love her. Rather it's the enthusiasm that she approaches everything with. Be it work, relationships, attempts at cooking . . . '

He let the crowd respond to the slight with the customary 'Oooh!' and touched Yas affectionately on the head. She wiped under her mascara, where tears were threatening her foundation. 'To quote Clem, her lifelong best friend, "Yasmin doesn't muck about".'

Everyone laughed, and Emma knew Clem almost certainly didn't say 'muck'.

'She knows what she wants, and she gets it; she works harder and with more passion than anyone I know. She has inexhaustible supplies of enthusiasm and for me, that's just the most valuable gift in the world. When we're together I feel like I could do anything, no matter how scary or insurmountable it may seem. That I could go anywhere, no matter how far away or hard to get to. I know that I will spend the rest of my life being braver, because Yas has my back. She also has my head, my heart, and my undying love. So, friends and family, please be upstanding, raise your glasses, and allow me to introduce you to my best friend, the love of my life, my wife, Mrs Yasmin Harley.'

From her place at the top table Clementine caught Emma's eye. Yasmin kissed Adam and they whispered at each other, the small voices of people in love, people sharing something that nobody else will ever know. Then they kissed again and sat down and everyone took a deep breath and tidied away their tears.

The first dance was 'Sweet Like Chocolate' and they laughed their way through it. Clem and Emma stood on the sidelines with equal parts happiness, envy and relief. Clem called it the wedding emotion cocktail and sighed into her fourteenth glass of champagne.

'So what's your exit strategy?' Emma asked.

'Bitch, I've got a room upstairs. If I don't get lucky with one of these filthy granddads you are more than welcome to the other half of my king-sized suite.'

'Are you sure? I think I see Timmy giving it some welly on the dance floor. That's him, right?' She pointed at a cherub-faced businessman doing something resembling the twist with a classic dad-dance overture.

'Sure is. I bet he has sex like he dances, ' Clem said. From across the dance floor they watched as Timmy lassoed and reeled in Erica, who flung her hair wildly around and shimmied closer to him, moving with actual grace.

There was a midnight cheese buffet. Lots of dancing, lots of heartfelt chat with Yasmin, possibly some with Adam. There were lights and shots and then there was a bathroom and the curtains fell.

Clem and Emma woke up in a bright room with a massive bed. Emma peeped under the duvet – she had tried and failed to take her dress off and now it was wrapped around her like a toga. Her shoes, tights and accessories were in a rough pile nearby. She checked the state of her hangover and decided she was still drunk and feeling pretty chipper. Clem rolled over and tucked the duvet under her chin, grinning at her. Emma correctly diagnosed her as equally hung under.

'Water,' Emma whispered, pointing at the glass next to Clem, who passed it over.

'You and Paul are so cute together. Don't you secretly think he's the one?' she said.

Emma sniggered and turned to face her with a furrowed brow.

'What makes you say that?'

Clem laughed. 'You threw up in the hedge and he held your hair and rubbed your back. It was adorable.'

Emma had no recollection of an interlude with a hedge.

'Honestly, it's like someone going on about me and you being perfect for each other. He's going to marry Lucy anyway, he said so yesterday. He said I could be the best man though.'

'He was drunk.'

'He's never said that before and he's been plenty drunker.'

Clem yawned. 'Maybe you and I *are* perfect for each other.' Her arm emerged from the duvet and she squidged the general area of Emma's boob. 'Honka.'

They giggled.

'I thought you were perfect for the tall groomsman. Why isn't he getting honkered right now?' Emma asked.

Clem rolled her eyes. 'Gorgeous but boring. Unfortunately.'

'That's your problem, Clem – you'll always be the interesting one.'

'I know, darling, it's a curse. Surely it shouldn't be that hard to find someone who isn't a complete yawn.'

Emma turned and lay on her back. 'I just want someone to laugh with instead of at.'

'He was also an estate agent, though, so I made him fall in love with me – in case he comes in useful.'

'Sterling work, Clem. You're a saint.'

'I know, I deserve a medal.'

Clem reached over the side of the bed, picked up the

phone and dialled zero, ordered coffee and breakfast for two and turned back to Emma. 'Conversational highlights?'

Emma thought about it. 'Probably Adam's sister – we had a pretty blinding chat about fridge space at Christmas, which must take the boring brownie. She went on to tell me about booking online shopping from Tesco three weeks in advance because the slots fill up.'

'You got off lightly; she was at the spa yesterday and took great pleasure in recounting her bikini wax experiences. I had to shut her down when she referred to it as her Hairy Fun.'

'Good grief,' Emma cringed.

'I know. I told her I call mine a Fusty Maud.'

The bed shook with their laughter.

'Holy crap; that might take the brownie.'

Clem nodded wryly and pressed her head back into the pillow, still chuckling. 'Anyway, she'd already used her Tesco material at the rehearsal dinner.'

'No way.'

'True story. Maybe she should novelise it.'

'Tesco Chicken Soup for the Soul.'

'Catch 22 Bargains.'

'Love in the Time of Ocado.'

'A Tale of Two McVities.'

Emma groaned; her hangover had made a wave into her brain. 'This is much too highbrow for this time of day, Twist.'

There was a knock at the door and Clem bounded over in her bra and pants and let in a blushing bellboy pushing a trolley full of continental breakfast.

'Thank you, darrrling,' she said, clambering back into bed as he left.

They lay in silence for a few moments until Clementine sighed.

'Good wedding, though,' said Clem.

'Yeah, it was much funnier than I would have expected from them.'

'I think they bring out each other's inner funny. But let's be quiet because my hangover is trying to track me down and I'm going to hide from it,' Clem whispered and crawled further under the covers.

Cheers

Emma enjoyed her journey to work. Her monotone indifference was replaced by an excited terror.

She met Hilary by the coffee machine.

'How was the wedding and other Monday morning banalities?'

Emma stirred her coffee with a mischievous grin.

'That good, huh?' Hilary said.

'I have a meeting with Adrian today. I accidentally sent him an email meant for your eyes only.'

'That sounds ominous.'

'Sackable offence, mate.'

'Yikes, what did it say?'

'The subject was "Stupid Shit Machine" . . . '

Hilary gestured to the corridor. Adrian was marching grim-faced towards his office. He had the countenance of a general on his way to the White House situation room.

'Good luck, honey,' Hilary whispered and headed back to her desk.

Emma took a long deep breath, trying to convince the knot in her belly that she was a righteous crusader. With her head down she sat at her desk and powered up her computer. She opened her desk drawer and peeped at the bottle of champagne lying innocently in the bag. Adrian stood up and moved purposefully towards his office door, and Emma's heart leapt briefly into her mouth.

'Emma, a word.' Adrian stood in the doorway of his office with his face firmly furrowed into bollocking mode.

Emma got up and followed him in. Sitting down, she tried to strike a pose that occupied the space between austere and sorry.

Adrian placed his hands together on the desk in front of him and looked at her purposefully. 'Who was it meant for?'

For all the sardonic dialogue with Paul over the weekend, Emma hadn't considered her answer to this obvious question. She silently cursed Paul for not thinking of it either, and there found her scapegoat.

'My flatmate.'

'Your flatmate?'

'My flatmate. Paul.'

Adrian harrumphed in his chair. He seemed relieved; Emma wondered whom he had thought it was meant for.

'You remember signing the confidentiality agreement, don't you?'

She didn't.

'There wasn't anything confidential in it,' she replied, trying to remember the message in its entirety. Adrian threw her a look that said his fat head might be considered confidential.

'So?' He looked at her, ready for her apology.

She tried not to look too cheerful as she said, 'I hope you know how sorry I am. Obviously I subconsciously sent it to you. I really didn't mean any of it, I was just venting.'

'It was hurtful.'

'I know.' She nodded in acquiescence.

'I really thought you were on board, Emma. I really thought you valued your role here. I know you've been through a lot recently, and I hope that partially explains this, but you've put me in quite a difficult position.'

Emma sat and stared out of the window. She had been through a lot. She may have changed, but APRC was not helping her, not making her better at anything. APRC was just a way to hide from life. She was thinking of Erica, her tropical dress, her enthusiasm. She braced herself, and when her heart lurched expectantly she took a deep breath.

'I think it might be time I bowed out.'

Adrian looked surprised. 'That's not where this is headed. I've talked to HR. We've agreed that it doesn't warrant more than a verbal warning. This is it. We're not going to ask you to leave over something this trivial. Don't be so dramatic, Emma.'

Yeah, EMMA. Don't be so DRAMATIC.

'I'm not trying to be dramatic, Adrian. I gave it a lot of thought over the weekend, and I'm a writer. The work I do here doesn't really use the skills I think I have. I can't feasibly engage with an industry that I don't value. I'm a creative writer; I don't know how far I can advance in advertising without losing a valuable part of myself.'

He scoffed.

Bring it, Adrian.

He tapped the table with his pen and held her gaze. Emma could see he was figuring out his play.

'Maybe we haven't been using you to the best of your ability or maybe you don't think you get enough credit, but I do know how important you are in putting our presentations together. You're the only person here who cuts through the marketing spin. I understand that email was simply venting spleen and I'm not a fool, I know I'm the boss and some animosity towards authority is to be expected.'

He turned his gaze out towards the office. After a couple of moments he turned back to her with an earnest expression that shot a sting of guilt through her. 'But I thought we were friends, Emma.'

Emma's instinct was to assure him that they were friends, but the sentence stuck in her throat. The notion of their friendship was a testament to his ability to see the world through his singular focus. Friends? Of course they weren't friends. No more than she was friends with her dentist. Their presence in each other's lives was completely arbitrary, a necessity forced by a systematic obligation to pay rent and buy beer.

'I have learned a lot here, Adrian, from working with you. But it's not what I want to do. Even if I was the head copywriter and in charge of a department ...'

Adrian grunted. Emma changed tack.

'I shouldn't have written that email. It was rude and unprofessional, and I am genuinely mortified that you saw it. But as a catalyst for this conversation I kind of think it was necessary. I don't want to leave because of APRC, I want to leave for me. It's scary and maybe it's naïve. But I think I should take a real swing at being a writer, and that working here, for all the perks, is a bit of a cop-out. Artistically speaking at least.'

Her face was glowing and she felt shy, but not unsure. She had the marvellous feeling of being the most sure she'd ever been. *It's out there, what I want; it's definitely not in here.* She folded her leg over and caught sight of her trainers. Forget kitten heels – she could run in these, she could run away.

'Well, Emma, I read your blog. You are talented, you have a very unique voice. I don't love your emails, obviously, but I could see you being reasonably successful. We'll of course wish you the best of luck in whatever you do next.'

Emma got up authoritatively and her body felt lighter; she had lost a lot of weight in the last fifteen minutes.

'Thanks Adrian . . . Thanks for everything.'

She returned to her desk and tried to concentrate on the presentation she wouldn't have to look at for much longer.

At lunch she sat with Hilary, who cheered when Emma told her what had happened.

'High five for Emma Derringer! I am so proud of you. Congratulations. What will you do with your new, fabulous life?'

'I've got a meeting with this woman who works for a start-up publishing house. She thinks I've got a good shot at joining a features department. I've got loads of ideas and I've let them slide working here . . . I'll miss you. But I won't miss the rest of it.'

'Hell no you won't. And we can still hang out. I'll be your resident grown-up.'

'God knows I need one, H.'

'I'm proud of you, Emma. I never thought you were right for APRC, and I mean that as a compliment.'

Back at the office the news had spread. The Eds sent identical emails.

Sorry to see you go, Emma! ☺

Ross stuck out his bottom lip and whimpered at her, and Gemma didn't even look up from her magazine.

At the end of the day when she left the building, she already felt nostalgic towards it, despite having to be back the next day.

She called Clem, who answered with a gruff, 'Yup.'

'I quit, Clem.'

'Fuck off!'

'I handed in my notice this morning.'

'You did not.'

'I definitely did.'

'Emma.'

'Clementine?'

'I'm so proud of you, buddy. And we're going to be fine. I just got paid from the Onion; I owe you ten years of pints anyway. Welcome back, my love.'

'Thanks, man.'

She called her dad.

'Hi, Pops.'

'Emma! Nice to hear from you. You'll be pleased to know the washing-up is done already and guess what, Em?'

'You've also cleaned the oven?'

'No, well, that's not due yet, is it? No, Tumnus came back! You were right. He didn't like the state of the place. He's back anyway, still a grumpy git though.'

'That's excellent news.'

'Well it isn't really – now I have to feed the bugger.'

'In other news, Dad, I just quit my job.'

'You did! Congratulations. Sounded awful. Have you got something new?'

'Very tentatively, but I've got a month to figure it out.'

'You'll be fine, Emma. Well done – that's very brave. I'm proud of you.'

'Thanks, Dad.'

They hung up and Emma set off towards her house, deciding to walk, enjoying the sense of an ending. It was a long walk and she did it slowly; she was looking into the future and it was changing colour. She had something to look forward to for the first time since she had signed up to the APRC way of life.

She could have had an illegitimate kid and worked at APRC until she had a company car, a corner office and a pension. But she was taking control. Fear was not going to make her decisions any more. She would write her future, it would not be arbitrary.

Take that, world.

When she got home she marched happily past the handbags. Her rent was cheap, her skills were ample, she had as many free handbags as she could carry.

Emma pushed open the door expecting the flat to be empty, so it scared the shit out of her when Paul and Lucy leapt out with a bottle of champagne and party poppers that exploded in her face.

'Holy crap, guys,' she yelped.

They group-hugged her, jumping up and down and whooping, and ushered her into the lounge.

'How do you even know?' she asked.

Paul poured the champagne. 'Clem called and told us to do you a ticker-tape parade. We've been lying in wait for an hour – what took you so long?'

'Ah sorry, I walked.'

'Into the sunset?'

'Exactly. Thanks for this, guys. I'm so excited, I get to be free and poor!'

'Are you worried?' Lucy asked.

'Liberated mostly; nervous, optimistic, insta-skint, headed gently towards euphoric, maybe.'

'If you send me some work samples I'll make sure they get to the people at my office in case any freelance writing work comes up. You're going to be fine.'

'I'm proud of you, Em – you big *writer*, you,' said Paul softly, raising his glass. Lucy raised her glass with him. 'Me too.'

'Me three.' Emma sighed, and a pent-up, year's worth of relief escaped with it.

They touched glasses solemnly.

'Cheers.'

In her room Emma opened her blog. She had 7000 followers, which was small by internet standards, but that number was growing daily. She sipped champagne and stared happily at a blank post. Then, typing with a new sense of professionalism, she started what felt like her first post in a new era: 'Living The Dream . . . '

Acknowledgements

The writing of this book was made possible by the generosity of family and friends who have committed time, space and patience to the project. Heartfelt gratitude to Pamela Kemp, an ever mysterious benefactor without whom I would still be a secretary with a pencil; to Marion, Alan and Matt Kemp, the Joneses, Anne Steenhauer, the Durkin-Nobles and the Halfpenny-Duffys for letting me sit in their houses, drink their coffee and stare wistfully out of their windows; to the Mankins and the Miltons for putting up with my terrible attitude and to all the people I've worked with who thought that attitude was funny as opposed to unemployable.

Professional thanks for the votes of confidence and excellent input go to Jon Elek and Millie Hoskins, Ailah Ahmed and Caroline Zancan.

Love and thanks always to Claire Wilson for pulling the first draft back from the brink and for your seemingly bottomless lake of faith.

And a special thank you to Hannah Lanfear for the drink(s).

virago

To buy any of our books and to find out more
about Virago Press and Virago Modern Classics,
our authors and titles, as well as events and
book club forum, visit our websites

www.virago.co.uk
www.littlebrown.co.uk

and follow us on Twitter

@ViragoBooks

To order any Virago titles p & p free in the UK,
please contact our mail order supplier on:

+ 44 (0)1832 737525

Customers not based in the UK should contact
the same number for appropriate postage
and packing costs.